D0962233

Con Ed

Con Ed

MATTHEW KLEIN

WARNER BOOKS

NEW YORK   BOSTON

Copyright © 2007 by Matthew Klein, LLC
All rights reserved.

Warner Books
Hachette Book Group USA
1271 Avenue of the Americas
New York, NY 10020

Visit our Web site at www.HachetteBookGroupUSA.com.

Printed in the United States of America

First Edition: March 2007
10   9   8   7   6   5   4   3   2   1

Warner Books and the "W" logo are trademarks of Time Warner Inc. or an affiliated company.
Used under license by Hachette Book Group USA, which is not affiliated with Time Warner Inc.

Library of Congress Cataloging-in-Publication Data

Klein, Matthew, 1968—
    Con ed / Matthew Klein.—1st ed.
        p. cm.
    Includes bibliographical references and index.
    ISBN-13: 978-0-446-57955-1 (alk. paper)
    ISBN-10: 0-446-57955-6 (alk. paper)
    1. Middle-aged men—Fiction. 2. Swindlers and swindling—Fiction. I. Title.
    PS3611.L449C66 2007
    813'.6—dc22   2006018438

Book design by Giorgetta Bell McRee

For my father,
And for my son, Jackson:
I think now finally I understand.

AUTHOR'S NOTE

The events in this book are fictional, except one.

On April 27, 1998, a publicly traded company that specialized in manufacturing meat casings and fish oil announced that it was going to change its name to Zap.com and become an "Internet portal" and "e-commerce business."

Because of this news, shares of the company on the New York Stock Exchange rose 98 percent.

Today, eight years later, the company is again a meat casing and fish protein company.

"It should be no reflection upon a man's intelligence to be swindled."

—DAVID W. MAURER, *The Big Con*

PART ONE

THE ROPER

CHAPTER ONE

It's the world's most simple con, and any idiot can do it, even the one sitting next to me.

He's twenty-five years old, dressed in khakis and a pinpoint Oxford shirt. He has soft hands and wears glasses. I'm guessing a dot-commer, college-educated. Probably he read about this con in a book, or maybe on the Internet, so he wants to try it out. A story to tell his friends. Here in the Blowfish he has found the perfect place to give it a whirl: a friendly bar without obvious thugs who might break his fingers, but far enough from home that he'll never have to walk past the door again.

So here he goes. He's sitting at the bar, one stool over from me. He's talking to the guy on the other side of him, a beefy fellow in a badly fitting suit. The beefy guy has one solid eyebrow across his forehead and a big signet ring on his pinkie. I'm guessing that he has stamped that signet into the cheeks of one or two men that have tried to fuck with him. Maybe the Dot Com Kid doesn't have such good instincts after all.

Dot Com says to Monobrow, "You know what? I'm feeling lucky. You want to play a friendly game?"

Monobrow is holding a glass of JD near his mouth. His hand is so big that it wraps entirely around the glass and makes it seem like a trifle. He chews on an ice cube and looks at the kid. He measures him in about a second. "All right," he says.

Dot Com says, "It's called the Pot Game. We each put some

money in a pot. Say, I dunno, twenty bucks." He takes a twenty from his pocket and drops it on the bar. "Then we both bet on the pot."

Monobrow thinks about it. He takes a money clip out of his jacket. A fat wad of cash. That's another bad sign. No one carries that much cash unless he's in a certain line of work. Work where checking accounts are frowned upon. Now I'm thinking that I ought to break in, stop the kid before he gets hurt. But before I can act, the big man peels a twenty off his roll and drops it on the bar. "I'm in," he says.

"Okay," the kid says. His face is a mixture of fear—will he be found out?—and excitement—that he's actually trying the con. He has probably thought about doing this for weeks, maybe months. What a great story he'll be able to tell his other dot-com friends. "It's simple. Each player gets to bid on the pot. Whoever bids the highest wins the pot. Got it?"

"Yeah, okay," the big guy says. From the look on his face, math was never his strong suit. But the rules are simple, and the kid doesn't seem very threatening . . .

The Dot Com Kid says, "All right. There are forty dollars in the pot. So I guess I'll start off the bidding by offering to buy the pot for twenty bucks."

Monobrow thinks about it. The pot's worth forty dollars. The kid's willing to pay twenty for it. Still room for a profit. Monobrow spits his ice cube into his glass of JD, rattles it around like a craps die. "Yeah?" the man says. "I'll give you twenty-five dollars for it."

This is where the kid should stop. He should wave his hand magnanimously, take twenty-five dollars from Monobrow's hand, slide him the pot, and then he should walk the fuck out of the bar with a five-dollar profit, and fast, before Monobrow warms up his synapses. But the kid's greedy. Not for money—he probably has more than enough of that, maybe millions of dollars of stock options in some company that sells something useless on the Internet. No, the kid wants a better *story*. He's already envisioning it: getting together with his friends tonight, at a SoMa bar, and telling them how he took this blue-collar guy—those are the words he'll use, *blue-collar guy*—for a wad of cash—enough to pay for a round of drinks, and so—hey?—why don't I treat tonight, gang?

So Dot Com says, "You're bidding twenty-five, huh?" He makes a show of rubbing his chin, thinking about it. "You're a tough one, mister. All right, I'll offer twenty-eight dollars."

Monobrow chuckles. He's already worked out the math, so he doesn't even need to think. Any bid under forty dollars means a profit. "Thirty bucks," he says to the kid.

The kid pretends to flinch. He sucks in his breath, as if he just ate something spicy. The kid says, "Ooh. Too rich for my blood. You win. I'll take your bid. You win the pot." He holds out his palm. Monobrow peels a twenty and a ten off his personal roll and hands it to the kid. The kid pockets it and graciously waves his hand over the forty-dollar pot. He says, "The forty dollars is yours."

Monobrow takes the pot, adds it to his roll. Did you catch what happened here? Monobrow put in twenty dollars in order to play the game. Then he paid the kid thirty dollars to "win" the pot. So in total, he paid out fifty dollars, in order to win a forty-dollar pot. The kid took him for ten bucks in two minutes. This is the old Change Game. There are a hundred variations on it.

Now, though, Dot Com Kid is making a big mistake. He's hanging around the bar. The first rule of cons is: Never let the victim know he's been had. The second rule is: If you break the first rule, then run like hell. But the Kid is sipping his beer, watching the Giants game on the bar TV. Finally, he gets up from his stool and settles his tab in a leisurely fashion, dropping a few singles, one at a time, on the bar. God, he's hopeless. Your tab should always be settled before you start. You need to be able to leave the moment the con is done.

I can see the wheels turning in the big guy's head. He's obviously a criminal; criminals can smell a swindle faster than straights. It's all the years of ripping everyone else off: If the big man had spent thirty years dancing ballet, chances are he'd know a good plié when he saw one, too. Meanwhile Dot Com is watching Barry Bonds on the television. Dot Com is standing behind his bar stool, gaping up at the television, without a care in the world. He's about to be disillusioned. Fast.

"Wait a second," Monobrow says. He's blinking, as if he's bothered by sweat. But the bar is cold as a meat locker. "That ain't right."

Dot Com looks down from the TV, realizes his mistake. If he had gone straight home, he could have watched Barry Bonds highlights on *SportsCenter,* and he would have kept his ten bucks and his pretty looks. But now, none of those things is certain.

Monobrow says, "You trying something funny, pal?" Monobrow rises from his stool. He's nine inches away from Dot Com. Dot Com grasps that, for a lousy ten bucks, he's about to get beaten up. Or worse.

"Sorry?" the kid says. Which is the right move. The three rules of running a con: deny, deny, deny.

Monobrow is in the kid's face. The kid probably smells scampi. The big man says, "I paid out fifty! You gave me forty. You think you're smart?"

The kid goes white. Now the story he will tell his friends won't be as charming as he thought. And it may be recounted not from a SoMa bar over a chardonnay, but from a hospital bed with an IV drip.

"No, listen—"

Too late. The big man sends a right hook up into the kid's jaw. The kid's arms windmill around as he goes flying and crashes into the bar. He arches his back and lies on the bar top, soft like a bartender's rag, with his feet on the floor. Monobrow reaches down and clutches the poor kid's throat. He pushes down, hard. The kid's eyeglasses are crazily askew, one earpiece off the face completely, and his eyes bulge behind the lenses. "You little fuck," Monobrow says. "You wanna fuck with me? You picked the wrong guy, pal." He reaches into his too-small jacket and pulls out a gun. He presses it against Dot Com's jaw. Surely this is not what the kid expected when he read about this Change Game on the Internet, or when he practiced it in the mirror last night.

A patron with a gun always attracts a bartender's interest. He was at the far side of the bar, twirling a swizzle stick in a glass, when the ruckus started. The bartender is a young man himself, early twenties. He calls out, but not too loudly, "Whoa there." It's clear from his tentativeness that he doesn't own the place—he's just a worker bee in the middle of a four-hour shift between classes at Santa Clara or Stanford. He'd prefer no trouble in the bar while he's in charge, but, then again, he'd also prefer not to be shot. If he has to choose, he'll take trouble over being shot. So he says, holding up both hands as if he's the one being stuck up, "Let's all just calm down." Yes, good idea. Let's *all* calm down—as if the kid lying on the bar and turning red, with his eyes bugging out of his head, is acting unruly. If only Dot Com would calm down, by not gurgling so loudly, then everything would be fine.

Now's a good time for me to step in. I'm only a few feet away from the kid who's choking, so I don't have to speak loudly. I say, "That's enough." This action sums me up perfectly: I wait too long for everything, and then it's too little, too late. Celia, my ex, would agree.

Monobrow turns to me without releasing the kid or lowering the gun. He has a *you-gotta-be-kidding* expression: He can't believe some fifty-four-year-old guy with salt-and-pepper hair, a paunch, and tired eyes is approaching him in a Sunnyvale bar while he's in the middle of *killing* someone. He gives me a one-second glance, then turns back to Dot Com. He says to Dot Com, "Now I'm going to teach you a lesson." He pulls back the trigger with his big thumb. It makes a click.

Dot Com's fingers scrabble feebly at the beefy hand clutching his throat. It is implacable. I can tell the kid is trying to say something, but he can't breathe and no sound comes out. I'm guessing the general idea of what he wants to say is, "I'm very sorry."

I stand up from my stool so that Monobrow can't ignore me. I say, quietly, without menace, "Come on, he's a just a kid. He didn't mean anything by it."

"Mind your own business, pal." And then, still staring at the kid: "The kid tried to rip me off."

"He learned his lesson. Look, he took you for ten dollars. I'll pay you twenty bucks to make it up to you." I reach into my back pocket, pull out my wallet. I look inside, hoping that I do indeed have twenty bucks. Unfortunately, I have only a ten and six sad-looking singles, wilted like day-old lettuce. Whoops. I say, "Here, take whatever I have. It's sixteen dollars. You still come out ahead. Plus the kid knows never to mess with you again. You taught him a good lesson."

The big man turns to me. He lowers the gun from the kid's jaw. It's not clear if he's standing down or repositioning to take a shot at me. He says, "What are you, a fucking guardian angel?"

"Just a busybody who doesn't know when to keep quiet," I admit. I take the bills from my wallet, hold them out to him. He releases the kid, who slides off the bar and falls to the floor. Monobrow swipes the money from my hand, counts it. He stuffs it in his pants pocket. He drops his gun into his coat, turns back to the kid. Dot Com is rubbing his neck. He has five purple bruises around his throat, one for each garlicky finger, like a well-worn page in a precinct fingerprint book.

"Your lucky day," Monobrow says to the kid. He's obviously a pro, because he knows the exact lesson the kid failed to grasp: Always walk away when you have a profit. He's not going to hang around the bar and wait for the police, who are surely on their way. Come to think of it, neither am I.

Monobrow smiles at the kid with a face that indicates absolutely nothing in the world is funny. He gives me a little nod and walks out of the bar. The kid's eyes follow him and then stare at the door for a good ten seconds, to see if Monobrow is going to change his mind and return. When it's clear he won't, the kid looks up at me. He whispers, "Thank you."

I kneel down beside him. His eyes are watering, maybe from choking, maybe from crying. I don't think he's going to join his South of Market friends tonight. I feel I should give him some advice about how to run a con. Teach him to get out before the mark figures it. But then I decide his conning days are over, and tomorrow he'll go back to writing performance reviews, or breaking bread with venture capitalists, or whatever it is he really is good at. Running Change Games isn't one of those things.

So I decide against giving advice. I have something else I want to say to the kid. I say it softly, so that no one else in the bar will hear. When he sees I'm about to speak, the kid turns his ear to me, as if he's ready to receive golden wisdom. But I'm thinking about my empty wallet, and the fact that I gave the mafia goon my last sixteen dollars. I say to the kid, "Hey, you mind reimbursing me sixteen bucks?"

By the time I leave the Blowfish, I have forty dollars in my wallet. That's all the kid had left, and he was happy to give me whatever he had. In fact he offered to write me a check for more—"I'm good for it," he assured me, as if I had any doubt—but I refused. Half because I'm a good guy, and half because I prefer not to leave a paper trail.

You may wonder if I helped the kid because I thought I'd make a profit. I entered the bar with twenty bucks (then spent four on beer), and I left with forty. But I walked up to a guy brandishing a gun. He was a guy who looked comfortable with guns, as if he had some practice with them. So ask yourself: Would *you* walk up to a guy with a gun and try to stop a fight for forty bucks? It would take a certain desperation for a man to do that, for forty bucks, wouldn't it? So just what kind of guy do you think I am?

But, okay, yes. The thought of a small profit *did* cross my mind. Briefly.

After I walk out of the bar, it's time to go home. It's six o'clock, and so I've timed peak rush hour perfectly. I will now spend the next hour driving eleven miles to my apartment in Palo Alto. Had I left Sunnyvale an hour earlier, or an hour later, I could have cut my commute in half. But that would indicate good common sense, something I lack.

I walk to my car and press the key-chain remote. The Honda chirps brightly. I hear footsteps running toward me. Without turning, I know they are women's heels.

I turn. She is half-walking, half-running. I remember her from the bar. She was at a table in the back, barely visible in the dark. The only reason I noticed her was her big Jackie O sunglasses. Not many people wear sunglasses in a dark bar.

She's blond, in her twenties, rail-thin, with big breasts that cannot possibly be real. She's wearing dark glen plaid pants—with loose cuffs but tight around the thighs and rear—and a beige ribbed sweater. She's obviously trying to dress down and look inconspicuous, but she's fashion-model gorgeous. It's impossible for a woman like her to be inconspicuous.

She says, by way of introduction, "That was nice of you, back there."

I guess she didn't see me take forty bucks from the kid. Or maybe she did, and she has low standards. I say, "Thanks."

"You ran out so fast. I nearly missed you."

I give her a little smile. Polite, but not too interested.

She says, "Can I buy you a drink?"

Here's another lesson for you men. Never in the history of the entire world has a woman offered to buy a strange man a drink. Unless she wants something. So don't flatter yourself. You're not *that* good-looking, or *that* rich, or *that* funny—or whatever you think you are. If a woman offers to buy you drink, you are only one thing: a sucker about to be fleeced.

"All right," I say. I can't help myself. She's pretty. A little too young for me, but what else do I have to do? Sit in traffic? Drink alone in my apartment? "But not at that bar."

"We can go somewhere else."

"You're on."

We walk down the block to another bar, McMurphy's Irish Pub. There's nothing Irish about it except for the "Mc" on the sign outside. Even that rings false—painted in a different color than the rest of the sign, an owner's bright afterthought—probably inspired by a last-minute discovery that there's another Murphy's on the east side of town. The pub is filled with young kids who just got off from work. They dress messy, in jeans and T-shirts. This being the center of the Internet Universe, at the height of the Internet Boom, I suspect these kids are programmers, and each one of them is worth more than I ever was—even at the height of the Kip Largo Boom. You don't remember the Kip Largo Boom? It was a brief glorious period in the life of Kip Largo—that's me—before I went to prison. I was worth maybe twenty million dollars. Now I'm not. You want to know the whole story? Have patience; I'll tell you soon.

Jackie O and I sit at a table in the back, far from the programmers. She goes to the bar and orders drinks. Soon she returns with my scotch on the rocks. For herself: a martini, dirty. She's still wearing her big dark sunglasses. I suspect that underneath them, I will discover two things. One: a pretty face. Two: purple bruises. Like I said: Most women don't wear sunglasses in a dark bar.

When she sits down she says, "So are you a cop?"

I laugh.

"Why are you laughing?"

"Because I'm the furthest thing from a cop you can be."

"What does that mean? Are you a criminal?"

"I was," I say. I've learned to get this part of the conversation out of the way as early as possible. The longer you wait, the more cheated the other person feels. You spring the fact that you're an ex-con on someone more than a day after meeting them, and they feel violated. It's better to set expectations low and then exceed them. "I was in prison for a little while. I've been out for a year."

"What'd you do? To go to prison?"

I can tell from her face that she's asking if I killed anyone. If I'm dangerous. "White-collar stuff," I say, vaguely. The way I say that, it sounds like I took a few boxes of paper clips from the supply closet at work. "Nothing too colorful." Which is not exactly true. I served five years in a federal penitentiary for securities and mail fraud. It was pretty colorful, by the time I was caught.

"I see," she says. She's trying to reconcile this new information with what happened in the Blowfish, where I was a Good Samaritan and saved a young kid from getting his face broken, or worse. How can I explain to her that I'm a con man? That I've always had a passion for cons? That if I see a badly run con going down, I always want to step in and give advice. It's like what would happen if Renoir went to one of those art schools advertised on the back of a matchbook. He'd see a kid painting a portrait of Dumbo the Elephant, and he'd be horrified. He'd throw up his hands and shout, "No, no! Zat is not how it's done!"

I say, "Those days are long gone. I'm just a plain guy now, trying to get on with my life."

She stares at me. Something is bothering her. "You seem so familiar."

Here it comes. This is when they try to place my face. It takes most people a few minutes. Then, after they give up, and I tell them, a look of relief washes over them. *Of course,* they say. *I knew it.* Then they stare at me a bit longer, comparing my current face to the one they remember. Inevitably, I see their expression change to one of sadness. I'm a poster child for the phrase *Time Is Kind to No One.* I used to be on TV hours every week, usually late at night, on infomercials touting a diet plan in the form of a deck of playing cards. It was called the Diet Deck. Maybe you remember it? You would deal yourself a card at random—say, with a picture of a steak—and then you got to eat a steak. If you dealt yourself a picture of steamed broccoli, you got to eat broccoli. There wasn't much science behind it. Except that there was only one steak in each fifty-two-card deck, and there were five broccolis and five apples. I suspect that when a fattie dealt herself a broccoli, she called a misdeal and dealt herself another card, again and again, until she got what they wanted: the Popcorn Card, or the Chocolate Card.

I say, to put her out of her misery, "I was on TV. The Diet Deck?"

"Oh," she says. "That was *you?*" Now the comparison begins. I was in the low-security part of Lompoc. But low-security is not what you think. It's not a country club. Not unless you belong to the kind of country club where the golf pros perform rectal searches regularly, where the tennis courts are locked down for head count twice a day, and where you get stabbed for accidentally taking someone's bar of soap. Five years of being out-of-control—of being on someone else's schedule, of being able to take a crap only when you're allowed to take a crap, of being visible to guards twenty-four hours a day, of being fed strange slices of meat with arterial cross-sections around the edges—five years of this have changed my face from B-Actor handsome to C-List has-been. You're never the same after you get out. Ask any ex-con. He'll tell you.

"My television days are behind me," I say. "Like I said, I'm just an honest man trying to earn an honest living."

"Really?" she says. "That's too bad."

I smile. The line is so perfect, so surprising, I have to bite. "And why is that?"

"I have a job for you."

"I'm not interested," I say.

"You don't know what it is."

"I don't need to. Look, lady, you wanted to buy me a drink. I never turn down a drink. I've enjoyed it." I hold up the glass of scotch, to show her how much I've enjoyed it, and also to see what's left. I'm surprised that a few gulps remain. I throw it back into my gullet and put down the glass. "But I already have a job. I'm very happy with it."

I work at Economy Cleaners—a dry-cleaning and laundry shop—in Sunnyvale. I get paid ten dollars per hour, plus tips. You ever leave a tip at a dry cleaners? That's what I thought. In a year of working there, I've gotten tipped three times. Twice was loose change that accidentally dropped from someone's slacks.

"I'll pay you a hundred," she says.

"Dollars?"

"No."

"Hundred *thousand?*"

"Yes."

"That's tempting," I say. "But no."

"Don't you want to know what the job is?"

"No."

"Do you know who my husband is?"

"No."

As if to answer her own question, she takes off her sunglasses. As I suspected, she has a black eye the size of a crumpet. "His name is Edward Napier. Do you know who he is?"

I do. He's a Las Vegas magnate. What the media call an *impresario.* I guess that's because he impresses people. And why not? He owns The Clouds casino, on the Strip. He's tall and handsome. He's worth maybe a billion dollars. No exaggeration. He also has mob connections. Nothing has ever been proven, mind you. It's just that people who negotiate too hard with him tend to disappear. So deals get done.

Now that he has conquered Las Vegas, Ed Napier has come to Silicon Valley. Recently he has fancied himself a venture capitalist. He's been throwing money around, investing tens of millions of dollars in Internet companies. He was quoted in the *Wall Street Journal* as saying that, when the dust clears, he's going to own a small percentage of the New Economy. Not many people doubt him. Out loud.

"No," I say. "Who is he?"

She smiles. "It's a simple job."

There's no such thing as a simple job that pays one hundred grand. Unless you're a newscaster or a senator. "Like I said, no thanks." I stand.

"You're leaving?"

"Yup."

"Why?"

"Because I don't believe you. I don't believe you just *happened* to run into me in a bar. I think you know who I am, and this is a setup."

"But I swear to you."

"Oh, you swear? Well, in that case . . ." I sit back down.

She looks surprised.

"Just kidding," I say. I stand up again. "Last chance. Who sent you?"

"No one."

"Goodbye."

I turn to leave.

"Wait," she says. She tugs my pant leg. "Here."

She hands me a business card. It says, "Lauren Napier." Just a telephone number. No job title. No address. "That's my private cell phone," she says. "You can call the number anytime."

"Why would I do that?"

"Maybe you'll change your mind."

"Don't hold your breath," I say. "Thanks for the drink." I leave Ms. Lauren Napier sitting at the table, and I hurry out to my Honda. If I'm lucky, my trip home will consist of exactly one hour sitting on Highway 85 in the hot sun.

I get home at seven o'clock. It's summer, still plenty of daylight left.

I live in a four-plex apartment in downtown Palo Alto. It's not exactly run-down, but it's not up to neighborhood standards, either. On all four sides are beautiful gated condominium buildings where one-bedrooms go for half a million dollars. My place is old, cheap stucco, with an open carport in the front, like the neighborhood cold sore. My landlord—who lives in the apartment above mine—is ninety years old. He bought the building in 1958, long before the area was known as Silicon Valley. For the first ten years he owned the place, he kept a chicken coop in the backyard. Nowadays he charges me four hundred dollars to rent my one-bedroom, when the market would command twelve hundred per month. It's not clear if his policy is the result of stubborn decency or senility.

In return for the low rent, I help out. There's not much to do: clip hedges, bring the recycling out to the curb each Tuesday, call the Sears man when the communal washing machine conks out.

Today, Mr. Santullo meets me in the driveway. He's wearing a wife-beater undershirt and a terry-cloth bathrobe. He shuffles over to my car and says, "Kip, can you change the light bulb upstairs?" He's a little man, shrunken and worn like a well-chewed dog toy. He speaks with an Italian accent. I've heard his life story dozens of times: came over from Italy during the Depression, worked at the Swift meatpacking plant in San Francisco, made good union wages, started buying real estate while the rest of his family mocked him for paying too much for rural land in the middle of nowhere—Palo Alto. Now the land under the apartment where I live—downtown, at the epicenter of the biggest economic boom in the history of capitalism—will fetch a million dollars whenever he wants to sell. Chances are, he never will. So his heirs will get the money. In fact, they've already started to circle, visiting him more frequently now, as they sense impending death. Nothing like money to inspire love.

I say, "No problem, Delfino."

He leads the way, slippers scuffing concrete. I follow as he circles to the back of the apartment and climbs the stairs. There are two units on the first floor—mine and that of a young divorcée—and two upstairs—Delfino's and a Stanford professor's. It takes Delfino a good minute to climb the thirteen stairs. Finally he reaches the second-floor landing. He points to a ceiling-mounted exterior light. "Here," he says. He reaches into his bathrobe and produces a light bulb, as if he's part of a magic act. He hands it to me.

I look at the ceiling light fixture. On my toes, I might be able to reach. So I stretch, hands high above my head, to unscrew the glass cover from the fixture. I am precariously near the edge of the concrete staircase. I unfasten the fixture cover. My body strains.

From the bottom of the stairs, a voice calls, "Delfino, no!"

I nearly drop the glass cover. I look down. It's Mr. Santullo's grandson, trotting up the stairs toward me.

Even though Delfino calls him his grandson, he is not actually related. He is the husband of Mr. Santullo's granddaughter. Which means: He married into Delfino's family, just in time. For years, I seldom saw the granddaughter visit the old man. But now that Mr. Santullo is approaching death, and his assets are about to be distributed, grandson has been making frequent appearances. Perhaps he smells a payday?

The grandson is from somewhere in the Middle East, maybe Egypt. He has dark wavy hair, a swarthy complexion. He speaks perfect English, hardly an accent. He's a commercial real estate broker. He always has the look of a man measuring how much something is worth.

Recently Delfino told me that his grandson has been helping with paperwork—bills, bank account statements, taxes. It's not merely because I'm an ex-con that I smell something fishy. I would not be surprised if Mr. Santullo's will is rewritten, perhaps without his knowledge.

But like all elderly marks, Mr. Santullo suspects nothing. He affectionately calls his grandson his "Arabian," like the kid's a horse. I think the kid bristles at that, but he does a good job hiding it. *Just a year or two more*, he must tell himself.

The Arabian flies up the stairs, to make sure I stop helping grandfather. No one can be invited into Mr. Santullo's inner circle now, not when wills are being rewritten. He joins us on the landing. "Delfino, how many times have I told you?" he says, angrily, as if to a child. "You can't ask tenants to do your chores."

"It's really no problem—" I start to say.

He ignores me. To Mr. Santullo, as if I don't exist: "You call *me* next time."

Mr. Santullo laughs good-naturedly. He's hard of hearing, so it's not clear he heard or understood what his Arabian said. He turns to me. "That's my grandson," he explains. "He's my Arabian."

"Yes," I say gently, "I know."

Grandson holds out his palm in front of me. It takes me a moment to understand that he's asking for the light bulb. I hand it to him. "I've got it now," he says to me. Whether he means the light bulb or the real estate under our feet is unclear.

"Sure." I turn to Mr. Santullo. "Take care, Mr. Santullo."

Mr. Santullo chuckles. Maybe he knows what's going on; maybe not. Without a further word to the Arabian, I head down to my apartment.

My apartment contains: one bedroom, a galley kitchen, an old GE electric stove with three of the original four eyes still functioning, green carpet that was laid down when Eisenhower was president, and two broken windows patched with Saran wrap and Scotch tape. There's a bathroom with an exhaust fan that sounds like the engine room of the QE 2. When something breaks, I don't bother Mr. Santullo with it. Like I said, he charges me only four hundred dollars each month for rent.

In my living room I keep a computer and dozens of cartons filled with vitamins. I run a business selling nutritional supplements over the Internet. It's called MrVitamin.com. It's totally legitimate. Unfortunately.

I net about twenty dollars each month.

I had to order eight hundred bottles of vitamins from the wholesaler in order to receive any kind of reasonable discount. My living room looks like a warehouse, stacked high with cartons of vitamin E, beta-carotene, multivitamin pills, and selenium tablets. In the unlikely event that the world ever switches to a selenium-based economy, I will become a very rich man.

Until then, it's slow going. I stumble over the vitamin cartons to the computer. It's set atop an old rickety card table. I asked my programmer to write a program that displays up-to-the-second sales results. He created a screensaver that shows a little vitamin pill bouncing around the screen. Inside the vitamin is the daily sales total. According to my bouncing vitamin, while I was at work today, I sold $56.23 worth of vitamins. My gross margin is about 7 percent. That means today I earned $3.94. It costs me about ten dollars per day to run the Web site. Like the old joke, I lose money on each sale, but I hope to make it up on volume.

In the kitchen, I play my telephone messages. There are two. The first is from Peter Room, my programmer. I met Peter back in my Diet Deck days. When sales started to take off, I was taking hundreds of orders each day. Our telephone operators scribbled down orders on index cards. I realized I needed a professional computer database to store all of my fatties' names and addresses, and to keep the orders straight. Anderson Consulting offered to write me a piece of custom software and install it for seventy-five thousand dollars up front, plus a ten-thousand-dollar monthly maintenance fee. That sounded a little steep, so I biked over to the

Stanford campus and I posted a handwritten sign on a tree that said, "Computer Programmer Wanted. $10/hr." I got twenty responses. One came from Peter Room. By the time I got sent to Lompoc, I had paid Peter a total of twenty thousand dollars. I'm sure nineteen thousand of that went to Peter's pot dealer. If I could have set up some kind of direct deposit with Miguel, it would have made everyone's life easier.

In his telephone message, Peter tells me that he finished the software project I requested for the Web site: automatically recurring orders. Here's the idea. People take vitamins every day, so a jar of thirty pills should last exactly one month. So why should customers have to return to MrVitamin.com to reorder each month? I asked Peter to allow customers to request automatic monthly shipments of their vitamins. Once per month, their credit card gets billed and a new jar of multivitamins gets shipped. Automatically.

I know what you're thinking. In my old, pre-Lompoc days, I may not have told customers that they were signing up for this convenience. And maybe the billing would have been more regular than the shipping. But that's the old me. I'm a new man. Straight as an arrow.

On his message, Peter tells me the good news, that recurring orders are now available on the MrVitamin.com Web site. Then he clears his throat. "So, um, listen," he says. "Maybe we can settle up the bill soon?"

Peter's a good guy. I haven't paid him a cent since I got out of prison. I guess his generosity is coming to an end. I probably owe him a few thousand dollars. At $3.94 per day in gross profit, I should be able to settle my debt with him in two and a half years. From the hopeless tone in his voice, he seems to have run the same calculation.

The answering machine beeps and the second message plays. I'm surprised by the voice. I haven't heard from him in six months—since Christmas. Toby seems to always come around when gifts are being distributed.

"Hey, Dad," Toby says. "Just checking in." His voice sounds casual—too casual. I know my son. He wants something. "Called to see how you're doing. Nothing important." He pauses, thinks about whether to leave further details on the machine. He decides against it. "Okay, then. Catch you later." He hangs up.

I cook myself the usual dinner: Ronzoni spaghetti ($1.19 at Safeway) and Ragú tomato sauce ($2.30 per jar). As I eat, I think about the day—about Ms. Lauren Napier's surprising offer to hire me for a mysterious job that pays a hundred grand, and about my son's alarmingly vague telephone message.

Guys like me get feelings in their bones. My bones say this story is just beginning.

CHAPTER TWO

The Pigeon Drop works like this.

You're walking from the supermarket, heading to your car. You see a pretty girl coming toward you and you smile at each other. As you pass, she looks down at the ground. She stops suddenly and says, "Whoa, look at this."

You follow her gaze. She has found a brown paper bag. Even without examination, you can see twenty-dollar bills practically falling out of the bag; it's stuffed full of cash.

She bends down, picks up the bag. She removes a wad of twenties, thick as the Sunday paper, and flips through it. "Jesus," she says.

She looks inside the bag and finds a folded piece of paper. She hands it to you. She says, "Mister, you read this. I'll count the money."

While she's counting the cash, you unfold the note and read it out loud. It says something like this: "Tyrone—Here's your cut of the deal. I've already paid off the cops. You pay off the DA like we agreed. See you in Cabo—Juan."

After you read the note, you put two and two together. You say, "This money must be from a drug deal."

The roper (as the female con artist is called) has finished counting the cash. She announces, in a half-whisper, "There's over five thousand dollars in this bag! What should we do with it?"

Before you can answer, a well-dressed young man in a suit walks up. This is the cap—the second con artist. He says to the girl,

"Listen, I don't mean to intrude, but I want to warn you folks not to wave that kind of cash around. This isn't exactly the safest neighborhood."

The girl says, "Actually, we just found it. We don't know what to do with it." She says to you, "Show him the note."

You hand the note to the young man in the suit. He reads it. "This is illegal drug money," he announces.

"Should we return it?" the girl asks. "Maybe we should bring it into the supermarket over there, in case someone claims it."

The man smiles at her simplicity. "Lady," he says, "I don't think many drug dealers are going to come forward to claim this."

"Well," the girl asks, "can we keep it?"

The guy shrugs. "I don't know." He thinks about it. "But I'll tell you what. I'm a paralegal. My boss is a pretty big lawyer. He'll know the answer. My office is three blocks down the street. If you want, I'll go ask him what to do with the money."

"All right," the girl says.

The cap takes off, ostensibly to talk to his boss. In reality, he heads to the nearest coffee shop and buys himself a donut and a cup of joe. While he's gone, the cute girl says to you, "Listen, mister, I don't want you to get the wrong idea. I was brought up to treat people fair and square. You were here when I found this money. So half of it is rightfully yours, okay?"

You thank her for her sense of decency.

After a few minutes, the cap returns to the parking lot. "I have some good news, folks. I spoke to my boss. He says you can definitely keep the money. If you want to be totally legal about it, you'll need to report it on your income tax at the end of the year. But otherwise, you're free and clear."

While you're thinking about whether you're actually going to bother reporting your half of the five thousand dollars on your tax form, the young man adds one more bit of information. "The only thing is," he says, "you have to wait thirty days before the money is rightfully yours. So you can't spend a cent of it until a month from today."

"That's fine," the girl says. "Me and this gentleman"—she

means you—"will just hang on to the money for a month." She thinks about it. "Hey, listen," she says to you. "I'm new in town. I don't even have a bank account. Why don't you hold on to the money?" She hands you the brown paper bag.

Before you can claim it, the young man pushes the bag out of your hands and back toward the girl. "Whoa," the young man says. "Wait just a second." He's looking at the girl as if she's the stupidest person on the planet. "You never even met this guy before. How do you know he won't just keep the money for himself?"

The girl is angry. "Look, mister, I appreciate your help. I'll even give you some of my cut in return for your time and trouble. But I resent that you're talking about this nice gentleman that way. He helped me find this money. I happen to trust him completely."

The cap looks apologetic. "All right, sorry. It's *your* money. Do whatever you want with it." He pauses. "It's just that, if you're going to hand a guy a few thousand dollars in cash, you ought to know whether he's trustworthy. He should show some good faith, that's all."

You're staring at the bag full of cash. It's only inches away from you. The girl is *this close* to handing it to you. So you say, "What do you mean 'good faith'?"

"Look," the cap says, "chances are, you're a decent guy. But how does this lady know you're not some kind of scam artist? Sure, you're dressed in nice clothes. But maybe you don't have a single dime to your name. Maybe you're just a poor hustler, and you're going to spend all the money on your own—"

"I have money," you say.

"But how does she *know* that? Can you prove to her that you're a trustworthy guy? That you have your own money?"

At this point one of two things will happen. Either you will volunteer to show them that you have money, or you won't. If you remain silent, the girl will start to agree with the cap. "Yeah," she'll say, "you're probably right. I don't know if this guy has any money. I guess I should keep the bag . . ."

In either case, you quickly will be convinced of the need to demonstrate your financial resources.

So you lead your two friends to the nearest ATM machine, or—
if the con men decide your daily ATM withdrawal limit is too
low—they'll convince you to make a personal appearance at your
bank branch. To "prove" that you are a man of means, you'll withdraw five thousand dollars from your account.

You return with five thousand dollars of cash and show it to the
young girl and her suspicious new friend. The girl is suitably chas-
tened. "All right," she says, "you convinced me."

"Yeah," the cap admits, sheepishly. "Me, too. Sorry I doubted
you."

You say that you understand, that you probably would have
done the same thing.

The girl takes your cash and stuffs it into the brown paper bag,
alongside the drug money. Now the three of you exchange names,
addresses, and telephone numbers. You agree to hold the bag of
cash for thirty days on their behalf and then to call your two new
friends when the month is up.

What you don't know is that, while telephone numbers are
being scribbled and traded, the girl switches the brown paper bag
with an identical one containing newspaper. Before parting, she
hands it to you. She says, "Keep this safe. I'm trusting you."

The young gentleman looks around the parking lot, ever suspicious. "Be smart," he warns. "Keep that bag closed. Don't flash the
money around. Keep it hidden and closed until you get home. You
promise?"

"Yeah," you say. "I promise."

Maybe, depending on your own level of greed, you have given
your two friends a fake name and contact information. Maybe
you've already decided how you're going to spend the entire five
thousand dollars.

Or maybe you're an honest guy, but a stupid one. Maybe you intend to divvy up the money after thirty days, fair and square.

It doesn't really matter. Because when you get home, you open
up the paper bag, and you discover that, because of your own stupidity and greed, you've been had.

CHAPTER THREE

The next morning I leave for work at six o'clock, in order to arrive by seven. It's my job to open the shop for my boss, Imelda. Dry cleaning is an unpleasant business. Half your customers show up before eight in the morning. The other half show up during lunch. For the rest of the day, you sit around an empty store, smelling perc fumes and worrying about those state-mandated signs on the walls that ominously warn that the State of California Believes Dry Cleaning Fumes Will Make Your Forehead Sprout a Third Testicle. What you're supposed to do with this information is unclear.

When you finally do see customers, they're not nice. Everyone's in a hurry. No one's happy to see you. You're the guy who handles their blouses with underarm stains, ties with pasta splatters. No one likes seeing their clothes in this state. You're a walking, breathing reminder of the customer's own filth and imperfection.

But an ex-con eleven months out of Lompoc doesn't have many employment choices. I interviewed at nine places before Imelda agreed to hire me. She never asked if I had been to prison. So I made a point to volunteer that fact ten minutes into my interview. She said, "Sweetie, you're not getting out of here that easy. I don't care if you were a Catholic priest. You're hired."

God bless Imelda, even if she pays only ten bucks an hour. Plus tips.

This morning, traffic on 85 is brutal. I arrive at the store five minutes late. By the time I unlock the door, there's a line of four angry customers.

"I'm sorry," I say, jangling the keys in the lock. I push open the door, flip on the lights, circle around the counter. Before I can put down my keys, a man shoves a bundle of shirts into my arms. He grunts his last name.

I try to smile. "Thursday after one," I tell him. I write a receipt and hand it to him. Without acknowledging me, he takes the receipt and leaves the store.

The next customer, a woman in her forties, dressed like a lawyer, is worse. She's annoyed that she had to wait five minutes for me to open the store. Her look says, "My time is billed at three hundred per hour. What's your time worth?" I feel like telling her, *Ten dollars an hour, plus tips,* and pointing at the "Tips Please" jar. She slides a crumpled blouse and a pants suit across the counter to me. When I hand her the receipt, she doesn't make eye contact. That's my job in a nutshell: I'm invisible to customers, an inanimate piece of dry cleaning machinery, like a cog or a rotator drum.

I serve the other two customers and make it through the morning rush. Imelda shows up at nine-thirty. Imelda is forty years old, of indeterminate Asian ancestry. I'm guessing Filipina. I'm also guessing that Imelda is a transsexual. She's five foot ten, with a deep voice and an Adam's apple the size of a Braeburn. More important: Her hands are huge. When she lifts plastic-wrapped hangers from the ready-rack and offers them, with bulging biceps, to customers, you can't help staring at those hams, huge as oven mitts.

She waltzes into the store and says in a singsong man's voice, "Hello, my dear!"

Imelda either wears an auburn wig or is the victim of a ghoulish hair coloring accident. In the early morning light that streams through the shop window, I catch a glimpse of dark facial hair. "Good morning, Imelda," I say.

"How's my favorite man today?"

When Imelda tries to flirt with me, I can't help glancing at those huge hands and feet of hers, and I get the heebie-jeebies. "Not bad," I say.

"You got a call yesterday, after you left. Some guy."

"He leave a name?"

"Nope." She looks me up and down, smirking, as if I have a delicious secret. "Anything you want to tell me?"

Imelda thinks everyone is secretly gay. I say, "No."

"Well, he said it wasn't important."

I recall the telephone message my son left me at home. Now I'm sure. He's in trouble. As usual.

Imelda disappears behind the clothing storage racks, into the back bathroom. There's a moment of silence, and then I hear a long, manly fart reverberate in the porcelain bowl. I sit down on my stool and stare thoughtlessly out the window, as well-dressed professionals go about their business outside.

I return to my apartment at six o'clock that evening. Mr. Santullo is waiting in the driveway for me, dressed in his bathrobe and holding a rolled-up newspaper as if to swat me on the ass.

When I climb from my Honda, he says, "My grandson wants to talk to you." He chuckles.

"Oh?" I look around. I don't see the grandson anywhere.

Then I hear his voice behind me. He appears from around the side of the apartment. He's holding a paintbrush, dripping with white paint, and a bucket of Glidden enamel.

"Hi, Kevin," he says.

"Kip," I correct him.

"Right." He lays down the paint canister and puts the brush inside. I notice wet patches on the exterior stucco wall behind him. The grandson has been doing some touch-ups. This is not a good sign. "Listen," the Arabian says. He walks closer. "I've been talking with my grandfather. He wants to raise your rent."

I look at Mr. Santullo. He's smiling brightly, as though delighted that he's finally managed to get two of his favorites together for a chat. I say, "Is that true, Mr. Santullo?"

Mr. Santullo answers a different question. "My grandson is Arabian," he says.

The grandson says, "Of course it's true."

I don't have a lease with Mr. Santullo. Everything has been informal, month-to-month. I've been living in the building and paying four hundred dollars monthly since I got out of Lompoc.

I turn to the grandson. No use even pretending Mr. Santullo is in charge. "What's the new rent?"

"Twelve hundred," he says. He waves his hand magnanimously. "But my grandfather can wait a month. Why not start in June?"

"Okay," I say.

I have the sudden urge to retreat into my apartment and check today's Mr. Vitamin sales. I'm hoping for a miracle.

Before I even reach my apartment door, I know something is wrong. Years of always watching my back—first, when I was a free man and ripping people off, and later, when I was incarcerated and afraid of a sudden shim in the ribs—have increased my sensitivity to threat. Today I feel it as I walk past the rosebushes along the path to my apartment. The hairs on my neck tingle, electric. When I get to the door, I see something amiss: the door ajar in the frame, not locked tight the way I left it this morning.

I push open the door with my finger, ready to hit the pavement if a lead pipe swings at my face.

None comes. I walk inside. The curtains are closed. It's dark. I can barely make out the outlines of vitamin cartons along the wall. At the other side of the room, my screensaver vitamin pill is happily bouncing around the cathode-ray tube. I can't help but notice today's daily sales total in the center of the vitamin: $9.85. Somewhere in the back of my mind, I have a depressing thought that, if there is an intruder in my apartment who wants to kill me, the pathetic sales total inside a dancing vitamin will be the last thing I ever see.

I close the door behind me. I ask, "Who's here?"

I hear breathing. My mind does a quick inventory of potential weapons in the house. On the kitchen counter: the knife block. A pair of cuticle scissors in my bedroom. A screwdriver under the bathroom sink.

I take a step into the darkness. I think about the odds. Can I run into the kitchen and lunge for the knife block before the intruder can act? It's *my* apartment: I know the layout better than the intruder. If I hurry . . .

The lights switch on. I blink at the brightness.

A young man is sitting at the kitchen table, leaning back in his chair, his fingers fiddling with the wall-mounted light switch behind him.

"Hi, Dad," he says.

Toby has the stupid *Gotcha!* grin of a fifteen-year-old boy. Unfortunately for both of us, Toby is twenty-five years old. He's a good-looking kid, with dark hair that is too long, a stoner moptop, and a big bright smile. He says, "Did I scare you?"

"I could have killed you," I say.

"Yeah, right." He laughs. "Oooh, I'm scared." He waves his fingers near his face to indicate fright.

"Jesus, Toby, what are you doing here?"

"Nothing. I haven't seen you in a while. I thought you might miss me."

"Of course I miss you."

I last saw Toby six months before my release from Lompoc, the one and only time he visited me in prison. Five minutes into the visiting hour, he asked to borrow money so he could open a coffee shop in Seattle. When I explained that my incarceration and bankruptcy made it difficult to fund new business ventures, he got that mopey look I was so familiar with. After a few minutes of further pleasantries he left. He has called me a few times since I got out, either when he's mad at Celia—his mother—or when he needs cash. I try my best to help him whenever I can, no questions asked. Last thing I heard, he was living in Aspen, working as a ski instructor.

I say, "Are you still in Aspen?"

"Not really."

"Not really? Where do you live?"

"Here and there."

"Let's say you had to choose one: here or there."

"I'm sort of hanging out with friends. Mostly in San Francisco."

I swallow, try not to seem angry. "You mean you live right *here*?" San Francisco is thirty miles away. A half-hour drive without traffic. I'm tempted to show my hurt, that my son has been living so close to me, but hasn't bothered to come by, or call, or even let me know he lives in the area. But acting hurt with Toby is unproductive. So I say, as happily as I can make my voice sound, "Well that's terrific."

"Yeah, you know, it's whatever."

I nod. *Yeah, it's whatever.*

I say, "How's the ski instruction business?"

He shrugs. "You know, it's kind of . . . Well, I'm sort of done with that."

"Done with it?" I conjure a vision of my son carving up the slopes, speeding downhill at sixty miles an hour with a terrified toddler in tow and a doobie hanging from his lips.

"It didn't really work out," he explains.

"Okay," I say agreeably.

"Dad, why do you always have to attack me?"

I hold up my hands in surrender. "No attack," I say. "I think you're great."

"Now you're being patronizing."

"No, I'm not. I love you." Which is true. Who doesn't love his son? No matter what the son does? And, if Toby is a bit lost in his life, whose fault is it but mine? When he was fourteen years old, I divorced his mother after she caught me cheating with her best friend, Lana Cantrell. Five years later, I was sent to the slammer for mail and securities fraud. Toby's father is an unfaithful, womanizing, corrupt criminal. What kind of kid can he expect?

I say, "I'm just glad to see you, Toby." I walk over to him, give him a hug. He sits stiffly in the chair. As I hug him, I look down at his scalp. He's balding. Even more than me. Now, in addition to feeling hurt and unloved, I feel halfway dead.

*   *   *

We cross the street to have beers at the Blue Chalk Café. Toby chooses a table on the second-floor balcony overlooking the diners. He chooses it, I suspect, to ogle the Stanford girls on the floor below.

The waitress brings each of us a pint. We clink our glasses together and I say, "I'm glad to see you, Toby."

"Me, too, Dad."

I sip my beer.

Toby drinks. Not delicately: He gulps—again and again, loudly—until three quarters of the pint is gone. He slaps down his glass and says, "Ahh."

I say, "So can you spend the night?"

Toby tilts his head, looks at me quizzically. For a moment I think I have gone too far and am suffocating him. But he says, "Oh. Well, I was sort of *hoping* to stay. For a while."

"For a while?" I say. "Great." I lift my beer. Try to drink. I don't want him to feel like I'm attacking him. I need to slow down. To pause. So I count to myself: one, two, three. Okay. Now: "So how long can you stay?"

"I'm not sure. Until things, you know, kind of blow over."

"I see." I smile pleasantly. I wait for him to volunteer more information about what needs to blow over. But he's silent, sipping his depleted beer, staring at a table of cute coeds down below. He finishes the remainder of the golden liquid in his glass and slides it toward the center of the table.

"Come on," he says. "Drink up."

I drink. When I decide that Toby will volunteer nothing further about the crisis in his life, I say, "So what's going on? That you need to get away from?"

"It's no big deal. I really don't want to bother you about it."

I have a vision of the next six months: Toby sprawled on my living room floor in a sleeping bag, empty beer bottles beside him, and my tripping over him during my thrice-nightly urinations. I say, "You're not a bother, Toby."

"Well, it's like this. I think maybe I made a little mistake."

I nod. I wait. One, two, three . . . Okay: "What kind of mistake?"

"You know how I've been *cleaning up* on sports? I mean, absolutely *rocking*. I must have made ten grand during football season."

"I didn't know that."

"Well, it's not like we ever talk." He waves his hand to attract the waitress's attention. When she sees him, he holds up his empty glass and two fingers. Just in case she doesn't understand, he jitterbugs his fingers back and forth, from me to him.

He turns his attention back to me. He says, "Anyway, I was doing really awesome. It's like I have a knack, you know? So I made a couple of pretty big bets."

"How big?"

He answers another question. "The point is, I didn't even have to put up the cash. They knew I was good for it." He looks at me, as if I should be impressed.

"How much did you lose?"

"Well, it's not just how much you lose." His voice suddenly quiets. He leans forward in his chair. His eyes focus on mine. His face and posture take on a new seriousness. I've never seen him like this. He's so . . . *adult*. If we weren't talking about his impossible gambling debts, I might even be proud of him. He says: "When you can't pay what you owe on the first bet, they let you borrow and put it on the next bet. The idea is to win and then pay back everything you owe."

"But that didn't happen."

"No." He shakes his head. "No it didn't."

"How much do you owe?"

The waitress appears and puts down two more beers. My first glass is still full. She lays my new one beside it, and replaces his empty. Cheerily, she says, "Would you like to hear about our specials? We have delicious chicken fingers!"

"Chicken fingers," Toby says, with sudden childlike enthusiasm. "That sounds great."

The waitress says, "Would you like an order?"

Toby looks to me. "I'm starving. You mind, Dad?" He's not asking if I want to share them; he's asking if I'll pick up the tab.

I say, "Sure, go ahead."

"Anything else?" the waitress asks.

"That's fine for now," I say.

The waitress nods and disappears. I wait for Toby to continue
talking about his gambling debt. But he's looking around the
restaurant, scoping the women.

I say, "Toby, how much do you owe?"

For a moment, it's as if he doesn't know what I'm talking about.
Then it all comes back to him. He focuses, snaps to attention,
bears down in his chair. "Sixty," he says.

"Sixty thousand dollars?"

He shrugs and makes a little *What can you do?* smile.

I ask, "Who do you owe?"

"Well, it's these guys. Like I said, they trusted me."

"Toby—"

"I think they're mob guys. The one I deal with is named Sergei
Rock."

"Sergei the Rock?"

"No 'the.'"

"I've never heard of him."

"Well why would you?" He feigns sudden realization. "Oh, of
course. Because you're a master criminal. A con man, turned TV
star, turned con man again."

I ignore him. "Who does this Sergei Rock work for?"

"Andre Sustevich."

"Oh," I say. I *have* heard of Andre Sustevich. After La Casa
Nostra was decimated by RICO and federal prosecutions, the
Russians from Brighton Beach moved into California. Now they
run the state's prostitution and loan-sharking business. They are
smarter and more ambitious than the Italians—and a thousand
times crueler. Italy, after all, was the heart of the Roman Empire.
Some of that civilization rubbed off, even on the crooks. Sure,
the Italians are tough, but at least they have rules. The Russians
are from the cold and brutal steppes, land where civilization

never alighted, where evil is a long dark season, where you can be killed simply for looking at the wrong person at the wrong moment, where your son, and his son, and his son after that, can be sentenced to death for an intemperate remark, or a thought-less gesture.

The leader of the Armenians—or *khan*—in Northern California is Andre Sustevich. Sustevich is Russian-Armenian—and so able to command the loyalty of both groups. He's known as the Professor—either because of the Ph.D. in economics he earned from Budapest University, or because of his lifelong study of the effects of torture on the human body. I'm guessing more of the second.

I ask Toby: "Did they threaten you?"

Toby waves his hand dismissively. He smiles brightly. "Who? Guys like Sergei Rock and Andre Sustevich? Threaten? Just because I owe them sixty thousand dollars? Come on, Dad, get a grip! What kind of guys do you think they are?" In case I miss his sarcasm, he says, more quietly, through clenched teeth, "Of course they threatened me. I think they were going to mess me up, big-time. I got out of town just in time."

"You're only thirty miles away. You're not out of town."

"But they don't know I'm here."

I shake my head. I know my son. Within twenty-four hours, everyone—even people who have no idea who he is—will know he is here.

"What's your plan?" I ask.

"My plan? I'm coming to you."

"That's your plan?"

"I need your help, Dad. *Please.*"

I sigh. "Toby, I don't have sixty thousand dollars."

"Mom says you do. That you squirreled it away."

Celia is convinced that I have sequestered a fortune in Swiss bank accounts, that I have secret real estate in Florida, phantom yachts on the Riviera. I wish I were half the crime lord she thinks I am. Maybe if she entered my apartment and stepped into my bathroom, with the crap-crusted toilet bowl; or if she saw that my

TV remote is missing the Lower Volume button, forcing me to listen to everything at the same deafening loudness; or if she spent a few tedious hours with me at the dry cleaners, shrink-wrapping shirts and slacks, then she would know that I have nothing, that I am nothing except what I appear: an honest man, trying to get by. And not succeeding.

I wish she would stop telling Toby otherwise. The poor kid is doing cartwheels across a high wire, counting on a safety net that doesn't exist.

I say, "Your mom is delusional. I don't have anything to give you, Toby."

"Then what should I do?"

There is only one thing Toby can do to avoid having his brains knocked out of his skull by Russian goons. He must build a time machine in my garage. When he has done so, he must travel backward in time and then erase his bet with the bookies that work for Andre "The Professor" Sustevich.

Precluding that unlikely option, Toby must run like hell.

"You need to go somewhere," I say.

"Where?"

"I don't know. Someplace far."

"Dad, I can't run. You and Mom both live here."

For a moment, I am touched. Then I realize that ten seconds ago, Toby was asking for sixty thousand dollars. His love for me is erratic.

"Toby, if you stay here, they're going to find you."

"I was thinking maybe you can talk to them."

"Who?"

"Andre Sustevich. The Professor."

"And say what?"

"You know, that I'm good for it."

"Are you?"

He looks to me as if to ask: Are *you*?

I say, "I don't really know Sustevich."

"He knows you."

"Oh?"

"He says you were a classic."

"You talked to him?"

"Not really," Toby says, quickly. "I just heard. The thing is, I need your help."

"I want to help you, Toby. I just don't know how."

"At least let me stay at your apartment."

"Of course you can stay," I say. But I'm wondering: For how long?

I'm expecting some sort of thanks, but the kid is looking around the room for the waitress. "You want another beer?" he asks me. I'm surprised to see that he has finished his second. Before I can answer, he locks eyes with the waitress and makes a series of hand gestures like a trader in the Chicago futures pits. In seconds, another round is on the way.

CHAPTER FOUR

When I wake at five in the morning, I have suddenly become the Amazing Largo, the World's Greatest Mentalist, and all of my predictions have come true.

Start with: Toby is in the living room, sprawled across the floor in a sleeping bag, snoring. Next: that I am forced to jump over him in the dark, to empty my bladder. That when I return from the bathroom twenty minutes later, having showered and shaved, Toby has not moved. For a moment, when I hear no snoring, I fear he is dead. I imagine explaining to his mother that Toby passed away on my watch, after drinking four beers and ogling Stanford girls in a bar. But his snoring starts up again, and, relieved, I decide that, if the time ever comes, I will invent an alternate story for Celia—that Toby passed away after an edifying night at the opera.

The sun won't rise for a half-hour yet, but I must leave for work now. The competition for space on the highway has become so brutal that a narcoleptic arms race has broken out. People in California leave their homes ever earlier, just to beat the rush. Which in turn makes the rush start sooner. Which makes people leave earlier. It's a maddening cycle that has spiraled out of control. We need a UN mandate of some kind, or humanitarian intervention by Jimmy Carter, to stop this insanity, or else soon the entire Peninsula will be forced to rise at two in the morning.

In the darkness, I stumble to the kitchenette. I sweep my hand across the fridge until I find the pad of notepaper. I scribble: "Toby— See you here at six. —Dad."

I leave the apartment quietly. I don't bother locking the door behind me, because I want Toby to sleep. Jingling keys, snapping deadbolts, testing doorknobs—all will make too much noise. So, instead, I leave the apartment unguarded, accessible to anyone who cares to enter, with my son asleep inside.

In Sunnyvale, my day begins with a donut and cup of coffee at the bakery near work. I linger with a *San Jose Mercury News*, then wipe my fingers on a paper napkin. I leave a quarter as a tip. I hope that, like karma, it comes back around.

When I get to work, it's a little before six. I unlock the door and jam the doorstop to air out the perc fumes before Imelda arrives. I rotate the paper sign in the front door so it says "Come in, we're OPEN," and then retreat behind the counter.

After I serve the morning rush, Imelda arrives at ten. She wears a yellow floral dress that accentuates her facial hair. She waves a big hand at me and says, "Hello, my love!"

"Good morning, Imelda," I say. "You're perky this morning."

"Am I?" She touches a hand to her face, turns red. "I can't hide a thing, can I?"

"I guess not."

I haven't asked, but she volunteers anyway. "I'm in love."

I don't want to encourage further conversation. Imelda's sexuality—indeed, her biological sex—are her own business. Like so many other things in life, here ambiguity is delicious, certainty suffocating. I say, "I see."

"He's a terrific man," Imelda continues. "A dancer."

I try to picture a lithe Russian ballet dancer, in bed with Imelda. She adds, "A *tap* dancer."

Now Imelda's lover turns black. Gregory Hines in tights.

"We met at the Bay to Breakers. Did you know that I ran all seven miles?"

"There's a lot about you I don't know, Imelda," I say, hoping to keep it that way.

I'm relieved when the telephone rings. It's a rare occurrence at a dry cleaning shop. Customers have little reason to call. No one dials to ask, "Do you do shirts?"

Imelda places the phone on the counter. She wraps her massive hand around the receiver, as if a trinket, and lifts it to her ear. "Hel—*lo*," she sings into the phone. She listens to the voice at the other end. She says, "He's right here." She turns and hands me the phone. Her face is ashen. "It's for you."

I take the phone. "This is Kip," I say.

"Mr. Largo?" a woman's voice says.

"Yes." I have a bad feeling. "What is it?"

"Mr. Largo, this is Stanford Hospital Emergency Room. Your son, Toby, has been injured. We'd like you to come see him."

I fly up Highway 85 and cross over to 101. When I get to Palo Alto, speed limit signs become suggestions. I take Lytton across town, to avoid running over venture capitalists, who this time of year dart across Palo Alto roads like squirrels with nut on the brain.

I get to Stanford Hospital, follow the signs to "Emergency," and leave my Honda jacked on the curb in the entry circle. A black man whose job is to allow parking only for real emergencies decides, from my pallor and sweat, that I qualify. He lets me pass.

I run through the automatic sliding doors and am hit by chilled air that smells like pine oil. Before I get far, I come to the nurses' station.

"Can I help you?" a nurse asks.

"You called me. My son has been hurt. Toby Largo."

She types something into a computer, looks up. "He's okay," she says. It's as much a relief to her as to me. And I thought *I* had a lousy job. Shrink-wrapping slacks is nothing compared to telling fathers that their kids are *not* okay. "He's in room 108. Down the hall, to the left." She points.

I go to room 108. Toby is lying in bed, with his leg in a cast, raised in traction, and an IV drip in his arm. He has a huge black eye. He's awake. My ex-wife, Celia, stands over him. Somehow she always manages to beat me to Toby's side. It was the same when we were married. Even though she was the emotional and erratic one—throwing tantrums, tossing guilt like plates at a Greek wedding—Toby always remained closer to her. I was the rock, but he loved her softness.

When I enter, Celia looks up at me. I would prefer that she ignore me instead of the face I get: a combination of anger (that I let this happen to Toby), disappointment (that I'm late), and familiarity (that I'm late *as usual*). There is no empathy, that we share a love of our son. Only bitterness.

I go to Toby's side. He says in a weak voice, "Hi, Dad."

"What happened?"

"I got visited."

"Sergei the Rock?"

He tries to nod, but the gesture obviously hurts. He says, "Yeah. But no 'the.' Just Sergei Rock."

Celia pipes up. "They broke his leg and two ribs." She says it accusingly, as if I personally banged Toby around.

When I look at her, I remember why I thought she was pretty once. She has long dark hair that falls in waves past her shoulder. She's slender, with dark eyes that sparkle like firecracker fuses about to go off. Her nose is thin, with a small bump in it. But twenty-five years after I married her, the qualities that once attracted me have curdled. Long ago, her face radiated strength. Now I see circles under her eyes, and she looks tired—as if all that strength, which I loved once, took a lot out of her. Her posture, which long ago was lithe and elegant, has changed, and now looks aggressive, like a panther's, coiled and ready to strike.

I say, "Hi, Celia," as kindly as I can.

A young man in a white lab coat enters the room. He looks my son's age, with smooth baby skin. I remember that Stanford is a teaching hospital, and suddenly I feel half-dead again—shocked by the realization that the next generation of doctors, those who will soon begin treating my final-stage ailments, whatever they prove to be—heart disease, cancer, diabetes—are younger than my own child. The world moves on, relentless.

"Mr. Largo?" the young doctor says. "I'm Dr. Cole."

I shake his hand. "Hi, Doctor."

"Your son is going to be fine. He was beaten up a little. Lucky that your landlord found him so quickly."

Toby chimes in, "The young guy."

Great, I think. *Now, in addition to rent, I owe Mr. Santullo's Arabian grandson my son's life.*

Dr. Cole continues, "He's going to be okay. I was telling your wife—"

"Ex-wife," Celia says.

"Sorry. I was telling Ms. Largo that we're going to keep your son overnight for observation, make sure there's no internal bleeding. He'll probably go home tomorrow."

"That's great," I say.

Dr. Cole turns to Toby. "The police are going to come by and ask you some questions."

"Okay," Toby says.

Dr. Cole says, "I'll check in later today." To Toby: "Hang in there."

"Thanks, Doc," Toby says.

When the doctor leaves, I say to Toby, "Of course there's not much you can tell the police, since you have no idea who did this to you, or why they would want to. Since it was a random mugging."

"Okay, Dad," Toby says.

Celia shakes her head in disgust. "Can I talk to you?" she says to me. Before I can answer, she heads out of the room, supremely confident that I will follow. I raise an eyebrow at Toby and then do.

She leads me down the hall, to an alcove near the soda vending machine. We're standing near the machine's refrigeration vent, so it's hot. I immediately start to sweat.

Celia says, "What are you doing?"

"What do you mean?"

"What have you gotten him involved in?"

"Nothing. I swear. He came to me last night. I had no idea he was in town. He said he owed people money."

"What kind of people?"

"Bad."

"Why don't you give him the money?"

"I don't have it."

She shakes her head, laughs. "You expect me to believe that?"

"Celia, how many times do I have to tell you—"

"Aren't you supposed to be some master con artist? Why don't you—"

She stops. A middle-aged woman walks into the alcove, pretending not to hear our conversation. We stand aside as she goes to the soda machine. She slides a limp dollar bill into the bill reader. The machine grabs it and sucks it in. After a moment, it changes its mind, and disgorges the bill with a spiteful *whirr.*

The woman takes the dollar bill, turns it around in the other direction. Again she inserts it into the machine. The motor *whirrs,* takes her bill. The machine thinks about it. Then, again, it spits it out.

Celia and I are standing and watching the latest generation of man-machine interface. Apparently the woman decides that the third time is the charm. She flips the dollar bill over, inserts it again. *Whirr.* The machine accepts it. Longer thought this time. I have high hopes. But then, with robotic stubbornness, the machine *whirrs* and the bill shoots back out.

"Can I help you with that?" I say. I step up to the machine, reach into my pocket, and feed in four quarters. To the woman: "What would you like?"

"Diet Coke."

"You got it," I say. I press the button. A can thumps to the bottom of the machine. I reach inside, hand her the soda.

"Thank you," she says. She turns to go.

"Hey," I say.

She stops. She turns to me, looks confused.

I hold out my hand. It takes her a moment. Either out of slowness or embarrassment. I'm guessing embarrassment. Finally, she places the crinkled dollar bill in my hand.

"Thank *you*," I say.

I spend two more hours at the hospital, waiting first for the police to come and go, and then for Celia to leave. I insist on out-lasting her. Toby needs to know who loves him more. I figure I have less to rush back to—five more hours behind the counter at Economy Cleaners—while Celia can choose among lunch with the girls, a day spent shopping, maybe a game of bridge. Like a master stock investor getting out at the market top, Celia di-vorced me at just the right time, removing half my money—just months before federal prosecutors convinced the courts to dis-gorge my illegally gained profits, leaving me with zero. Somehow, she refuses to believe that I am now poor, and insists that I must have secret assets *somewhere*. I probably have a few dimes in the crannies behind my couch, but that is the extent of my secret holdings.

Toby does a fine job with the police. The Palo Alto cops send a lone detective, a young woman named, appropriately, Detec-tive Green. She takes Toby's statement, challenging nothing, asking no follow-up questions—simply accepting his story: He was heading out of my apartment for a cup of coffee when he was mugged by two black men. While it's not politically correct to admit, I'm proud of Toby's touch: He understands racism la-tent in police officers, and knows that a story about mean black men will be believed faster than a story about a mugging by two white Stanford kids. Maybe Toby has some of my street smarts, after all.

After Detective Green leaves, it takes Celia another hour before she throws in the towel. With resignation in her voice, practically admitting that I've won, she says, "Well it looks like you'll be able to stay here longer than me. So I'm going."

"That's fine," I say.

She kisses Toby goodbye, and, leaning over his bed, whispers to him, "I love you. I'll call you later."

She passes me as she leaves. She says, "Don't do anything stupid."

I'm not exactly sure what she means by this, but it's hard to object. It seems like a good rule to live your life by.

I return to my apartment at three o'clock in the afternoon. I step over blood drops on the carpet, near the entry. I look around the room, figure out the story. Muddy shoeprints, two different sets. The Professor delivered his message using two guys. Maybe one of them was Sergei Rock, his muscle. Toby's sleeping bag is on the floor, tossed open as if he just got up. I'm guessing: He heard the door open, woke, and rose to greet the men. They carried a baseball bat. They shoved him back into the room, closed the door behind them. They delivered their message. They left Toby lying unconscious, on the floor, with the door ajar.

I walk into the kitchen. There's a message on my answering machine from Peter Room, my computer programmer. "Just checking in," he says. "Call me." Which means: When will you pay me for the programming work I've done for you?

I check the bouncing vitamin on the screen in my living room. Sales since I left for work: zero. Silently, I curse American Capitalism. I try to calculate the odds of a sudden revolution, a violent overthrow of the system and redistribution of the nation's wealth. Slim, in my lifetime. I glance at the cartons of multivitamins stacked along my living room wall. There is a lot of inventory to liquidate before the Day of Reckoning comes.

There's a knock on the door. I open it to see the Arabian Grandson. He has an uncertain look.

"You come from the hospital?"

"Yeah."

"Everything okay?"

"Yes." As much as it kills me, I add: "Thanks for helping. For calling the ambulance."

"No problem," he says. He peers into the apartment behind me, at the vitamin cartons. "What's all this?"

"Nothing. Vitamins."

He thinks about it. He's trying to decide if I'm being facetious by using the word "vitamins." It sounds like a punch line. Like I'm implying: *cocaine.*

"You running a business in here?" he asks. From the way he asks, it sounds like I should say no.

"No," I say. I think about it. "Well, it's a nonprofit," I add.

He looks around the room. I can tell he wants me to invite him in, but I refuse. I stand up straight in the door frame, to block his view.

Finally, the Arabian says, "Does my grandfather know you're running a business in your apartment? I'm sure you need a license."

I'm sure you need a punch in the stomach, I want to say. But instead I say, "I wouldn't worry about it."

"I need to talk to my grandfather about this."

"You do that," I say.

There's an uncomfortable silence. Finally, he says, "I'm glad your son's okay."

"Thanks," I say, and close the door in his face.

It takes me five minutes, alone in my apartment, thinking about money I can't afford to give my son, before I call Lauren Napier's cell phone number.

It rings once, and she picks up right away. "Hello?"

"This is Kip Largo. We met at the bar a few days ago. The Blowfish."

"Right," she says. She tries to keep her voice neutral. "Well, that sounds good. But I'll need to call you back about it. Let me talk to my husband. He's right here."

"Whatever," I say. I hang up.

I go to the fridge to grab a beer. My note from this morning is still posted: "Toby— See you here at six. —Dad." It's written in a childish scrawl. I wrote it in the dark, before the sun rose. Already, this morning seems like forever ago.

I try not to think about what I'm about to do. I know I'm making a decision that will haunt me. The first danger sign: getting involved in something because you're desperate. In the history of the world, has a plan conceived in desperation ever worked? Look around at the richest, happiest, most successful people. Can you imagine any one of them gambling recklessly? It's the mark of a loser—to start a venture because you have no other choice. That's the funny thing: Winners never actually *need* to win.

But what is my choice? Toby is my son. He needs my help. In my life, I have already let him down too many times to count. What would you do, if you were me? What would you do, for your son?

I open the can of beer, sit at the table in the kitchenette. I check my watch. A little past three. Too early to drink, but with the end of my world coming, I decide to drink anyway. The beer goes down cold and easy.

In another minute, my phone rings.

"Hello," I say.

"It's me," Ms. Lauren Napier says. "Sorry about that."

"You're very naughty."

"Who told you?"

"Can you talk now?" I ask.

"I want to see you in person," she says. "We need to meet. Somewhere safe. Somewhere my husband never goes."

"There's a church around the corner from me," I say, joking.

"That sounds good," she says. She's serious.

"Fine. St. Mary's, on Homer Street, in Palo Alto. It's Catholic. I hope that doesn't bother you."

"It's not the Catholics who bother me," she says. "It's just the dirty wops."

I smile. Another danger sign: I'm starting to like her. That's when all hell breaks loose. You start to fall for a woman, and can't even see the stupid truth an inch in front of your face.

I change my clothes to get rid of the hospital smell. Maybe also because I remember Lauren Napier was an attractive woman, and you never know. I put on my best button-down shirt, blue gingham checked; a pair of linen pants; loafers. I brush my teeth, comb my hair. As I look in the mirror, I curse myself. *What are you doing, Kip? You should know better.*

I drive five blocks to St. Mary's, park around the corner. St. Mary's is built of white clapboard, with a single spire holding aloft a tasteful crucifix. It looks more Episcopalian than Catholic. That's what happens if you live in Northern California too long: No matter how radical you start out, you end up quiet, moderate, and plain. I know a Black Panther who settled here in 1972, with an Afro the size of a cosmonaut's helmet; now thirty years later he's a white man who shops at Whole Foods for organic barley.

In the church, it's dark and cool. I look around for her in the pews, but she hasn't arrived. The church is empty.

I take a seat in a middle row and stare at the altar. Above the proscenium there's a big Jesus in agony. I've been to this church four times. The first time was two weeks after I got out of prison. I went weekly for the next three Sundays. It was all part of my plan to become a different person—someone better. I ran out of steam after a month. I'm still the same person, just less ambitious.

I hear her footsteps behind me. I turn. She's wearing sunglasses again, but not Jackie O glasses. Now she has small blue lenses. Like John Lennon. With her bruises healed, she has nothing to hide.

I don't remember her being this pretty. When I saw her last, at the bar in Sunnyvale, I wasn't interested. First, she was trying to hide her face behind those ridiculous glasses. Also, she seemed out of my league: too wealthy, too beautiful—in a different class than I usually associate with.

Today she's different. She's dressed casually, in jeans and a yellow T-shirt. She looks about five years younger. Now she's one of the girls. Maybe this is the real her: blond hair pulled back in a loose ponytail, well-toned arms, little makeup.

She sits beside me in the pew. "So you've reconsidered?" she says.

For a moment, it sounds like she's talking about how I feel about her.

"Maybe," I say.

"It's a simple job."

"I'm sure at some point you'll tell me what the job is."

"You do what you're good at. You keep a hundred thousand dollars."

"And what am I good at, exactly?"

She smiles. She opens her purse, takes out two photocopied sheets of paper. She hands them to me.

It's a copy of an article from *San Francisco* magazine, from six years ago, called "The Return of the Big Con." It was published during my trial. It was a puff piece about me and some of the cons I've run: the fake antique shop in Cape Cod, the swamp land timeshare in Florida, the unclaimed funds scam in Knoxville. Any other businessman welcomes a glossy profile in a magazine. But in my kind of business, it's the kiss of death. Also, it doesn't help convince the jury that they have the wrong man.

"That article isn't even halfway accurate," I protest. Which is true. The author didn't know about half of the scams I committed, before I hit the big time with Diet Deck. She had some of the details right: that my dad was a grifter, that I grew up running Pigeon Drops with him, that I put it all aside to enroll in CUNY when I was twenty, to become a lawyer and go legit, but that—finally—with my father dying and my mother alone and helpless, I turned to the only career that was a sure thing: parting people from their money, by any means possible.

"I thought it was romantic," she said.

Everyone thinks cons are romantic. They see too many movies. In real life, cons are about ripping off old people, swindling workingmen out of their pensions, pretending to be in love with the ugly girl to get her bank account. There's nothing romantic about them. Except that suitcase of cash under your bed.

I fold the article in half, stick it in my shirt pocket.

"What do you want me to do?"

"My husband," she says, as if that explains everything. She sees I need more. "I want you to take money from him. I want you to steal it."

"You know, this is why I always put down the toilet seat when I was married. Women hold grudges."

"Do you know much about my husband?"

"Just that he's the kind of guy you shouldn't mess with."

"No," she says. "He's the kind of guy you shouldn't get *caught* messing with."

I shrug.

"I met him four years ago," she says. "I was eighteen. Modeling. Just runway, nothing exciting. We met at a Galante show. He was forty-six. He swept me off my feet. Picked me up in limousines. Flew me across the country in his private jet. To his own hotel. A huge suite. I gave up everything for him. *Everything.*" She says the word through clenched teeth. I try to imagine what kinds of things a naive eighteen-year-old girl gives up to a forty-six-year-old man. When I figure it out, I decide I'll need to shower again when I get home.

I ask: "And now what?"

"He's not the man I thought he was."

I think to myself: *So he hits you. Tough luck. Leave him.*

As if she has read my mind, she says, "I want to leave him, but I can't."

"Why's that?"

"I signed an agreement. If we divorce, I leave with nothing."

"You *came* with nothing."

"The reason I can't leave is because of what he said."

"What'd he say?"

"He told me what would happen if I left."

"What would happen?" I ask, even though I know.

"He said he'd spend every cent he had tracking me down. Then he'd—"

She stops at the sound of footsteps approaching behind us. I turn and see an old woman, with a cane, hobbling up the aisle to the apse of the church. We wait for her to pass. She reaches the altar, kneels, lays down her cane. She bows her head in prayer.

Lauren continues. More softly now: "He said he'd track me down. Then he'd kill me."

"And so you want to steal all his money."

She smiles. "I'm no angel. I never said I was. But I need that money. To get away. You don't know my husband. He's a monster."

"How can that be? *People* magazine named him one of the Sexiest Men Alive."

"Not to me," she says, dreamily, as if remembering some of the instances when he acted less than sexy. "I need money to get away from him. I'll go someplace, maybe back east. Maybe Paris. I'll start somewhere new. I still have a long life ahead of me."

"How much do you want me to steal?"

"I don't know. Twenty million dollars?"

"Oh, sure," I say. "That sounds reasonable."

"But he's worth billions . . ."

"So let's see. I steal twenty million. And I get to keep a hundred grand. That's mighty generous."

She waves her hand. "Fine. What's fair? I mean, in your . . ." She thinks about it. "In your line of work?"

"Think of me like a waiter. You know, the guy that brings your dinner in those fancy restaurants? How much do you tip him?"

"Ten percent."

"Come on. The waiter at Evvia."

"Twenty percent."

"Now you're talking."

"On twenty million dollars . . ."

"Right."

"That's a lot of money."

"It's a delicious dinner."

She smiles. She has big white teeth, perfectly straight. She takes off her sunglasses, snaps them shut. Finally I see her eyes. Blue and yellow, feline. "You drive a hard bargain."

"Not hard enough," I say. "That's always been my problem."

"Will you do it?"

"You know, I could take his money and not give you a cent."

"But then you'd never have a chance with me."

"A chance? For what?"

Our eyes lock, and for the first time, I realize I'm infatuated with her.

CHAPTER FIVE

In a con man's lingo, the roper is the person that interests the mark in the story. The roper ropes the mark into the con. Usually this happens by appealing to the mark's greed, or vanity, or genitals. Or all three.

CHAPTER SIX

Pulling off a Big Con is like climbing Mount Everest. It's all about logistics. Whether you succeed has little to do with how you climb; it has everything to do with preparation. Once you start the ascent, your success or failure has already been determined. Did you stock your base camp adequately? Did you hire the best sherpa guides? Are you in good health? Is your equipment top-notch? Can you trust your fellow climbers to guard your lines?

So before I steal twenty million dollars, I need to make sure things stay copacetic at base camp. I can't have my son beaten up or killed while I'm in the middle of the con. Before anything else, I need to make sure Toby is safe.

How do you convince a gangster not to kill your son? Easy. Make it worth his while. The first step is to get face time. In the case of Andre Sustevich, the Professor, nothing can be simpler. All I need to do is ring his doorbell.

Sustevich lives in an estate in Pacific Heights. He settled in San Francisco, he told a reporter once, because it reminded him of Moscow: cold, gray, and depressing. This afternoon, when I drive up to his compound, I think that, living here, I would not be depressed. The house was built by one of San Francisco's railroad barons in the 1890s and escaped the earthquake and fire of 1906. It occupies an entire city block. The house is a Queen Anne Victorian, with elaborate wooden gables, a circular corner tower, and ostentatious ornamentation. The exterior wood is painted lemon yellow, perhaps to ward off the depression that must come when you live in a sixteen-room mansion with unobstructed views of the Bay and the Golden Gate Bridge.

I park my car at the end of the block and approach the house. It is surrounded by formal gardens with topiaries shaped like animals—a swan, a boar, an elephant—all things you want to kill or eat. The gardens are separated from the street by a black wrought iron gate. A bruiser of a man, dressed in a suit that fits him like a sausage skin, stands guard. He wears a delicate featherweight headset with a microphone. The getup looks out of place, like a linebacker with a tiara.

"Hello," I say to him. "I'm here to see Andre Sustevich."

"Do you have an appointment?" He speaks with a thick Russian accent.

"No," I say, "but could you kindly tell him that my name is Kip Largo. I'm the father of Toby Largo and I want to pay Mr. Sustevich one million dollars."

The man nods as if this sort of thing happens all the time: a stranger stopping by offering a million dollars. He lowers the headset microphone to his mouth and says something in Russian. I hear the names Kip, Largo, and Toby, but am not sure if they are attached to Russian words for *ridiculous old man* and *hopeless load of a son*.

After a moment, the Russian bruiser lifts the microphone from his mouth and turns to me. "Mr. Sustevich will see you," he says. "Please come with me."

He pulls the black gate and it creaks open. I step inside the garden. From the house another big Russian emerges. He has short blond hair and shoulders like ham hocks. I feel like I've stumbled into Goldsky's Gym on the Dnieper.

The blond man says, "Please lift your arms." I raise my hands above my shoulders. The blond man pats down my shirt, my rib cage, the small of my back. He gingerly cups my testicles. I feel like telling him not to worry—now *there's* a weapon I haven't used in about six years. Satisfied that I'm not packing heat, or wearing a bomb vest, the blond man escorts me into the house.

First stop, a huge foyer, two stories tall, with alternating black and white square marble floor tiles. Because—for two months of my former life, when I was rich, I shopped for a house like this— I know that these tiles are Italian Carrera, $13 per square foot. A grand circular staircase sweeps up to the second floor, where a balcony with a sitting area overlooks the entry.

The blond man stops in the foyer and turns to me. "Do you have a cell phone?"

At first I think he's asking to borrow it, maybe to make a personal call to Minsk. Then I understand. Cell phones can house all sorts of electronics. Bugs, homing devices, cameras. I take out my Motorola, hand it to him. "I'll return it when you leave," he says.

Damn right you will, I think, recalling the two hundred dollars I laid out for it, back when it was the latest model.

I follow the blond man into a large living room, with panoramic windows that look onto the garden, and then, further out, past a steep hill, onto the San Francisco Bay. Through the fog I can see the Golden Gate Bridge.

The blond man gestures to a couch and leaves. I sit down and stare at the walls. They're stark white, hung with large canvases that I find inscrutable: shapes and colors, black and white, splatters of red. These are either pieces of modern art or police sketches from a crime scene.

After a few minutes, I hear footsteps behind me. I turn to see a middle-aged man—thin, bespectacled, with closely cropped gray hair—stride into the room. The first thing I think is that he really does look like a professor, and that the only menace he can muster is the threat of giving me a D on a final exam. The second thing I think is that he is responsible for roughing up my son, breaking his leg, and scaring the shit out of me.

The man strides toward me with an outstretched hand. "Mr. Largo?" he says. I rise from the couch, shake his hand. He says, with a Russian accent, "This is a pleasant surprise."

"I was in the neighborhood," I say. "So I thought I'd drop by for blini and caviar."

He looks genuinely surprised, as if I really did want refreshments and he had rudely neglected to offer them. "Oh? Would you like something? Really? Perhaps tea?"

"No," I say, "I'm just kidding."

"I see." He gestures for me to sit. He remains standing. "Now, let me see. You are *who* exactly?"

I have a feeling that he knows who I am. Exactly. Surely a Russian so obsessed with security that he demands to have your balls fondled and your cell phone confiscated would not let a complete stranger walk into his house without an appointment, on the strength of a vague promise of a million-dollar payoff.

But I play along. "My son is Toby Largo," I say. "I understand he owes you some money."

He shakes his head and waves his fingers around, as if these petty details were literally buzzing around his face like gnats, annoying him. "So many people owe money," he says. It's unclear if he is apologizing for not knowing my son, or is lamenting the shiftlessness of society in general.

"My son dealt with a gentleman that works for you. Sergei the Rock."

"Sergei the . . ." his voice trails off. He seems puzzled. Then he understands. "No 'the.' Just Sergei Rock." He says it *Roke*—like egg yolk. With the Russian accent, it doesn't sound quite so ridiculous.

"Yes," I say. "Sergei Roke."

Sustevich turns to the doorway behind him. Without raising his voice, he says quietly, "Dmitri."

The blond man who got to third base with me appears in the room. Sustevich speaks quickly in Russian. I hear the word *Sergei*.

The blond man nods and disappears.

"I will get him," the Professor explains to me, as if I am a simpleton and cannot possibly understand what has just happened.

After a moment another man enters the room. It requires great effort for me not to laugh. Which part of what I see is most ridiculous? Is it that the man wears an expensive Armani suit, despite being shaped like a weightlifter, as squat and wide as he is tall? Or that a purple scar runs down his face, from chin to forehead, like a cheap Halloween appliqué? Or is it the scene in general: that a

Russian mobster called the Professor—who is quiet and effete, with Modern Art–bedecked walls, elegant spectacles, and a view of the Bay—is surrounded by beefy knuckleheads out of a Soviet gangster film?

Sergei the Rock, or Sergei Roke, or whatever he calls himself, trudges toward me. The Professor says, "Sergei, this gentleman is named Key Largo."

"Kip," I say. "Kip Largo."

Ignoring me, still addressing Sergei: "You do business with his son?"

Sergei smiles. He reveals a set of chipped teeth like a hacksaw blade. "Yes." He seems to have fond memories of yesterday's business meeting with Toby.

Sustevich turns to me. "Apparently you are correct."

"Good to hear."

Sustevich asks Sergei something in Russian. The huge gorilla answers in English: "Sixty thousand."

Sustevich nods. He says something to Sergei in Russian. Sergei grunts and leaves the room.

"Why have you come here?" Sustevich asks me. "Do you dispute this debt?"

"No. I'm sure my son owes it." I can't help myself: As I say it, my mind shuffles through memories of times Toby has disappointed me. Failing biology, summer school, dropping out of UCSC, the arrest for selling pot. "But I want to propose a business deal with you."

The Professor nods. "Ah, business," he says. He seems to like that idea. "Then let us walk in the garden."

He leads me across the living room, his footsteps echoing on the twelve-foot-tall ceilings. He opens a sliding door, and steps down onto the grass. We walk into the topiary garden. The afternoon is cool and overcast. I follow him for a few yards and then I am face-to-face with an elephant formed from English box.

"Do you know what this is?" Sustevich asks me.

I think he's talking about the topiary. "An elephant?" I say.

"No, I mean *this*." He sweeps his arm grandly, taking in the garden, the mansion, the view of the Bay. "Do you know what all *this* is?"

"No," I say. "What?"

"This is the result of very many business deals, all of them wise."

"Ah," I say. "I see."

"So what kind of business do you have for me?"

I sense a presence behind us. I turn and am surprised to see another beefy Russian, this one with hair as dark as the Moscow River. He hangs back, trailing us discreetly by ten yards. He wears another feather headphone. I did not hear him come from the house, nor see him in the garden when we entered.

"My son owes you sixty thousand dollars. I'll make good on it, and then I'll pay you several million more."

Sustevich has the look of a professor considering a novel academic theory. Yes, it might shake the foundations upon which the entire discipline is built, but he will have to consider it all the same, gentlemen! He keeps his face blank as he weighs the evidence, pro and con. He reaches into his pocket and takes out a Marlboro hard pack. He removes a cigarette and strikes a paper match. He lights the cigarette, takes a drag, and then throws the match, still burning, into the grass. It flares out and dies.

To my surprise, the dark-haired Russian goon scrambles over, bends down, retrieves the match from the grass, and then retreats to his spot ten yards away.

Sustevich sees me watching this. He looks amused. "You see? The science of economics at work. Comparative Advantage. David Ricardo. I am better at thinking about business than poor Hovsep is. Even though Hovsep is not particularly good at picking up matches from the ground, indeed doing a very incompetent job at it"—he shoots the dark-haired goon a dirty look—"he is *less* bad at it than I am. And I am better at using my brain." He says something in Russian to Hovsep. The words sound angry. Hovsep, with a frightened look on his face, scuttles back to the Professor's feet, sinks to his hands and knees, and searches the grass, separating the blades with his fingers as if hunting for a dropped diamond.

Finally he finds what he is looking for: a tiny nub of the match—just the head, now a black cinder. He shows the Professor the match head in his fingers and backs away once again.

"Fascinating," I say.

Returning to my business proposition, Sustevich says, "And why this generosity to me? Why offer me millions of extra dollars?"

"Because I'm going to ask you for two things in exchange."

"Yes," he says, as if he had expected that I would say something like this. "Economics is all about exchange, isn't it?"

"Right," I say. "Whatever." I walk on ahead, toward the swan topiary. I admire the level of detail: the thin beak, the raised left wing, as if the boxwood is about to take off in flight. I run my hand over the graceful, arched neck. I turn to Sustevich. "I think you know who I am."

I expect Sustevich to deny it, to keep up the charade that I am a random visitor off the street. But he is too smart for this, and his time is too valuable. He says, "Yes. You are Kip Largo. You are a con man. I know all about you."

"Then you know what I do for a living."

"No different than what I do. No different than what Gucci does, or Steven Wynn, or Ralph Lauren. Yes? You take people's money, in exchange for an illusion."

"I appreciate your kind words," I say, not completely certain they were meant to be kind.

"And so, my con man friend," Sustevich says, "what do you want from me?"

"It's what you want from me," I say. "I'm going to give you the chance to invest in one of my . . . business deals."

"I see."

"In exchange, you get a share of the profits."

"And what kind of business deal is this?"

"I'm afraid I can't tell you that. I can only tell you that the returns are expected to be quite significant."

He nods. "Ah," he says. He thinks about it. "I received a call the other day. A venture capitalist, investing exclusively in e-commerce deals. You know, books over the Web. Wine over the Web. Shoes over the Web. Toys over the Web. Web, Web, Web. Everything over the Web."

"I hope no vitamins."

Sustevich ignores me. "Anyway, this venture capitalist promised me thirty percent per year, minimum."

"I can beat that," I say quickly.

"Oh?"

"I'll double your money in two months."

"Double my money? In two months?" He turns to Hovsep, who is still pale and trembling from the match fiasco. "Hovsep, do you hear that? Mr. Largo offers to double my money in two months. Would you invest in such a deal?"

The Russian looks uncertain. Is this another test? He thinks about his answer. Finally, quietly, with uncertainty in his voice, he says—more like a question than an answer: "No?"

"No?" Sustevich asks, as if to a stupid student. *"No?"*

"No," Hovsep repeats. I know what he's thinking: that with a man like Sustevich, confidence in your answer is more important than the answer itself. So Hovsep repeats, trying to sound confident, "I say: Do not invest in this business deal."

"No?" Sustevich says again, raising his voice. "Come here." He gestures for the dark-haired Russian to approach. Hovsep sidles over, looking frightened.

The Professor puts his face just inches from Hovsep's. "You would not invest in a deal that promises to double your money in two months?"

"Well," Hovsep says, now sounding uncertain. "Maybe I would."

Big mistake. With a quickness that surprises me, the Professor swings his hand and slaps Hovsep across the cheek. The flesh makes a loud snap. "Are you stupid?" the Professor asks. "You would not invest in a deal that doubles your money in two months? Do you not understand? That is a six hundred percent annualized return!"

"Yes," Hovsep says. His cheek has a big red handprint. "Now I understand."

"Ach," Sustevich says, disgusted. He waves his hand, dismissing

Hovsep. "Go away. This is why you pick up matches and I do the thinking."

"Yes," Hovsep agrees. He looks relieved that he has been given his walking papers. He backs away, like a nervous courtier from an insane king.

Sustevich says to me apologetically, "You must forgive Hovsep. He is a very stupid man."

"But he's good with the matches," I volunteer.

Sustevich returns to the deal. "How much do I need to invest in this business venture?"

Even though I already know the answer, I pretend to think about it out loud. "Well, let's see. I basically need the start-up capital. To run the con. You know, setting up an office, IT infrastructure, legal and accounting. I have to hire about a dozen people. And of course there's the luxury speedboat I've had my eye on."

Sustevich looks at me. "Really?" he says. Apparently my sense of humor loses something in translation.

"No," I say, "just kidding. About the speedboat."

"So how much?" Sustevich asks.

"Six million dollars," I say.

"And you'll return twelve?"

"Of course."

"Fine," Sustevich says. His eyes flit out to the Bay, and already he is thinking about something else. "I hate this weather," he says. "Always gray."

"Fine?" I ask. His quick acceptance of my terms make me regret not asking for more.

"Yes, yes," he says. He waves his fingers. "And what is the second request?"

I'm so taken aback by the speed that things are moving I have no idea what he's talking about.

Sustevich reminds me. "You said you had two requests. For us to do business together."

"Right. Well, there's the money. And then there's my son. I want you to leave Toby alone while I carry out this business transaction."

"I see."

"So do we have a deal?"

"Yes," he says. "Is that all?"

I nod.

"Dmitri," he says quietly, as if the man were standing right beside him. Amazingly, within seconds, Dmitri strolls out of the mansion and across the grass toward us. Sustevich says to him: "We will invest six million dollars in Mr. Largo's new business venture."

"Yes, Professor," Dmitri says.

"And you will tell Sergei to leave Mr. Largo's son alone."

"Yes, Professor."

To me, he says: "You will call Dmitri when you are ready for us to wire the money into your bank account. Please open an account at Bank of Northern California. I have made special accommodations with them."

I sense that these accommodations involve payments to top executives to ignore money laundering laws, and incentives to IT managers to rewrite the watchdog software that flags suspicious account activity. I admire the Professor's audacity.

"Dmitri," the Professor says.

"Yes, Professor?"

As if he is a travel agent describing a potential itinerary for a pleasant day trip, Sustevich says, "If Mr. Largo does not return twelve million dollars to our account in two months, you will kill him. And his son."

"How, Professor?" Dmitri asks.

"However you like."

Dmitri smiles.

Sustevich thinks about it for a moment. Suddenly, his control-freak nature shines through. "No," he says, nixing the *however you like* idea. "You will use acid."

"Yes, Professor," Dmitri says. He looks disappointed. Whether this is because the use of acid is unpleasant and messy, or because the request stifles Dmitri's creativity, I am unsure.

"You are a pleasure to do business with," Sustevich says to me.

"Likewise," I say. But all I can think about is: not to forget my cell phone on the way out.

CHAPTER SEVEN

I leave Sustevich's and take I-280 out of the city. The highway meanders along foothills, overlooking ravines of junipers and blue gorged lakes. Its path is gentle; its views scenic. Few know that the route follows, with cartographic precision, the exact path of the San Andreas Fault. You actually needle your car through a narrow channel of space between two tectonic plates. On each side of you is an ancient undersea continent, a landmass more vast than all of North America; and each half of the earth is caught, like a bolt of satin on a tack, straining to rip free and fall to its natural place—on top of you. This realization, which comes to me each time I drive this road, is one more confirmation of my theory of life: that beauty always hides something, that everything you enjoy has a secret price.

Driving south, with six million dollars of funding backing my plan, I feel the game afoot, and the effect is physiological: My heart speeds, my breathing deepens. Like a sprinter stepping into the starting block, my reactions are involuntary, but not unwelcome. I know that I am doomed, that this venture is destined to fail, but—on the other hand—how many more years can I work at Economy Cleaners? How many more jackets and shirts can I retrieve from the motorized hanger racks, how many pasta stains can I mark carefully with fluorescent tape? I will call Imelda tomorrow and tell her that I must quit, that family obligations require my concentration elsewhere. She will cluck her tongue at me, and say knowingly, "Kip, my dear, what are you doing? Don't you know where this leads?" And I will have no answer, because she will be right. Where this leads is back to a prison cell, if I'm lucky, or to an earlier death than I have planned.

But it is the only path I see. My son needs me. Without my help, he will end up dead. For just a moment, I have a flash, a clarion realization, that my situation is not unique. That all the paths we choose are determined earlier, by decisions made years ago, sometimes before we are born; and that choices we seem to make are not really choices at all. My fate, to wind up back in Lompoc, with two strikes to my name, was written the day I was born to Carlos Largo, carny and small-time grifter, a man distant and reproachful to his son, because *his* father was that way to him. And so I am destined to either repeat his mistakes, or seek redemption for them—by stepping into hell for my own son.

The hurt will stop with me, I decide, and I will seek redemption for us all.

At Palo Alto, it's a straight shot from I-280 to Sand Hill Road. Maybe this is why I chose the route: not the views of the ravines, but because I know it passes a hundred yards from the Stanford Hospital, where my son, Toby, lies.

I park in the hospital's underground lot—no emergency today—and ascend to retrieve my son. The doctors said he would be free to leave this afternoon. Of course I will offer my apartment to him—even my bed, for he cannot sleep on the floor with a broken leg and two cracked ribs. It will be a small hardship, to tend to him—to help him bathe, and feed him, and keep him occupied—while also planning the con against Ed Napier; but I am willing. Now that I have extracted the Professor's promise that Toby is safe, at least for a while, keeping him around will be good for him, and for me. I am looking forward to the chance to be a father again.

The elevator ascends from the garage to the first floor. It empties next to the nurses' station. I start to walk past, to the room where I found Toby yesterday, but I am stopped by a male nurse. "May I help you?"

"I'm here for my son. Toby Largo. He's in room 108."

I turn, but the nurse says, "Toby Largo? He's gone."

I look up. The nurse is double-checking his computer screen, pecking on keys. "Yup," he says. "Checked out about an hour ago."

"Checked out? Can he even *walk?*"

"He had some help. His mother came."

Damn Celia. Once again, I do the heavy lifting—walking un-invited into a Russian crime boss's mansion, extracting a promise of safety for my son, signing my life as surety bond—but Celia claims victory by flitting into the hospital at the last moment and sweeping Toby away to a glorious homecoming.

My rage must show, because the nurse says, "Mr. Largo, are you okay?"

I try to smile. "Fine. I guess we crossed wires."

"They're probably home right now, waiting for you," the nurse says. He is trying to be helpful, but unfortunately he is only half-correct. They are home, but not waiting for me.

"Thank you."

I return to my car and pull back onto Sand Hill. I should not focus on Toby and Celia—there is too much else to do: I need to call work and quit; to begin planning the con, assembling my team; to start considering scenarios, and counterscenarios, and alterna-tives, and counteralternatives. But this rankles. I am about to give up everything, the normality and boredom I have for so long sought, and, at the very least, I hoped for some thanks.

I take my cell phone from my jacket and dial Celia's number. The phone rings four times, and her answering machine picks up. "This is Celia and Carl," she says, "we're not home, but please leave a message." I am surprised to hear the man's name. It has been a long time since I called her, and I had no idea she was even dating, let alone living with someone. I try to imagine what Toby will think of this, relegated to the couch while his mother and a strange man make love in the next bedroom.

I hang up without leaving a message. Another thought comes to me. That doing right ought to be its own reward, and that I shouldn't expect praise or thanks for doing it.

I mull this over for about a second, and then decide that, even so, it wouldn't have killed either of them to call.

CHAPTER EIGHT

Let me tell you how to run your own Bank Examiner Scam.

First, find a victim. The elderly are best, but almost anyone will do. The important thing is that they live alone. So: Widowers and widows are good—people without friends and family, people so lonely that a strange voice on a telephone is a welcome intrusion into their miserable lives.

Once you find a victim, you need to collect information. You want a bank account number, maybe a list of some recent banking transactions. Nothing high-tech here. Just open people's mailboxes when no one is around, and look for envelopes from banks.

One nice trick: Bust the mailman's lock on an apartment's communal mailbox. It will take two days for the landlord to notice and fix it. Return to the busted mailbox after the next mail delivery. You'll feel like an addict in the pharmacist's supply closet. Look for mailboxes with envelopes from the AARP.

Once you find a bank statement addressed to a widow or widower, bring it home. Make a copy of the contents. Reseal the envelope. Remail it to your victim.

Wait a week.

Now the fun begins. Call your victim on the telephone. Introduce yourself as, say, Frank Marley, bank examiner at Wells Fargo (or wherever your victim banks). Say something like, "Mr. Jones, we have a bit of an embarrassing predicament here at Wells Fargo. We suspect that one of the tellers at your branch is dishonest. She is stealing money from several customers' accounts, including yours."

My goodness, the victim will say. *How much was stolen?*

"Well, let me go through your records," you'll say. "First, would you mind confirming your identity for me? Does the following information ring a bell?"

At this point, recount to your victim all of the banking information you've stolen from him. "You're account number 444-555, right?" you'll ask. "You deposited $675 dollars on March 3rd, right? And you withdrew $400 on March 15th, right?"

Why, yes, your victim will say.

"Ah, that's what I was afraid of. It seems we *do* have a problem. The bank teller skimmed a hundred dollars out of your account during your last withdrawal. Overall, the bank teller has stolen about two thousand dollars from your account, since the beginning of last year."

"My goodness," the victim will fret. "How is it possible that I did not notice this?"

Ignore the question. Say: "Mr. Jones, we really need your help. We want to catch this bank teller in the act. This will speed up the process of returning the money that was stolen from your account. Also, I think I'm allowed to tell you that Wells Fargo will offer a reward of a thousand dollars for your help in catching this criminal."

The victim will now be perfectly played: upset at being ripped off, excited about the thousand-dollar reward. "What do I have to do?" he'll say.

"It's very simple. We have our suspicions about how the bank teller is stealing from customers, but we need to confirm them. As you know, the bank is monitored by closed-circuit television cameras. We'll need to study these videotapes very carefully. What I'd like you to do is to visit your branch at one o'clock today, and withdraw four thousand dollars in hundred-dollar bills. It's very important that you do not touch the bills yourself. Ask the teller to place the bills in an envelope for you."

I see, the victim will say.

"Mr. Jones, here's the important part. I am not sure how many employees at your branch are involved in this scheme. That is why you *must not mention a word of this to anyone*. If you tell anyone what you're doing, you will jeopardize our entire investigation."

"All right," Mr. Jones will say.

"Now then, once you withdraw the four thousand dollars, the cash needs to be examined. Please drive to the parking lot behind the Kmart. My partner, Examiner Sam Smith, will meet you there, and will inspect the envelope. Do you understand?"

"Yes, I suppose," Mr. Jones will say.

At one o'clock, you will send your accomplice to the Kmart parking lot. "Sam Smith" will pull up alongside the victim, and climb into the victim's vehicle. Smith will produce a business card that says something like: "Sam Smith, Internal Controls, Wells Fargo."

"Nice work," Sam Smith will say. He'll ask to see the envelope full of cash.

The examiner will inspect the contents of the envelope. He'll make a point to scrupulously record the serial number of each hundred-dollar bill on a piece of paper marked "Investigation Records."

He'll write a receipt for four thousand dollars and hand it to the victim. He'll say, "Make sure you hold on to this receipt. When the investigation is over, we'll return the four thousand to you, plus the thousand-dollar reward for your trouble. Don't lose that receipt, though."

"Okay," the victim will say. "What happens next?"

"Next you should return home and act like nothing happened. We'll call you later tonight to let you know how the investigation is going. But please, Mr. Jones, do not breathe a word of this to anyone. We've worked long and hard on this investigation. If it's disclosed now, it'll be ruined."

"I understand," Mr. Jones will say.

The victim ought to be good for two or three further plays. Want to take more cash from him? Call him again that night, posing as Mr. Marley, the bank examiner. Compliment him on a job well done. Tell him that, thanks to his help, the bank and police have narrowed down the list of suspected dishonest tellers to two or three. Only a few more withdrawals will be required to determine the identity of the thief with certainty.

Arrange a few more withdrawals, and a few more meetings with Sam Smith.

As soon as you've taken everything you think the mark is good for, or as soon as you sense the slightest doubt in the mark's voice, disappear for a few weeks. You'll be able to return later, for one more big score.

CHAPTER NINE

My night begins with a phone call to Peter Room, my computer programmer. Peter is surprised to hear my voice. I have been avoiding his calls for so long, unable to pay him for his work on MrVitamin.com, that my sudden reaching out to him, unprompted, is like a miraculous visitation by the angel Gabriel.

"Kip?" he says. "Why are you calling?"

"I owe you money," I say. "I'll have it in a few days."

"No, it's no big deal," he says. Peter is a member of the elite caste of programmers in Silicon Valley. Unlike their peers, who have permanent jobs at companies, these coding Marines parachute from gig to gig, hired as temps—brought in as expensive firepower to turn around a failing project, or meet an impossible deadline, or rewrite a program after a botched release. They command extraordinary rates—two hundred, three hundred dollars an hour—and some even have agents, like pro athletes, who wheel and deal to sell their clients' services to the highest bidder.

These programming jobs last for a month, sometimes two or three at most—and then the coders disappear from the real world of employment and paychecks for half a year at a time, to surf in Oahu, or hike through Nepal, or just sit and get stoned in their apartment in Palo Alto, until the money runs low and they are forced, despite their own wishes, to land another job, and start the process again.

Peter's calls to me, seeking to collect the several thousand dollars I owe him for MrVitamin, started three weeks ago. I suspect that it was around this time that Peter's hoard of cash ran out, and he was trying everything—even hopeless dreams, like collecting from me—to delay working for a few months longer.

Now, when I call him, offering to pay, he's suddenly no longer concerned. Which means he has a new job.

"It's no big deal, Kip," he tells me. "It's like, whenever you can, man."

His sudden indulgence is bad news for me and my plans. I want him hungry.

"You know I'm a man of my word," I say. "I owe you, and I'm ready to pay." Actually, I think to myself, I'm *almost* ready to pay. As soon as Sustevich's wire can be arranged, a few days from now. But I spare him the details. "Also, I want to get together with you," I say. "I have a new project. I need some advice."

"Uh-oh," Peter Room says. "Bad news, man. I just landed a new gig. You know that company that Linus joined? Totally top secret? How they're going to launch in three months?"

"Yeah, sure," I lie.

"Well, they're not," Peter says, as if this information will prove delicious to me.

"You don't say."

"Anyway, I've signed on with them until September. I'm off the market."

"That's fine. I wasn't really looking to hire you. This job isn't exactly . . ." I let my voice trail off. More softly, full of innuendo, I say: ". . . *Kosher.*"

"You're kidding me."

"I just need some advice. That's all. Maybe you can point me in the right direction. About technical stuff."

As I expected, the hint that I am planning something illegal titillates Peter. He has spent his entire life in front of a computer screen, writing code. The most illegal thing he ever did was a bong the size of a saxophone. I am his single tenuous link to a dark and exciting world. I suspect he brings up my name every opportunity he has to impress a woman. "You know that dude from the Diet Deck?" he says to his quarries at those depressing bars he frequents. "The one who went to prison? I worked for him for a couple of years. We were practically partners."

"We can meet," Peter says to me, a bit too excited.

"You sure?" I say. "I know you started another gig . . ."

"Well it's just a meeting, right? You're just looking for some advice."

"That's right."

"How about Zott's," Peter says, "in about an hour?"

Zott's is a bar that lies between Palo Alto and nowhere. That's a literal fact. At the edge of the city is a band of unincorporated land, neither Palo Alto nor nearby Portola Valley. It's a strip of grassland that runs along the foothills, an area quilted with state-mandated open-space preserves. Building anything, even a trail or a fence, is prohibited. The few structures that exist were grandfathered in when the fanatical green laws arrived from Sacramento twenty years ago. There is no building other than Zott's for hundreds of yards in any direction.

Zott's was originally a stable, where horses slept and crapped. During Prohibition, it was bought by the Zoteratelli family, and it became a saloon that served Stanford students. In an age when new Italian immigrants were considered dirty and dangerous, their language hopelessly exotic, the white-bread sons of the railroad barons who attended Stanford shortened the name of their new refuge to Zott's. For generations the name has remained, and so, too, has the bar, almost exactly the way it was in the 1880s. There's still a trough and hitches for your horse near the entrance. Inside, the concrete floor is covered with leaves and twigs and mud.

Tonight the bar is filled with Stanford types, packed into the booths, watching a Giants baseball game on the television behind the bar. I see Peter Room in the corner, waiting for me. He has long red hair, past the middle of his back, gathered in a loose ponytail. He has freckles, big white buck teeth like a rabbit. He wears a black T-shirt that says, "Code Warrior." The moment I see him, I think he is perfect for the part. You can't make guys like him up.

He sees me and waves. I sit down in the booth across from him. We knock knees.

"Kip, man," he says. I see he already has a beer.

"Can I get you a beer?" I ask anyway, secretly relieved that I may be able to get through this meeting buying only one drink. I have fifteen dollars in my wallet, which needs to last until I can get the new bank account set up and funded with Sustevich's start-up capital.

"Nah, got one."

"Okay," I say. "Hang on."

I leave the table, go to the bar. At Zott's, the bartender is also a short-order cook. There are beer taps on one side of him, a griddle with hamburgers frying on the other. He's a middle-aged man who wears a grease-stained apron over a fat belly. The stains on the apron are in the shape of swiped fingers. I have a suspicion that the apron is not removed during trips to the bathroom.

Nevertheless suddenly I'm starving. I haven't eaten since this morning. And now that I don't have to buy Peter anything, I feel flush. So I order a cheeseburger and an Anchor Steam.

"You want fries with that?" the bartender asks.

"They cost extra?"

"Fifty cents."

"No thanks."

I return to Peter with my beer and a tab of paper that serves as a claim for my burger. I see him eyeing the paper. "Did you want a burger?" I ask.

"I guess not."

"Anyway," I say, changing the subject, "thanks for meeting me."

"Sure. What's going on? How've you been? Since . . . *you know.*"

Peter means prison.

"Hanging in there."

"How's Mr. Vitamin? I love that idea."

"It's good," I say. I think about it. "Well, not as good as I hoped."

"You selling anything?"

"A couple bottles a day."

"That's a start," Peter offers.

I think that it is a start, all right, on the path back to Lompoc. "Yeah," I say. "I guess."

"I admire what you're doing. Starting over."

When I met Peter six years ago, he was a kid finishing his degree at Stanford, living in a dormitory with a paper globe over his light bulb, and I was a successful entrepreneur pulling in a million a month and living in a four-bedroom Tudor in Professorville. It was my job to encourage him. Now our roles have reversed. He can command a six-figure income any day he chooses to work. My life consists of trying to ignore BO when I am handed a well-worn suit.

"It's hard to start over," I say. I want to make some kind of effort to explain why I'm about to launch another con. I want to explain how you can't escape your fate, how your own nature is something you can't choose, how your entire life is already laid out for you the day you appear on the earth. But the best I can muster is: "Everywhere you go, there you are."

It sounds like lame pot-inspired philosophy. Which is something Peter is familiar with. "Yeah," he says, "tell me about it."

"Anyway, that's why I want to talk. I need some advice."

"Sure."

"First, I need your word. That what we talk about here, stays here."

"Yeah, okay."

Peter tries to keep his face nonchalant, but he can't help telegraphing his excitement: He leans forward in his seat; the skin around his eyes tightens.

"I'm thinking of trying to get some money."

"Money's good," Peter says.

"No, I mean, I'm going to *take* it. Take someone's money."

"Is this legal?"

I make a face at Peter. He quickly realizes the stupidity of his question. He asks: "Whose?"

"A very bad man."

"Who?"

I ignore his question. "So I'm trying to find some people who can help. I was thinking that, in your line of work, you probably know some guys, who know some guys."

"What kind of guys?"

"Computer guys. People who can talk about security . . . *issues.*"

"You mean hackers?"

"Well, here's the thing. They don't actually have to hack. They don't have to *do* anything illegal. They just need to pretend. They have to talk a good game. They have to *act* like hackers. It's more of an acting role than anything else."

This is the critical part of my story: explaining to Peter that his piece of the job does not involve anything obviously illegal. Guys like Peter still talk to their parents once or twice a week. You need to reassure these men that they will never have to explain anything unsavory, like, for example, why they chose to join an illegal scheme that will send them to prison. So far, everything I have laid out to Peter can be explained away in one apologetic phone call to the folks. "Mom and Dad, he *told* me I wasn't doing anything against the law. He said it was just an *acting* job."

Peter says, "What kind of thing are we talking about? Is this like the Diet Deck?"

"Oh no," I say quickly. I want to get the Diet Deck out of Peter's mind. He associates it—quite rightly, unfortunately— with my five-year stint in Southern California. "It's nothing like Diet Deck. Diet Deck was a horrible idea."

The funny thing about the Diet Deck is that I never meant for it to be a con. I was simply trying to run a legitimate business. It was my desire to succeed at a straight enterprise, no mat-

ter what, that caused my downfall. Running a con is much easier—less risky. You go into a con with a plan—an exact and un-
changeable strategy—and with an escape route. You stick to it.
Doing things by the book is harder. There is always temptation:
to do more, to pay less, to stretch the rules. Without a plan,
human nature takes over.

This is all too much to explain to Peter. I say instead, "The
Diet Deck was a mistake, because it was an ongoing enterprise.
This job I'm talking about is going to last for six weeks, tops.
Then it's done. It'll disappear before anyone knows about it."

"I see," Peter says. He thinks about it. "I guess I know some
guys."

"They have to be good guys. Trustworthy. Of course the
money will be good, so it'll be worth their while."

"How much money?" Peter says, trying to sound uninter-
ested.

"For the computer guys? I don't know. Maybe a million dollars."

"A million dollars?"

I pretend to misunderstand—that he's complaining about the
small payoff. "Well it's only for a month's work."

"I see," Peter says.

I look up and see the bartender with the greasy apron standing over our table. He's holding a paper plate with a cheeseburger. "Here you go," he says. He slides it onto the table.

"Thanks," I say.

He gestures to Peter's nearly empty beer glass. "You want
another?"

Peter is still thinking about the million dollars, and the
chance to get involved in my exciting world—with little risk to
himself. He's slow to answer.

I know I have another five dollars in my wallet; and that it's
looking increasingly likely that I'll get Peter to bite. So I can afford to be generous. I say, "Yeah, bring him another. I'll treat."

The bartender nods and leaves.

"Anyway," I say to Peter, "I don't want to pressure you for any names or phone numbers right now. Maybe you can go home and think about it. Ask around. Try not to give too many details about the job, though."

"Okay."

He's staring down at the surface of our table. He is wrestling with conflicting emotions. He's hurt that I did not ask him personally to participate; he's excited at the prospect of being part of my venture; he's shy about volunteering; he's frightened about the consequences.

I pounce. "Too bad you can't do it," I say. I reach for my burger and take a bite. Through a mouthful I say, "You would have been perfect."

"Why can't I do it?"

"You have another gig. You just told me."

"Yeah, but," he says. He thinks about it. "I've barely started there. I could leave."

"Besides, Peter, you don't want to get involved in these kinds of things." I gesture with my chin at his shirt. "You're a code warrior."

"Yeah, but I can do it."

"The thing is," I say, cruelly, "the job isn't only acting. The person needs to write real code. I'll need some pretty impressive software. It has to be built fast. We have to fool some smart people. It would require a combination of skills. Acting, coding, thinking on your feet."

"I can do that, Kip," he says. "I really can."

"I don't know, Peter. You weren't exactly who I had in mind."

"I'll do it," he says, again.

"You know, there's a chance . . ." I say. I leave the sentence unfinished. But he knows what I mean.

"That something goes wrong." He nods. "I know."

"There is an element of danger."

A bone to my conscience. In my world, those six words qualify as Full Disclosure.

"I know," Peter says.

"But it is a million-dollar payday for you," I say. "Or whoever does it."

"I'll do it."

"Once you're in, you're in. If you back out, you'll be hurting a lot of people. Including myself."

"I'm in."

"You understand what you're signing up for?"

For the first time he smiles. He's relieved that I'm allowing him to participate. "Not really," he admits.

I admire his honesty. I'll have to work on that—knock it out of him.

"All right," I say, "you're in."

At that moment, his beer arrives, and my last five dollars leave my wallet.

At ten o'clock I finally reach Toby and Celia. I'm in my apartment, watching an old *Cheers* rerun on TV, which—because of the missing Volume button on the remote control and my own laziness—is playing too loudly. I've been lying on the couch, dialing Celia's number once every ten minutes, hanging up when I hear her announce that she and Carl are not home, so would I please leave a message.

I'm perplexed about where they can be. If she is caring for Toby, who has a broken leg and ribs, she can't be very far. And yet she hasn't picked up the telephone for the past eight hours.

Finally, on my tenth call, she answers. "Hello?" she says.

"Hi, it's me." Suddenly I realize that the eight years since our marriage means further introduction is required. I add, "Kip."

"Have you been calling here?"

"No."

"I'm looking at my Caller ID. You've called . . ." She pauses. I picture her leaning over, peering at the satanic Caller ID box. "Jesus, Kip. *Nine times.*"

I damn modern technology, which—in its quest to perfect mankind—has eliminated cowardice and dissembly as viable strategies. I decide to go on the offensive. "Where have *you* been?"

"Nowhere. Here. Resting."

"Is he there?"

"Who?"

When I asked, even I wasn't sure who I meant: Toby or Carl. I say, "Toby?"

"Of course. They have him on Percodan. He's zonked."

I think that prescribing Percodan to Toby is like asking Willie Sutton to guard your safe-deposit key. A good idea on a conceptual level, bad in execution.

On my television, Sam—the ex-alcoholic, sex-obsessed bartender—delivers a smarmy punch line. All of Middle America laughs knowingly.

Celia says, annoyed, "What's that noise? Is that your television?"

"Volume button," I explain. "Missing."

"It's so loud."

"Yeah, I should fix it," I say. I feel like adding, *If only my wife hadn't bankrupted me.* Instead I say, "Pretty busy, I guess."

"What do you want, Kip?"

"I just wanted to talk to Toby."

"He's sleeping. Should I wake him?"

"No. I guess not." I think about it. "I'm calling to see if he wants to stay here. While he recovers."

"You *want* him?" She sounds surprised.

"Sure I do," I say. *I think. Maybe.* "I'll sleep on the couch. He can have my bed."

Despite the opportunity, Celia does not volunteer information about the current sleeping arrangements in her stately San Jose McMansion. Does Toby have his own bedroom next door to his mother and Carl?

"Well," Celia says, "ask him yourself. He'll call you when he gets up."

"Fine."

"I'm going to sleep now," Celia says. She is not sharing intimacy. She is warning me not to wake her.

"All right."

I think she is about to hang up. Then she says something unexpected. "It was good to see you yesterday. It's been a while."

"Yeah," I say. "Too bad, the circumstances."

"But he'll be okay."

I say, "Yeah."

A long silence as we both think about our son.

"Good night, Kip," Celia says.

"Good night," I say.

When I hang up, I'm surprised that for a brief moment I miss her.

CHAPTER TEN

Now let me tell you how to finish your Bank Examiner Scam.

If you've followed my instructions so far, you've cleared about ten Gs from an elderly victim, by calling him on the telephone and asking his help in catching that crooked bank teller.

Now you have the opportunity to fleece the victim one final time. Here's how.

First, wait a few months. This gives the victim time to mull over the crime. After the two bank examiners, Mr. Marley and Mr. Smith, vanish off the face of the earth, the victim will realize he has been conned. He may even go to the police, who will nod sympathetically while they take his statement, and then will bury the case in a dusty filing cabinet. (No violence + no hope of finding the crook = no investigation.)

But chances are the victim won't even report the crime. That's a benefit of running cons. Victims seldom tell anyone that they've been ripped off. In your case, the victim feels ashamed. How many times has the old man heard from his children that he's too trusting, that he's no longer responsible with his money, that he's an easy mark? This will only confirm his children's fears. Perhaps, if the kids learn how the old man was fleeced, they will declare him incompetent, put him in a nursing home, and take away his financial independence.

Whether he reports the crime or not, the old man will be miserable. How could he be so dumb? He'll obsess about the scam. He'll start dreaming about revenge. *If only there's some way I can get back at those bastards!* he'll think. *If only the police would catch them . . .*

That's when you come in. Best time: about two months after the initial con. Now you will run a Badge-Play Comeback. Here's how it works.

There's a knock at the victim's door. It's a new face—someone he hasn't seen before. He introduces himself as Detective Thomas. To prove he's a policeman, he flashes a big shiny gold badge.

He says he has great news for Mr. Jones; can he come in?

Inside the apartment, he reveals the good news. "We caught the two men who scammed you. They're in jail right now. Not only that, but they still have your money, so we'll be returning it to you in a matter of days."

Your victim's head spins. He can't believe his good luck. He's so happy, he barely even listens to what Detective Thomas says next.

"There's only one problem," Detective Thomas says. "The money they took from you, and the money you withdrew from the bank, is counterfeit. Apparently this is a fairly sophisticated operation they're running. But don't worry. The bank has promised to make good on your loss, so there's no problem."

Your victim sighs with relief.

"Now then," the detective says. "Would you mind coming down to the police station with me, so that you can look at a lineup and identify the criminals who stole your money?"

Of course the victim agrees. Detective Thomas leads the old man to his unmarked police car, which has a small plastic siren light Velcroed to the dashboard, and a CB scanner tuned to the police frequency. Detective Thomas drives the old man down to the police station parking lot.

"Wait here," the detective says. "I'm going inside to arrange a lineup."

The detective leaves the victim in the parking lot for a few minutes. In the meantime, he walks into the police station, uses the bathroom, maybe buys a Coke at the soda machine. After a while, he returns to the victim.

"Good news," Detective Thomas says. "Looks like we can spare you the unpleasant face-to-face confrontation with the suspects. My captain says I can show you a few Polaroids instead. If you wouldn't mind, please look through this pile and point to the man who stole from you."

Detective Thomas hands a stack of photos to the old man. He flips through them. One of them is a photograph of your partner, Bank Examiner Marley. The old man points at the photo. "That's him," he says.

"Just as we thought," the detective says. "Now listen, Mr. Jones, here's what we need you to do. We need to get to the bottom of this counterfeiting operation. The teller who is working with these men is still at large. This is clearly an inside job."

The victim nods. He's still thinking about the fact that he's about to recover his stolen money. Soon everything will be all right.

"So," Detective Thomas says, "I'm going to come down to the bank with you. I want you to repeat exactly the same steps those criminals told you to do. Stand in the same teller line. Go in and withdraw five thousand dollars."

Mr. Jones agrees. You drive him to the bank. He withdraws five thousand dollars from his account and returns to the unmarked police car.

Detective Thomas looks through the bills. He makes a point to hold each one to the light. He licks his finger, rubs it across the paper. "Yup," he says. "Counterfeit. Every one of them. These guys are *good*." He shakes his head in wonder.

He puts the cash in a manila envelope marked "Evidence." He hands a receipt to the victim. He says, "We'll replace these funny bills with real ones and bring them over to your apartment tonight. Will you be there at, say, seven o'clock?"

The victim agrees. You drive him back to his house, and thank him for his cooperation.

Needless to say, when seven o'clock comes, no one shows up at Mr. Jones's door.

CHAPTER ELEVEN

At two o'clock in the morning, I'm awakened by the ringing telephone. I reach across my bed, bobble the receiver, knock it against my night table. Somehow it makes the journey to my ear. I mutter something that sounds like: "Hello?"

It's a female voice. For a moment I think it's Celia; then I realize it's not.

"Kip," she says. "Are you sleeping?"

"No," I say.

"Remember me?"

"Of course I remember you."

"I've been thinking about you. It's been a long time."

Later, I wonder about the phone call. About whether it was a coincidence, or part of someone's plan. But for now, I'm just excited to hear her voice. It *has* been a long time.

Chapter twelve

Her name, as of today, is Jessica Smith, and the address she gave me is in the Mission District, in a loft building surrounded by Salvadoran restaurants and Web design firms.

I park my Honda near a street sign that reads like an inscrutable Zen koan:

No Parking Thurs
2 Hr Parking Mon, Wed, Thurs

I take a creaky lift up three floors and am deposited in a cramped reception area. On the wall hangs a sign with a voluptuous female silhouette, like the kind you find on the mud flaps of big rigs cruising down 880. The sign says: "Aria Video, Inc." Behind a desk sits a two-hundred-and-fifty-pound male receptionist. He's black, with a shaved head, a diamond-stud earring, a Vandyke, and rippling muscles visible under a skintight T-shirt. Although he's sitting, the posture seems temporary, as if he might spring upward, like some kind of terrifying gay boxer, and rush from his corner to kick my lily-white ass.

He says, "Can I help you?" His voice rumbles like thunder.

I say, "Jessica around?"

"You are?"

"Kip. She's expecting me."

He smiles, revealing a gap between his two front teeth the size of a Tic-Tac. "Okay, Kip. She said you'd be coming. Go on back. But stay quiet. They may be filming."

"Right," I say. "Understood."

I wander through a curtain of hanging beads. I am in a large space, half a football field in size, lit with halogen fixtures mounted on C-stands. A young Hispanic man holds a white light reflector panel down by his feet. He's staring off into space and seems completely unconcerned by the fact that, ten yards away, in the middle of the room, a gorgeous woman—blond, thin, with huge fake breasts—is lying, naked, sprawled on the floor atop a futon, fingering her pussy.

There's a gaggle of people at the other end of the room, also ignoring the masturbating girl. They mill about, glancing at their watches, checking their light meters, snapping batteries into and out of shoulder-mounted video cameras.

I see Jessica in the center of the hubbub. She's different than I remember. Actually, the way I remember her is like the girl currently on the futon—naked, on her back, and oozing, among other things, sexuality. But today Jessica is brunette, not blond; standing, not lying; and dressed in a conservative charcoal-gray Ellen Tracy suit that makes her look like a banker, not a pornographer. Today her hair is cut stylishly short, cropped and layered with an elegant bob; and her killer body has been tapered, through clothes and workout and diet, to look less like a boast and more like a promise. She radiates a quiet sexiness, like the voluptuous PTA mom whose comments about homework and field trips are met with clamorous applause by all the fathers in the school auditorium.

One of the cameramen offers his viewfinder to Jessica. She leans over and checks his shot. She nods approval.

As I walk toward her, a voice calls out from across the room, "We have wood!"

Like a shout of "Fire!" being relayed across miles of remote forest watchtowers, the cry of "We have wood!" bounces across the cavernous space. Another man frantically shouts, "Wood! Wood!" Cameramen scramble back to position. Lighting grips flick on their halogens. The Hispanic man lifts the reflector panel. The blonde stops playing with herself, and straightens up the hair on her cooch.

Now I see what all the excitement is about. A man rises, naked, from a chair, displaying an enormous erection. The entire production has been waiting for him to rest, and to return, engorged, ready to shoot the next scene.

"Wood!" Jessica shouts. "Let's go!"

"Rolling!" a cameraman calls.

The man with the huge penis struts into the center of the room, which is, I belatedly realize, a movie set made to look like a college dorm room. There are pennants hanging on the wall behind the blonde—preposterously, from Harvard—and a few books scattered on the floor. One, I notice, is Tolstoy's *War and Peace.* Never let it be said that surrealism in cinema is dead.

Jessica says, "Take it from 'Fuck me, Professor Johnson.'"

The blonde says, "Fuck me, Professor Johnson."

"Oh, I will," the naked man says, as he struts toward his recumbent student. "And I'm going to be a very firm grader today."

"Ooh, yeah," the blonde says.

One of the cameramen scampers into the scene with his Betacam. He kneels down beside the male actor, and—with the man's penis mere inches from his face—points his camera at the blond girl's genitals. She obligingly poses them with her fingers.

"All right," Jessica Smith says, matter-of-factly. "Let's make some magic."

I met her eighteen years ago, when she was a call girl, not even twenty years old.

I was desperate. I needed a way to keep a mark around town for a few days while I ripped him off. The safest way to make a guy stick around: the promise of pussy. Out came the Yellow Pages, and I began calling escort services, one after another, requesting that they send someone to my hotel room. I rejected the first four candidates who were unsuitable for various reasons—coked up, with track marks, black (doesn't play well in Boise), retarded—until luck smiled on me, and I finally met the woman whose office I visit today. Except, back then, her name was Brittany Diamond; and she had blond hair and double-D breasts; and she wore fishnets and smelled of bubblegum.

The night that she appeared in my hotel room, I told her that I didn't want to have sex with her. Instead, in return for a thousand dollars, I wanted her to pretend to fall in love with a balding accountant from Boise. She played her part brilliantly. The accountant stayed around town, giving me time to extract his banking information, and to set up the fake FBI raid that scared him back home. In the end, he retreated, a hundred grand poorer, scared out of his wits and certain that he was about to do hard time.

For me and Brittany, it was the beginning of a working relationship that lasted, on and off, for ten years. First we worked together on Pigeon Drops—she played the attractive girl who found the suspicious wad of cash. Later, we arranged countless Honey Traps, snagging lawyers and executives by placing classified ads in newspapers from a "lady seeking an unencumbered sexual relationship." (Few cons are as easy as this, in which the mark—usually a married man—sends you letters that will serve as fodder for his own blackmail.)

But over the years we grew apart. The first problem, of course, was my wife. Celia was innately suspicious of this beautiful woman whom I introduced as my "sales assistant." (For the first ten years of our marriage, Celia thought I worked for Caterpillar, as a regional sales director responsible for industrial equipment leasing in the Southeastern United States.)

But the more serious problem was Brittany herself. After the first few years, the novelty of conning middle-aged men out of their money wore off. She grew tired of worrying—about doing time or being killed. She wanted a real, legitimate career. So, without ever formally announcing that we were doing so, we parted ways. It happened gradually, as we saw each other less often, spoke less frequently, until finally, we realized that we were mere acquaintances, not partners, and that we owed each other nothing.

She darkened her hair, changed her name, and reduced her

breasts. Today, Jessica Smith, as she calls herself, is a business-woman—a porn entrepreneur: a director and producer of such classics as *Hindfeld* and *Bumpin' Donuts*.

It's been four years since I last saw her. She came once to Lompoc, but it was an uncomfortable visit. I could read her face as she looked around the prison's cold gray steel: She was glad that it was me behind the glass, and not her.

I have not seen her since then, or heard from her. Until last night's phone call.

Later, while the cast and crew wait for more wood, I meet Jessica Smith in her office, a small room with a ficus tree, an Ikea desk, and bookcases filled with VHS tapes, probably her own products.

"Would you like some water?" she asks.

I say, "From a glass, or a sealed bottle?"

"Very funny." She reaches under her desk to a mini-fridge, pulls out a Calistoga, and tosses it to me. She sees me examine the bottle. "It's sealed," she adds.

I twist the top and take a sip. I stare at her. "You look good," I say, finally.

"Do I?" She touches her hair, like a matron surprised by a compliment she hasn't heard for years, and for a moment I think she is being ironic. Then I see she is sincerely pleased.

"Really," I insist, since I'm making headway.

"And you?" she says. "How've you been?"

"So so."

"You're finally out."

"Can't keep a good man down."

"Are you a good man now?"

"Temporarily."

She examines me: my face, my hair, my paunch. "You look . . . good."

I ignore the obvious lie. "How's business?"

"Pretty good." She nods, trying to convince herself. "Yeah, good. I won an AVA award last month."

"For which movie? *Shaving Ryan's Privates?*"

"Very funny," she says. "That's a gay movie, by the way. I find it interesting that you even know about it."

"I was impressed with your directing out there." I wave my hand in the direction of the Harvard movie set. "Gosh, college sure has changed since my own university days."

"Don't be mean."

"Sorry." I genuinely am. Truth is, I'm jealous. She got out of the game and never went to prison. Instead, she went legit and is now making good money with Aria Video. In contrast, my first attempt at going legit landed me in Lompoc, and my second has me standing in a dry cleaning shop eight hours a day. I say, "I'm just feeling sorry for myself."

"Well don't," she says. "It's not becoming."

She smiles. She's still beautiful, but now the signs of age have crept into her face: the lines around her eyes, the skin under her neck. I wonder: Will she be adequate for the con? Will she be able to seduce Edward Napier, to attract his interest, to lie naked in his bed and win his loyalty?

"What are you looking at?" she says.

"Nothing."

"You're looking at me funny." She squints. "What's wrong? You think I look old."

"No I don't."

"Listen, Kip," she says, "*you* look old. Me—I'm still one hot piece of ass."

I raise my palms in surrender. "Okay."

"You understand?"

"Yes."

Even though it has been four years, it feels like we never left each other. Across the desk I see not a whore or a con artist, but the person (I now realize) that I want to settle down with—a thirty-six-year-old woman who is ready to order Chinese food delivery on a rainy night, to snuggle in front of the TV, to watch a movie, and to fall asleep in my arms.

I wonder: Is there any way to get from here to there? That has always been my problem. I know where I am, and I know where I want to be. It's getting from here to there that's the mystery.

"How's Celia?" she says.

"Divorced."

"How many times?"

"Just me. She's with a new guy now. His name's Carl."

"Better looking than you?"

"Probably. Definitely smarter."

"Well that's not saying much. You still rich from the Diet Deck?"

"Nope."

"Any money whatsoever?"

I shrug noncommittally.

"So *that's* why you're here."

"Wait a second. You called *me*."

She says: "But I know you, Kip. You would never drive into the city, unless you wanted something." She cocks her head, looks at me intently. More softly now: "Do you want something?"

What I want, at this exact moment, is to marry her.

I say: "No."

"Let me guess," she says. "A con."

"Well, okay," I say, since I guess a marriage proposal would be out of place. "There's a piece of business. I need a girl." I correct myself. "A woman." Then I correct myself again. "A girl," I say, finally, deciding this will flatter her most. "And since you called . . ." I let my voice trail off.

"I thought you were going straight."

"I am." I think about it. "Well I was."

"So what happened?"

"Toby."

"Toby?"

"My son."

"He's like—what?—twelve years old?"

"Sometimes," I say, and shrug. "But officially he's twenty-five."

"Jesus Christ," she says. "You're one old motherfucker."

"Thank you. Do you want to get married?"

I'll never know the answer, because—before she can continue the Nick and Nora routine—there's a knock at the door. The bald black receptionist pops his head into Jessica's office. "Jessica," he says, in the quiet and respectful tone someone might use to announce a visitor in the waiting room, "we have wood."

"Okay, Levon, I'll be right there."

Levon leaves. She turns to me. "Kip, I gotta go."

"Something pop up?"

"That's clever. Never heard that before."

"Really?"

"No," she says. "I've heard that about a hundred times. This week." She stands behind her desk. "It's good to see you, Kip."

"Is that it?"

"Is *what* it?"

"That's all? We're done?"

"I have to go back to work. These boners are precious . . . you know how it is."

Do I ever. I say: "Jess, in all seriousness . . ."

"Fine," she says. "I'll do it."

"Do what?"

"The job. The con. Whatever it is. That's why you're here, right?"

Not the marriage, then. Maybe I'll try again later.

I say: "Yeah, that's why I'm here."

"I know you wouldn't ask me if it wasn't important. You wouldn't want me to risk all of this." She gestures around her office: the Ikea desk, the ficus tree, the mini-fridge. As usual, I can't tell if she's serious or kidding. She pauses. "It *is* important, right?"

"Toby's in trouble," I explain.

"Then I'm in."

"Don't you want to know—"

"Just keep me out of jail."

I nod. "I promise."

"Good enough," she says. She walks to the door, opens it. "I gotta get this facial done. You wanna stick around?"

"Not really."

"I don't blame you," she says. She gives me a peck on the cheek and disappears onto the movie set.

You probably wonder if I've ever had a romantic relationship with Brittany Diamond, or with Jessica Smith. There was one evening, in Santa Barbara, thirteen years ago. The victim of our Honey Trap—the owner of a grocery chain in Nevada—lost his nerve and failed to show up for his romantic rendezvous with a "woman seeking an unencumbered relationship." Alone in the hotel, suddenly unencumbered ourselves, with a warm breeze rustling the palm fronds outside our window, we made love in the cool sheets and fell asleep in each other's arms. In the morning, I woke with a dull sadness in the pit of my stomach, and I knew that I had made a terrible mistake—that I had ruined everything, by treating the most important woman in my life like a one-night stand. She must have felt the same way. For, even though we never discussed what happened that night—never spoke a word about it—we never had sex again. It must have been a mutual decision.

Now *that* is the sign of an enduring, deep love—don't you think? To both have exactly the same thought, and to act upon it, without exchanging a single word? What else, besides love, can you call it?

But of course you have to wonder about the phone call.

You haven't heard from a woman in four years, and then suddenly, when you're planning a con, she calls to say hello. What are the chances of that?

CHAPTER THIRTEEN

I've tried to radically change my life three times, and have failed three times, and so maybe it's time to stop trying.

First try: When I was twenty, I told my father that I would no longer follow his path; that I was tired of cheating and swindling, of looking over my shoulder, afraid of being caught. So I enrolled in City University of New York, Queens College, to become a lawyer, because it seemed like the people who were hounding me were having a lot more fun than the person being hounded.

My father reacted with quiet fury, as if I had insulted everything he had ever achieved, and in a way he was right. He stopped speaking to me, but he still had the last word: He started to die, as if to spite me. Sallow, smelly, bedridden, he lay in his apartment for the last nine months of his life, leaving my mother to find a way to pay the debts he had racked up—the hopeless bills owed to dangerous men. Eventually I withdrew from college and went back to the streets: Pigeon Drops, Change Games, Honey Traps—until I finally paid what my mother and father owed. Within six months, they were both dead, and by then it was too late: I never went back to school, never tried again. My father won, smiling from the grave.

Second try: When I was forty-five, and finally self-confident—twenty years too late. I looked around at the successful men I knew—straight men, who never broke the law, who never feared the flash of red and blue lights in their rearview mirror—and I realized that I was smarter than every one of them. I decided I could have what they had: dull lives, suburban tracts in West L.A., pools in the backyard, two cars in the garage. If those men—plodding and unambitious—could succeed at business—*legitimate* business—then so, too, could I.

So I sat down, and I tried to think of the perfect business for an honest man: something that allowed me to profit from other people's imperfections—their laziness, their vanity, their lack of self-control.

The Diet Deck was born.

Imagine being paid $49.95 for a deck of playing cards that costs eighty-nine cents to buy from Shunxin Trading Company, Taipei, Taiwan! Then imagine being able to sell one of these decks to every American that is overweight, but too lazy, or too dumb, to do the obvious: eat less, exercise more.

That was the Diet Deck. In my first three months, I sold twelve thousand decks, which netted a profit of nearly $480,000. I never looked back.

Soon the pool came, and the suburban house, and the two cars in the garage. I could send Toby to a private day school in Los Angeles. My marriage with Celia grew stronger. My life, finally, was right.

So how did I blow it? This is the hardest thing to explain to people: that I never meant to cheat; that I wanted, more than anything, to succeed legitimately—but in the end, I was betrayed by a powerful and unrelenting force: my own nature.

It started simply enough. I discovered that I could sell Diet Decks by advertising through late-night television infomercials. I began to buy half-hour blocks of time in local UHF graveyards: 3:00 A.M. to 3:30 A.M. in Muncie, Indiana; 2:45 A.M. to 3:15 A.M. in Scranton, Pennsylvania. It was like magic. I had never before experienced the Euclidian perfection of capitalism, where every one dollar I spent advertising on late-night TV yielded exactly four dollars of profit. The math was unerring, the logic impeccable: Of course, I had to advertise more! And faster! Each block of television time meant another car, or a new addition to my house, or another year for Toby at St. Alban's Prep.

But I soon discovered there was a flaw in my perfect logic. I had to lay out money before I saw any profit. Television stations wanted cash, up front, three months before they would let me broadcast my advertisements. Mr. Jun Lee An from Shunxin Trading Company also wanted my cash two months before he agreed to stamp out ten thousand packs of playing cards with photographs of steaks and carrots.

It was a dilemma: Every block of television time I purchased meant fifteen thousand dollars of profit, but I needed to lay out thirty thousand dollars—at least temporarily—before I could claim it. That's when I hit upon my most brilliant idea yet: I would allow other enterprising businessmen to invest in my venture, alongside me.

So I began to solicit investments from neighbors and friends. They could come in as "partners"—investing twenty thousand dollars to buy a block of advertising time. In return, they would receive a percentage of every Diet Deck sold during their advertisement. It was good deal for everyone: the bald accountant who lived next door to me could earn six thousand dollars on a twenty-thousand-dollar investment, in just over three months time. In the meantime, freed from my cash flow problems, I could buy hundreds of hours of television time around the country, and then manufacture tens of thousands of decks of cards. The money kept rolling in.

In fact, the business of selling television advertising partnerships to wealthy partners soon superseded my business of selling playing cards to fatties. And what a business it was: The economics were so appealing that everyone wanted to invest, and soon I was receiving ten checks per month from eager partners—each check for twenty thousand dollars or more.

And of course I wanted to deliver on the promises I had made to my partners. That was the only decent thing to do. So the checks I received in March helped me repay the partners who invested in February. And the checks I received in February helped me repay the partners who invested in January.

Which meant: The problems began in June. Soon it was hard to find enough new investors to pay back the old ones. And the business of selling playing cards to fatties had plateaued. For some reason, the fatties never could keep the weight off, even if they dealt themselves a full house of three carrots and two broccolis.

You have to understand: I never tried to rip off anyone. If anything, I risked everything in order to *deliver* on my promises. But soon I began to delay paying back my investors. To save cash, I stopped shipping Diet Decks to fatties. From that point, it was only a matter of time. I was arrested on my way home from the Marina Del Rey Mercedes dealership. I had wanted to buy Toby a present for his eighteenth birthday—something sporty, to make him understand that I loved him. Instead, I went to prison, and he and Celia celebrated alone.

The third time I tried to change my life: when I took the job at Economy Cleaners, and tried again to go legit, for ten dollars an hour, plus tips.

It hasn't worked out so well. Not yet, anyway.

CHAPTER FOURTEEN

On Thursday I drive north forty miles into Napa Valley. It's ten degrees warmer here than the Peninsula, so on this June day I roll my windows down and open the first two buttons of my golf shirt. Route 29 empties into the city of Napa, which—despite the romance of its name and association with Wine Country—is an ugly blue-collar town with three trailer parks stacked high with shiny aluminum Algonquins. Half–labor pool, half–trucking terminus, the city of Napa sits at the mouth of the valley that bears its name; it's a place where truckers on their way south pull over to have lunch, their rigs loaded with live chickens from Petaluma.

Napa is home to the people who power the wine industry—those who do the actual work: the agricultural laborers, the vintners, the pool-cleaners, the waiters. A few miles further up the road, in the valley itself, you find the estates and wineries, where rich cardiologists and computer executives retire when they decide they've had enough of cruel city life and can instead find happiness by bottling wine with their family's newly designed crest upon it.

I take Route 29 past the city and leave the trailer parks behind. I pull my Honda off the asphalt onto a dirt road where few cardiologists venture. It takes me up into the mountains. I ascend Mount Vedeer along a dusty hairpin road. Big redwoods block the sun so that light is forced to poke through the canopy like insistent golden fingers.

When I reach the plateau, the sun returns. It takes me a moment to realize that I am driving along the lip of an extinct volcano. The crater is filled with soil, on which grow hundreds of acres of grapes arranged in rows of neat white trellises.

I pull up to an old stone farmhouse. A mangy dog lies in the dusty road, trying to squeeze his fat haunches into a circle of shade from an acacia tree. I get out of the car and close the door. The dog looks at me. After a moment he decides I can do nothing to solve his shade problem, so he lowers his head and closes his eyes.

"Elihu?" I call out.

From the farmhouse, footsteps. "Coming!" An old man appears in the doorway. He's dressed in a linen shirt, unbuttoned to the navel, jeans, work boots. His has two gray tufts of hair, one on each side of his head, remnants of a comb-over, but now hanging limply—too long—like deflated peaks from a jester's hat.

"Kip?" he says. He opens his arms, walks toward me. We hug. He slaps my back. He smells of sweat, oak, and wine.

He pulls back, looks at me. "My God," he says. It's unclear if this is an exclamation of thanks or sadness. "Look at you."

"Thanks," I say.

"I was just checking the barrels. Come in."

He leads me into the farmhouse. It's cool and dark. The walls are lined with racks of oak barrels. The room has the telltale odor of maltic acid, sweet and rotten.

"You want a taste?" he says. "I'm proud of this one." He grabs a wine thief—a long hollow glass tube—from a rack on the wall, and plunges it into a hole at the crest of a barrel. He covers the top of the tube with his finger and withdraws it. It's filled with ruby liquid. He holds the wine thief over a Dixie cup, releases his thumb. The wine pours into the cup. He hands it to me.

"Bottoms up," he says.

I drink. It tastes like grape juice, with an acid kick.

"What do you think?" he says.

"Not bad," I say.

"Like grape juice, right?"

"Sort of."

"Yeah," he says, suddenly weary. "I'm not very good at this."

"It's not bad," I say again.

"Maybe in a few years," he says. "Age makes everything better."

I hand him my Dixie cup. He tosses it into a trash can. I have no desire to argue, even though there is much evidence to the contrary.

We eat lunch outside, in the oppressive heat, on a picnic table beside the farmhouse. The dog finds his way over, and deposits himself with a grunt by our feet, under the table. Elihu serves: crusty French bread, soft Brie, olives, prosciutto, and a bottle of wine. He pours me a glass and raises his glass. "Cheers," he says.

"L'Chaim," I say.

I taste the wine. "Now, *this* is good," I say, hoping to compliment him.

"It's from that motherfucker on the other side of the mountain. The computer guy."

"I'm sorry."

"His wine's good," Elihu offers, finally. "Maybe someday."

"Something to aim for."

Elihu makes a pistol with his fingers. "Something to aim for, all right."

We eat in silence. Finally Elihu says, "So you're a free man."

"Yeah."

"I would have visited you," Elihu said. "But what a trip."

"I understand."

"I'm an old man now." He means it as an apology, for not seeing me in Lompoc.

I look into his rheumy eyes. "I know."

Elihu Katz was a friend of my father's. After my father died, Elihu watched over me, helping me set up cons, guarding my back, imparting valuable lessons. Once, when I stupidly conned the wrong man—a heavyweight political contributor to the San Francisco DA—Elihu cashed in a chip he had been hoarding for himself—a set of photographs of the DA with a young boy. Elihu saved me from certain jail, and I owe him everything that I have. Which is now, admittedly, not much.

Elihu retired fifteen years ago, retreating to the top of Mount Vedeer, to live off his earnings and to realize his dream of making wine. He told me then that times were changing, that the days of big cons were dwindling, that marks were getting too smart, police too aggressive, other criminals too dangerous. He wanted to quit while it was still his choice.

But he has kept his fingers in several pies, staying close to the groups in San Jose and San Francisco, sharing information, acting as a dignified elder statesman and a clearinghouse for the world of confidence men.

"So," Elihu says, "what can I do for you?"

"Toby's in trouble," I say.

"What kind of trouble?"

"He owes money. To the Russians. You know Sustevich? The Professor?"

"A gonif," Elihu says. He bites into his bread, tears off a piece.

"So I'm taking a job."

"Who's the mark?"

"Edward Napier."

"From Vegas?"

"He spends time here now."

"How much?"

"Twenty-five."

"Sustevich is in on it?" he asks.

I nod. "Something like that."

Elihu thinks about what I've told him. He leans over, takes a piece of prosciutto, piles it on a slice of bread. He takes a bite. "You know you'll get caught," he says, finally.

"What makes you say that?"

"Too many sharks. Sustevich, Napier. Between them, too much juice. Why not rip off the president of the United States while you're at it?"

I act surprised, as if I hadn't thought of that. "Wait," I say, "is he in town?"

"Even if you take the money, they'll find you."

"I'll use a button. Blow them off."

"They're too smart."

"It can be done."

"Anything can be done," Elihu admits. "The question is whether you want to be the one to do it."

"I don't have a choice."

"Sure you do."

"Toby needs me."

"Toby is a grown man. He makes his own choices."

"I can't let him get killed."

"Put him on a train. Have him disappear for a few months."

"You don't know Toby," I say.

Elihu shrugs, as if to say that he has no desire to, either. "What do you want from me?"

"Some names. Bit players. Guys for the button. They have to be convincing. FBI types."

Elihu says, "I can help, of course." He spits an olive pit into his hand, tosses it under the picnic table. The dog opens his eyes, hopefully. When he sees it's a pit, he shuts them.

Elihu says, as if he's continuing a conversation we've been having for twenty minutes, "Napier's been in the news a lot lately. That casino he's trying to buy."

"The Tracadero," I say.

"It's all people can talk about out there. 'Will Napier buy it?' 'Does he have the cash?'" He imitates the voices of Mr. and Mrs. White Bread, from Lansing, Michigan. "'Gee, I hope he wins the bidding war.' 'Gee, those Europeans are outbidding him by twenty-five percent!' You know what I say? Who cares? Who cares if one rich guy owns a casino, or another rich guy owns it? You're going to walk in and lose your money, no matter whose name is on the door."

"People love businessmen," I say. "They're the new celebrities."

"What happened to the old celebrities?"

"They're still around. They're the new businessmen."

"You know what it sounds like to me? Napier's overextended. He got himself into a bidding war, and he doesn't have the cash. Probably needs to raise some, fast." He gives me a sidelong glance. "But you figured that out already, didn't you?"

I shrug.

"Always a step ahead." He pauses. He spits an olive pit into his hand, tosses it. "So be it. I'll get you some names, for your button."

"Thanks, Elihu," I say. "And one more thing."

He stares at me.

"When the time comes, I'll need to borrow some money."

"How much?"

"It's only for five days. You'd be factoring. I'll already have the money in hand, just not liquid."

"How much?"

"Fifteen million. In diamonds."

"Jesus Christ, Kip, you're killing me."

"You'd get the usual. Five percent per day."

"What the hell are you going to do with fifteen million dollars' worth of diamonds?"

"I'm going to repay the money I owe to the guy I'm stealing from."

He shakes his head. He thinks about it. "You know you're going to get caught, don't you?"

I don't bother giving an answer. Then again, he doesn't expect one.

CHAPTER FIFTEEN

A button is con man lingo for a way to blow off your mark. The word *button* comes from the term used to describe the gold shield that a cop flashes.

But to a con man, a button means something else. A button is when you have a fake cop arrive in the middle of your con in order to start asking questions, or even to make an arrest.

Buttons are used to end a con—to scare off your mark, to preempt him from going to the real police.

It's much better to have a con end with an arrest by a fake cop, rather than with an arrest by a real cop. Trust me. I've done both. The fake cops are always easier to deal with.

CHAPTER SIXTEEN

Back in Palo Alto, I stop by the Bank of Northern California and open an account in the name of my company, newly incorporated in Delaware, Pythia Corporation. The account is empty save for one hundred dollars I transfer from my own personal checking account.

I arrive back at my apartment. I dial the phone number the Professor had handed me before I left him. A voice answers—Russian, familiar.

"Yes, hello?"

"Dmitri," I say, "this is Kip Largo."

"Yes," he says.

"You remember me?" I say. "The one with the acid?"

"Yes."

"I'm ready for the wire. You know what I'm talking about, don't you?"

"Yes."

"You have a pencil?"

"Yes."

I reel off the new bank account number and wiring instructions. When I'm done, Dmitri says, "Six million will be there tomorrow. You have two months."

"And then I get a chemical peel?"

"Yes."

"You take care," I say to Dmitri.

"Yes," he says.

I hang up. At last, the con is on.

Three minutes later, my kitchen phone rings. I think it's Dmitri, calling back to confirm the wiring instructions. I'm surprised to hear Toby's voice instead.

"Dad?" he says.

"Toby!" I haven't seen him since the day in the hospital. "How are you?"

"A lot better," he says dreamily. "They have me on this medicine. It's really nice."

I'm about to say something snide, but I recall my son's accusation that I always attack him. "Great," I say. *You're hooked on Percodan? That's fantastic, son!*

"Mom says you want me to stay with you?"

"I would love that."

"Can you pick me up at Mom's?"

"Sure." I think about it. "Is everything all right?"

"What do you mean?"

"Why are you calling? I mean, it's great; I want you here. It's just . . . out of character. Are you having problems getting along with Mom?"

"Yeah," he says. He pauses. I picture his biting his lip, as he does when he thinks about something troubling. Finally he says, "I guess I just feel more comfortable over there. With you."

It is these words—not Dmitri the Russian's agreement to wire six million dollars into my bank account—that are surely the best thing I have heard since I woke this morning, so long ago.

PART TWO

THE MARK

CHAPTER SEVENTEEN

On a Wednesday night in July, Ed Napier throws a party. He rents the Hillsboro Aviation Museum—a converted hangar in a thumbnail airport, where old Zeros and Spitfires hang by steel cables from the ceilings, and where an earlier technology revolution is celebrated with light-box displays, walk-through wind tunnels, and photographs of the Wright brothers.

The party is meant to celebrate the launch of Napier's venture capital firm, Argyle Partners. But what it really celebrates is how *fabulous* life has become, here on the Peninsula—where even the secretaries earn seventy grand, where college dropouts with a business plan can raise a million dollars after a five-minute lunch, where the only thing needed to get rich is a can-do attitude, and the belief that *the Internet changes everything,* a phrase that means both nothing and anything, but which has become, it seems, the official mantra of the state of California.

The party is also a celebration that Silicon Valley has arrived on the world stage, or at least that the rest of the world has arrived on our stage. Now, even people who have never used a computer—as Edward Napier proudly admitted to *Forbes*—have set up shop here, and have begun investing in technology companies. How does a man like Ed Napier choose where to invest his dollars, you may wonder, since he has no technical knowledge whatsoever? The answer is simple (as Napier explained to *Forbes*): Do the entrepreneurs in question understand that the

Internet changes everything? Are they can-do guys? Do they have a vision?

Tonight, I have my own vision. It is: to unspool some line—just enough to snag our mark and begin to reel him in. I show up at the party with Jess Smith and Peter Room. Without much difficulty, we have managed to wangle invitations from Peter's code warrior friends. It wasn't hard—all of Silicon Valley has been invited: lawyers; entrepreneurs; engineers; journalists; PR flacks; even other, competitive, VCs. And why not? There's plenty of wealth to go around. Competition and jealousy are so pre-boom; remnants of an old world that existed before the *Internet changed everything*.

Jess, Peter, and I each split up to cover the room. Peter and I are dressed in the Silicon Valley uniform: chinos and blue chambray shirts. I've asked Jess to wear something more provocative. She chooses a tight black dress, with a slit leg and plunging neckline. When I see her—particularly that flash of toned white thigh as she walks—my earlier doubts, that she could pull off a con, vanish.

The party sprawls across two stories, with a balcony that overlooks the hangar floor. In one corner a swing band plays, with an attractive blond singer and four men in porkpie hats swinging their brass instruments in unison. At each of the three other walls, crowds gather around the open bars. Drinks of choice tonight: cabernet for the men, chardonnay for the ladies. Real glassware, by the way—no chintzy plastic cups when Ed Napier foots the bill.

I see him at the far side of the room. He's movie-star tall, dark, and handsome. Because of his tan—acquired racing his sloop in the Pacific, or vacationing in St. Bart's—his teeth seem strangely white and sharp, like surgical instruments. He has pale blue eyes, which—even as he chats to a cluster of sycophants—predatorily sweep the room behind them, like a lion scanning the savannah.

"I think I know you," a female voice says to me. I feel my testicles shrink: Could the con be blown already, before it even begins, because some snarky *Wall Street Journal* stringer recognizes me as the Diet Deck King?

I turn around to the voice. It's Lauren Napier. She wears a navy dress, with her blond hair pulled back in an elaborate and sexy bun, held together with two ebony chopsticks. Her face has completely healed—no black eyes—or, if there are, they have been expertly covered with foundation.

"No, you don't know me," I say, as a piece of advice.

"What are you, exactly? A reporter? PR man?"

"I'm an entrepreneur," I say proudly. I point to my chinos and chambray shirt. "Can't you tell?"

"I thought entrepreneurs were all young and brilliant."

"What makes you think I'm not young?"

We're joined by a Chinese woman with a notepad and a micro-cassette recorder. "Ms. Napier," she says, ignoring me. "I'm Jennifer H. Chin, *Information 2.0.*"

"How do you do?" Lauren Napier says.

"What do you think of the party your husband is throwing?"

"I think it's fabulous," Lauren Napier says, into the recorder, without missing a beat. "We're just excited to be here, at the center of the technology revolution."

"Is there any difference that you notice between Silicon Valley and Las Vegas?"

"Yes," Lauren Napier says. "About fifteen degrees Fahrenheit."

Jennifer H. Chin laughs and scribbles the line in her pad. Finally, she turns to me. "And you are?" she says. Over her shoulder, I see Jess walking past Ed Napier. She wiggles her ass like a fly-fishing lure and heads to the nearby bar. I watch Napier's glance follow her.

"Franklin Edison," I say. "My company is called Pythia."

"Has Ed Napier invested in your company?" Jennifer H. Chin asks.

"Not yet," I say. "But we're hopeful."

"And what does your company do?"

Ed Napier says something to the gaggle of fans that seem to hang on his every word. Two of the young men—swarthy, geeky, probably Indian engineers—smile and nod enthusiastically at him, as if he's Ganesh imparting the secret of karma. Ed Napier gives his own thousand-watt smile, shakes a hand or two, and then walks away to the bar, toward Jess.

"What do we *do?*" I repeat, as if the notion that a company needs to do something is hopelessly outmoded. I stare at Jennifer H. Chin. "I'm afraid I can't tell you that."

"Stealth mode?" she says knowingly.

"Yes," I say. "It's very top secret. But I know for a fact that we are going to change the world."

"Can I quote you on that?"

"No."

"Really?"

"Really."

She is nonplussed. Apparently in her vast twenty-month career as a journalist, no one has ever refused to be quoted. She doesn't know what to do.

I say helpfully, "Maybe if you give me your card, I'll call you when I'm allowed to talk."

"Would you?" she says. Her eyes light up. Maybe the flabby old guy has a good story, after all. "I would appreciate that."

"My pleasure," I say. She hands me a business card. I pretend to examine it carefully. I stick it in my chinos pocket. Later, it will prove a convenient place to deposit used chewing gum.

"I need to go now," I say, mysteriously. "Pleased to meet you, Ms. Chin." I turn to Lauren Napier. "And nice to meet you, too, uh . . ."

"Lauren," she says.

"Lauren," I say.

Lauren Napier says, "Nice to meet *you.*" She shakes my hand. "Good luck with whatever you're doing. I hope it'll change *my* world."

I smile and leave her alone with Jennifer H. Chin, to answer the reporter's insightful questions about how parties differ between Las Vegas and Silicon Valley.

I head to the bar where Jess is waiting for a drink. In front of me, Ed Napier snakes his way through the crowd, ignoring well-wishers, trying to edge closer to her. He's a coonhound on the hunt, and the scent of Jess's booty is irresistible to him. Finally, when he is a foot behind her, he reaches out and taps her shoulder. Jess turns. Her reaction is perfect: a brief flash of annoyance—that some clown is trying to pick her up; then an instant of recognition; and a pleased smile.

I'm close enough now to hear their conversation over the noise of the swing music. "I noticed you were heading to the bar. Can I offer you a drink?" Ed Napier says.

"I'm having wine," Jess says.

"Allow me." Napier waves two fingers, slightly, to get the attention of the barman. He says, "Two chardonnays."

"Right away, Mr. Napier," the bartender says.

Napier takes the chardonnays and extricates himself from the crowd. He cocks his head for Jess to follow.

Now they stand ten yards from me.

"I think I've seen you somewhere before," Napier says. He has that loud, booming voice that all rich people have: It says I'm going to talk and you're going to hear me, whether or not you volunteer.

"I doubt it," Jess says.

Napier holds out his hand. "Ed Napier." They shake.

"Jessica Smith."

"Pleased to meet you, Ms. Smith. What do you do?"

"Marketing."

"Ah," he says, as if that explains everything: why she's pretty, and why she's here. "What company?"

"Pythia."

"Pythia? I haven't heard of that one. What do you do?"

"I could tell you," Jess purrs, "but then I'd have to kill you."

"I see. Not even a hint?"

"Massively parallel computing."

"Sounds good to me," he says. "You looking for funding?"

"Are you offering?"

He shrugs, as if considering the possibility of picking up the check at Denny's. "Sure. Why not?"

Jess pretends to notice me for the first time. "Speak of the devil. There he is. Franklin! Come here." She waves me over. "Ed, this is my partner, Franklin Edison."

I walk over, shake Ed's hand. "How do you do."

Napier says, "Mr. Edison. Your partner won't tell me what you do, but it sounds fascinating."

I glare at Jess. "My partner talks a little too much," I say.

Jess looks down at the ground.

"She didn't say anything, really," Napier assures me.

Jess says to me, as if apologizing, "Mr. Napier says he's interested in talking about *funding* us." When she says the word *funding*, it drips with innuendo.

"Really," I say. I turn to Jess. "Can I talk to you for a second?" Before she can agree, I grab her arm, a bit too hard, and lead her five feet from Napier. He's watching our little tête-à-tête. I whisper to her, "What did we agree? No outsiders."

"But he has money."

"We don't need it," I say. "Not yet."

She makes a face: that I'm wrong, but it's no use trying to convince me. Not here, not now. I lead her back to Napier. "Sorry," I say. "I guess we crossed some wires. We're not really looking for any outside funding at the moment."

Napier shrugs. "That's fine. If you change your mind . . ." He produces a business card from his pocket and hands it to Jess. "Call anytime. Be sure to tell my assistant who you are. She'll put you right through."

"Thank you," Jess says.

"Now, if you'll excuse me. It seems I'm wanted."

He looks over at the corner of the room where the musicians stand. They've stopped playing, and the blond singer is holding the microphone out, in Napier's direction.

Some voices from the crowd say, "Come on, Ed, speech! Speech."

Napier leaves us and makes his way to the far side of the room. He climbs on the raised platform, takes the microphone from the singer. He taps it twice. The speakers *pop—pop.*

He says into the mike, "Hello?" His voice echoes from the amplifier, a warm honeyed baritone.

He smiles radiantly. The crowd cheers.

"I'm glad you could all come tonight. I understand that as soon as I sent out the invitations to this party, a mysterious European competitor sent out invitations to its *own party,* to be held tonight—and they're offering twenty-five percent more alcohol than I am!"

The audience laughs.

Napier pauses, scans the faces in the crowd. He continues: "Well it looks like I've won at least one bidding war." More cheers. The drummer in the porkpie hat gives a rim shot. The crowd laughs.

"I promised my wife, no speech today," Napier says. "So I just want everyone to enjoy themselves. You're going to hear a lot about my firm, Argyle Partners, in the future. Now that we've conquered Las Vegas, we're here to conquer . . . *excuse me,* invest in, Silicon Valley. We're going to invest in great companies. Companies that change the world!"

More cheers. Napier raises his fist in a little self-deprecating salute. He hands the microphone back to the blonde. The band strikes up "When the Saints Go Marching In." I'm not sure if the irony of associating Napier—a Las Vegas gambling magnate with connections to the underworld—with sainthood is apparent to the band, or anyone else in the room. Or maybe it is, and the open bar helps everyone overlook it. Napier skips off the platform merrily and is immediately mobbed by well-wishers. That's what having a few billion dollars can do: turn you into a movie star.

Jess turns to me. "How'd I do?"

"I'd say he's hooked. Now we just reel him in."

But she's looking at me, and I know immediately what she's thinking. *Nothing goes this easily.* When things go too easily, it's a warning. To run like hell.

CHAPTER EIGHTEEN

We've set up our office in an industrial park near the salt ponds at the foot of the Dumbarton Bridge. We have seven thousand square feet of space. You may think that seven thousand square feet is too large for a company of three people. But if you think like that, my friend, then you do not have the proper can-do spirit that is required to *change the world*.

It has taken us seven days to set up a fully functioning office. This is one of the miracles of the Valley: that there are hundreds of companies whose job is solely to set up other companies. All you need is a bank account. Then you make a phone call and say: "Please create my company." Within days, your company has sprung to life like a giant fungus that explodes, one rainy night, from an invisible spore.

So: The real estate agent finds us space near the Dumbarton. The office was previously occupied by a biotech company that itself moved into larger offices that were previously occupied by an Internet shoe retailer. *Where did the Internet shoe retailer go?* I ask the real estate agent, as we drive along Bayfront Expressway to see our office for the first time.

"Where did it *go?*" the agent repeats, as if I asked him to answer an impenetrable riddle. "What do you mean?"

This sums up the difference between the New Economy and the Old Economy. In the Old Economy, of which I am a proud card-carrying member, every winner creates a loser. Every new office tenant requires an old tenant to leave, to disappear, to die. In the New Economy, there are no losers. Nothing is finite. Not only can you have a free lunch; you can also have free breakfast and dinner. And a cappuccino with that, too.

The day after we sign the office lease and pay three months security deposit, the furniture arrives. This includes: ten desks and cubicles, ten Aeron chairs ($1,400 apiece), five gun-metal gray filing cabinets, a new foosball table ($800), and an old Ms. Pac-Man arcade game ($495, not including freight). I have been told by Peter Room that these last two items are required if we hope to hire competent computer programmers.

After the furniture arrives, we bring in the computers. Because we are racing the clock, we have little time to actually interview people and hire computer experts. No matter: All it takes is one phone call. Peter Room and I get on the speakerphone with a Silicon Valley temp agency, whose principal, Bo Ringwald, proclaims that he is a talent agent to "the world's smartest people." I say to Bo Ringwald, "I need five IT guys to help me set up a computer infrastructure for a brand-new company."

"Five IT guys?" Bo Ringwald says. "Done."

"How much?" I ask.

Bo Ringwald laughs, as if such a question is ridiculous. "Do you *care?*" He is used to dealing with entrepreneurs flush with cash from their first round of VC funding. In a world where profitability is not expected or sought, how can cost be a concern?

"Not really," I say, getting into the spirit of it.

The five computer guys amble into the office the next day at various times during the morning. Engineers regard *9-to-5* as a helpful suggestion. As long as you show up before noon, you are ambitious.

When enough of them arrive that we have achieved some kind of critical mass, Peter and I lead them down the hall and show them an empty windowless room with its own air-conditioning unit.

"I need an impressive-looking server room," I say.

Their leader, a lanky dude with a soul-patch, asks, "What do you need the computers to do?"

I shrug. "Blink lights, mostly."

The soul-patch dude nods, as if he gets this kind of request all the time. "How many computers?" he asks.

"How many can you fit in the room?" I say.

His eyes light up. It's like asking Dale Earnhardt Jr. to soup up your car however he sees fit.

While the computer guys excitedly discuss their upcoming trip to Fry's Electronics—the geek retail mecca in Palo Alto—arguing about what to buy, I take Peter into one of our three conference rooms.

I lay out the general outlines of the con. I trust Peter, and he is a good man, but details are dangerous. So I stick with broad strokes. I describe the piece of software I want him to build, which we will use to snare Ed Napier.

"Can you do that?" I say.

"Sure."

"In three days?"

Peter smiles and points to me, as if to say, *Whenever I talk to you, there is always a catch.*

"Three days," he says. He runs his fingers through his long red hair, dreamily, like a girl in a shampoo commercial. He thinks about it. "Yeah," he says, finally. "I think so."

"Then get to work."

I wander around the vast offices. The place feels like the Astrodome after everyone goes home and they turn off the lights: creepy and empty.

At one end of the cavern, the computer geeks are still arguing at the door of the server room, debating the merits of Linux versus Windows. To call the debate academic, since the computers they are about to install need not actually do anything, is to belabor the point. This is what computer people like to do—argue about operating systems. Asking them to stop would only raise suspicions that something is not quite right here at Pythia Corporation.

I find Jess in another dark corner, playing Ms. Pac-Man. A can of Coke rests on the game table, which is helpfully equipped with a cup holder. Without looking up, she says, "Did you know that a cherry is worth a hundred points?"

"Whose cherry?" I ask.

She smiles.

I say, "I think you'll run into Ed Napier on Thursday."

"That's fine."

"Are you willing to go through with it?"

Still not looking up: "Go through with what?" She slams the game joystick left, then up. The table shudders. The Coke shimmies in the cup holder.

"Whatever it takes."

"*Whatever it takes,*" she repeats. "That's mighty Silicon Valley of you."

"I mean, you don't have to do it."

For the first time, she looks up at me. "If I didn't know any better, I'd think you were jealous."

"I'm not jealous," I say. "Just concerned."

"Don't be." From the game: a *wah-wah-wah* melting sound, as Jess's cheese gets fatally gobbled.

"That's fine." I turn and walk away.

"But I appreciate it," she calls after me. "You being jealous."

I am about to protest that I am not jealous, but I realize the words will be hollow—and untruthful. So I say, "Thursday," and leave to rejoin the debate over Linux versus Windows, which suddenly seems quite compelling.

When I arrive home in the evening, Toby is lying on the couch watching a professional wrestling match on the television, in which two near-naked men slap and grapple each other to the frantic screams of the announcers.

I shut the door behind me and say, "Hi, Toby."

He doesn't turn around. He's been living with me the past week. What originally seemed like a good idea—an opportunity for father-son bonding—has lost some luster. Toby is waylaid by a half-length leg cast and crutches, medicated with Percodan and beer, and has a hard time moving. So he spends his time on the couch while I am in the office. Wrestling is his new hobby.

Watching wrestling.

He says, as a greeting, "Did you know you can't lower the volume on this TV?"

"I'm aware of that."

"Annoying," he says.

"You want to go out?" I ask. "For drinks?" Alcohol may be the only way to lure Toby from the apartment.

"Gee, Dad, I'd really love to go out on the town with you," he says, deadpan. "It's just that I can't actually, you know, *move.*"

I shrug, throw my keys on the table near the entry. I head for the bathroom.

Toby says, "That Mexican fella came by."

I stop in my tracks. "Mexican?"

"Your landlord."

"The young guy?"

"Yeah."

"He's Arabian," I explain. "Maybe Egyptian."

"Interesting," Toby says to the TV, not sounding particularly interested. On the screen, to the jeers of the crowd, one of the wrestlers climbs atop the ropes of the ring and prepares to launch himself, airborne, onto the windpipe of his supine opponent. "Anyway, he was real nosy. Asking a lot of questions."

"What kind of questions?"

"Who I am. What you do for a living."

I wait for Toby to continue. He does not. On the television, the wrestler flies off the ropes and lands with a thud on the canvas, barely missing the gullet of his opponent.

I say, "What did you tell him?"

"Tell him? That you're a con man and that you cheat people out of their hard-earned money."

"No you didn't," I say, suddenly appreciative of his dry sense of humor. But then I realize I'm not entirely certain he has one. So I say: *"Did* you?"

"No, knucklehead. I told him you're an entrepreneur."

"Much better," I say.

"And *that's* how you cheat people out of money."

I leave Toby and his roomful of irony to go to the bathroom, where I piss and wash my hands and face. I stare at myself in the mirror. I look beat. The days of preparation before the con, where your time is spent waiting and planning, are the most exhausting. Once you're on stage, adrenaline kicks in, and everything takes on a nervous edge. Until then, you fight boredom and torpor. I splash cold water on my face.

I return to the living room and join Toby, squeezing beside him on the couch.

"Anyway, I was thinking," Toby says.

"Oh?"

"Maybe I can help."

"With what?"

"Whatever you're doing. Your—you know . . . your *job.*"

"My job?" I repeat stupidly. I'm so amazed that he's proposing it, I don't know what else to say.

He thinks I don't understand what he's talking about. That he needs to be more specific. He says: "The con job you're doing. I can help."

I shake my head. "But . . . you're . . ." I wave at his cast. "Injured."

"I have crutches. I can get around. I'll say it was a skiing accident. Lots of people have casts."

I shake my head. "But the whole point of this," I explain, "is to protect you. To help you get *out* of trouble."

"Is it?"

"So I don't want you involved in something that could . . . go wrong."

"You asked that woman to help. The hot one."

He means Jess. "But she's a friend."

"What am I?"

"You're my son."

For the first time, he turns to me. "Dad, you're risking your entire life for me. I haven't told you how much I appreciate it."

"You're my son," I say again.

"So let me help. You're doing something for me. Let me contribute. I'm a grown man now, as much as you refuse to believe it. I can make adult decisions."

"Toby, if something goes wrong . . ."

"Then we're going down. I know. But at least we'll go down *together*. Father and son. Isn't that how it's supposed to be?"

No, I want to say. The way it's *supposed* to be is that the father *protects* the son. That the son climbs atop the father's shoulders, so the son can reach further. That the son leaves the father behind.

But I am overcome by selfishness. I relish the chance to show Toby my world, which I have hidden from him for so long. I never realized I possessed it, but his request unlocks the floodgates of my desire, and suddenly I want to show Toby everything: the weeks of preparation, the care, the planning, the skill. For so long, Toby has known me as the loser in Lompoc, the white-collar criminal who cheated Midwestern fatties out of their money. Now I can show him who I really am: a professional, someone who has worked for years—his whole life—perfecting an art.

I say halfheartedly, "Toby, it's not a good idea."

But he and I both know the same thing: that this argument is like the wrestling match now on the television in front of us—not even remotely a fair fight—and, like the blond muscleman with the glistening oiled pecs, Toby won the match even before he stepped into the ring.

CHAPTER NINETEEN

It's Thursday morning and I'm following Ed Napier in my Honda, twenty yards back. I've been tailing him all week, so that now we're old friends. Like a lover, I know his schedule, his peccadilloes. Each morning, he rises at six, exits his Woodside estate by the north gate, and chats for a minute with a security man who looks like a former linebacker. Then Napier, dressed in gray sweats, sets off down Skyline Boulevard and jogs a three-mile loop. He returns home at six-thirty and disappears into the mansion, presumably to shower. At eight o'clock he pulls out of the driveway in a cherry-red Mercedes SL convertible, top down, and heads over to Buck's for breakfast. Three out of the four days that I have followed, he has a meeting while he eats.

What I see through the restaurant's big front window is this: Two young men sit across from him, too nervous to touch their pancakes, while they walk Napier through a PowerPoint presentation on their laptop. Napier chews contentedly while they *tap—tap—tap* the spacebar of their keyboard to advance the presentation to the next slide. Each time they peer intently at Napier to divine his reaction: Should they advance to the next slide? Talk more about this one? Move on to the next section? Speed up? Slow down?

In case you ever have an opportunity to present to Ed Napier, here's a hint: *Speed up.*

Like a churlish teen, Napier can't control his display of emotion.

Typically that emotion is boredom. So as the young men talk about their company, describing no doubt how they will become the next Microsoft, Napier's eyelids droop. His chewing slows. His body slouches.

Inevitably the entrepreneurs don't notice. So they go on talking, about Internet this, or IP that—about monetizing eyeballs, or eyeballing money—about portals and gateways—until, mercifully, the check comes, and Napier grabs it and says his goodbye.

After Buck's, Napier heads to his office, a low-slung building near the Redwood City Marina. He parks in the underground lot and disappears from my view for the next three hours, which he probably spends on his speakerphone, his voice booming through the office, driving his receptionist and assistant crazy.

At twelve noon, like clockwork, he reappears, and pulls his Mercedes out of the garage and hightails it to lunch. Usual destination: Zibibbo's, in Palo Alto. Typical duration: two hours. Typical beverage: a bottle of Sancerre.

More meetings at lunch. Most of them seem to be with fawning reporters, since they take copious notes while they converse, and some carry their own cameras. However, I also witness one meeting with an attractive young redhead who, I suspect, never went to journalism school. I doubt that Mrs. Lauren Napier will ever learn about this lunch.

After lunch, Napier typically calls it a day. He heads back to his Woodside house, where he disappears from view, or over to the Menlo Club for a round of golf before having drinks on the veranda.

Not exactly a tough life. And not a workaholic's. But if I had a couple billion dollars in my bank account, I'm not sure I'd work any harder—or even, come to think of it, at all.

Now it's eight o'clock in the morning, and I'm following Napier as he pulls his red Mercedes out of his estate. As soon as he turns left on Woodside and I'm sure he's heading to Buck's for breakfast, I take out my cell phone and dial Jess. She's already stationed at the restaurant, waiting for Napier's entrance.

She picks up my call on the first ring. "Yes?" she says.

"He's coming. He'll be there in five."

"I'm ready," she says.

"Good luck."

"I'll see you in an hour," she says, and hangs up.

I follow three car-lengths behind Napier as far as the Buck's parking lot. When I see him climb from the Mercedes and head into the restaurant, I speed off toward Pythia's offices. I know exactly what will happen to Ed Napier next. It has been scripted and planned. This is the pickup. This is where Ed Napier thinks he is in charge, that he is making all the decisions, that his life is under his own control. But a con man knows something different: that your choices are never your own, that when you choose your own path, you are actually walking into a trap that has been laid for you. Walking happily. In a big rush.

Here is what happens next.

Napier walks into the restaurant, perhaps intending to meet young entrepreneurs for a pitch, or perhaps simply to eat alone. No matter: When he sees Jess sitting by herself at a table in the front of the room, looking at her watch, annoyed, he jettisons whatever plans he has.

He saunters to her table. "Hi," he says to her. "Jessica Smith, right?"

She looks up. "Yes." For a moment her face remains blank. She knows him from somewhere, but *where?* Then, a flash of recognition, and a bright smile, big and white, enough to melt any man's heart. *"Yes,"* she says again. "Mr. Napier."

"Please," he says. "Mr. Napier was my dad. Call me Ed."

"Ed."

"Coming or leaving?" he asks.

"Here for a meeting," she says. She looks at her watch again. "But I was stood up. You VCs. So selfish."

"Tell me his name and I'll have him killed."

"Wouldn't that make me an accomplice?"

"It's not a crime if you don't get caught," he says. Pulling up a chair, sitting down, he asks, "Can I join you?"

"Sure."

"Have you ordered?"

"No."

"My treat." He waves his hand at the waitress. She comes and takes their order. Napier requests his usual: a Lumberjack—two eggs over easy, three silver-dollar pancakes, bacon. Jess orders the same.

When the waitress leaves, Napier leans over the table, as if to confide in Jess. He says, "I looked up Pythia in the encyclopedia."

"Sorry?"

"Pythia. Isn't that the name of your company? I looked her up. She was the prophet at Delphi. In ancient Greece."

"Very good."

"But I still don't get it," he says.

"Get what?"

"What the name means."

Jess says, "The Greeks believed she could see the future. Men traveled hundreds of miles to hear her speak."

"I see," Napier says, though he doesn't. He thinks about it. Then he says: "So what does your company do, see the future?"

Jess smiles. "What we do is—" She stops mid-sentence, shakes her head. "Franklin would kill me if he knew I was talking to you."

"Franklin?"

"My partner."

It takes Napier a minute to recall me. "Oh, the older guy."

"He thinks we shouldn't tell anyone what we do."

Napier nods. "A lot of people are like that. Too secretive. Like I'm going to walk out of the meeting and run into my secret laboratory, to reproduce what they've spent years working on. As if I *could.*"

"Franklin's a very suspicious person."

It is at this point, I suspect, that Napier asks: "You and Franklin—are you . . ." He gestures vaguely with his hands.

"Together? Oh no. We're just business associates."

Napier's face shows relief. Maybe he leans over the table, with lupine grace. "I can't say I'm disappointed to hear that."

Jess says, "What are you doing after breakfast?"

Napier shrugs. Is it possible? Is she coming on to him?

She continues, "Come over to my office. I'll show you what we do."

At which point Ed Napier is quick to agree, although of course the choice was never his to make.

So he follows her in his cherry-red Mercedes, over to Menlo Park. They shoot down Willow and trace the curve of the Bay to the Dumbarton Bridge. They park in the Pythia lot and get out of their cars. I watch them from between the slats of my office window shade. It's only ten o'clock, but already eighty degrees, and the asphalt has started to bake. Napier squints into the sun.

Jess points to the entrance.

I hear them in the vestibule near my office. Jess is rattling her keys around, searching for the right one. Finally the door opens, and I hear Jess finishing her sentence, ". . . just moved in. About a week ago."

"Where were you before?" Napier asks.

"Oh it was all very glamorous. Working out of our apartments."

"You entrepreneurs. I admire what you do."

"Let's see who's around," Jess says. She calls out, "Franklin? Peter?"

That's my cue. I start toward the reception area. When I turn the corner, I lurch to a stop and pretend to be surprised to see Napier.

"Jess," I say, "what's—"

"Relax, Franklin. I ran into Mr. Napier at Buck's."

Napier says, much too loudly and much too friendly, "Hi, Franklin. Good to see you again!"

"Good to see you, too," I say, though my tone suggests otherwise. "Jess, I thought we agreed—"

"That we shouldn't talk about Pythia. We did. But we can trust Ed. He's offered to help."

"Oh," I snip. "Well why didn't you just say that?"

Napier's voice is as warm as an old sweater. "I've seen a lot of business plans, Franklin. I know what works, what doesn't. Even if you don't want my money, maybe I can help." He shrugs. "And who knows? Maybe I'll be interested. Wouldn't a million dollars or two help you guys out? Bring you to the next level?"

I pretend to think about it. Finally I say: "Give me your word."

"On what?"

"That whatever you see here, stays here. You don't tell a soul. Not your partners, not the press, not even your wife."

Jess says, "Franklin, you're being rude."

Napier waves her off. "No, no, he's not. He's being cautious. I admire that. Okay, Franklin, I give you my word. Whatever you show me today will be our secret."

"Okay, then." I turn and walk out of the room.

Behind me, I hear Jess say, "I guess that means we should follow him."

The tour starts at the server room. I unlock the door and swing it open so Ed Napier can take a look.

Peter Room is there, sitting on the floor, pecking at a keyboard, a can of Dr Pepper by his feet. My son, Toby, hanging off a pair of crutches, stands beside him, chatting. I'm keeping Toby on a short leash. He can hang out at Pythia, I've explained, observing and listening—part of his con education. But his assigned role is computer geek. *Quiet* computer geek. I have instructed him to keep his witty repartee and winsome personality to himself. So far, so good.

I step back to allow Napier an unobstructed view of the room. The space, which was empty when we moved in, has been transformed. Metal racks, mounted with computers, fill every inch of wall space. Hundreds of orange patch cords hang down in hopeless tangles like cyborg hair. Dozens of router switches display rows of blinking green and yellow lights. The effect of the blinking lights—thousands of them—in ruler-straight lines, is psychedelic, trippy. Then there's the noise, of a hundred computer fans—surprisingly loud, like rushing water.

I say over the noise, "This is the brain of Pythia. All the software runs here, in this small room." I look at Peter. "Ed Napier, this is Peter Room. He's our lead programmer."

Peter scrambles to his feet. He steps over his Dr Pepper, shakes Napier's hand. "How do you do?"

I say, "Peter, can you give Mr. Napier a brief description of what's going on here?"

"Sure." He gestures at the wall of computers. He raises his voice over the rush of the fans. "You're looking at one hundred Xeon-class Pentium machines, running the Linux operating system. Each machine is rated at one gigahertz. That may not sound like a lot, but the computers are networked together. You can think of it like one big mainframe. The effective processing speed, for software that has been properly designed to operate in parallel, reaches one teraflop."

Napier nods sagely.

I say to Peter, "Why don't you put that in terms us normal people can understand, Peter?"

"Right," Peter says, "okay. Let's put it this way. The computers in this room are able to perform one trillion floating point operations per second. Just to give you a sense of what that means, the National Weather Service recently bought a Cray supercomputer to help predict the path of hurricanes. That single Cray computer cost twenty-five million dollars. The machines in this room, all together, cost around two hundred fifty thousand dollars. But this room contains four times the computing power of the Cray."

"Fascinating," Napier says.

"Basically, this is the world's most powerful pattern-matching software. We use genetic algorithms and neural networks to analyze massive amounts of data."

I say, "Thank you, Peter. Why don't you go to the conference room to get a demo set up for Mr. Napier."

Peter nods and scampers down the hall, ahead of us, toward the large conference room. Napier, Jess, and I leave the server room, and slowly follow.

I say, "The only reason we stopped at one hundred computers was lack of space. If we added another hundred computers, the processing power would increase by a factor of ten."

"And what do the computers *do?*" Napier says.

"Come," I say. "I'll show you."

We make our way to the conference room. Jess powers up the video projector and presses a wall switch. A motorized white screen whirrs down from the ceiling. Peter is hunched over a keyboard on the conference table. Pecking away, he says, "I'll be ready in a sec."

I offer Napier a seat facing the screen. I gesture to the light switch. "Jess, would you?"

Jess cuts the lights. The only thing visible on the screen is a single blinking cursor.

I walk to the head of the table, stand in front of the screen. The cursor blinks on my cheek. I say, "It's taken us twelve months to develop the software that Pythia uses. The idea behind Pythia is to assemble hundreds of off-the-shelf computing components, and then to write software specially designed to take advantage of them. The software models real-world chaos by breaking down complexity into tiny, simple equations. Anything that seems complicated—that seemingly can't be represented in a linear fashion—Pythia can model accurately. From simplicity comes complexity."

"I see," Napier says. He glances at his watch. We've lost him. He's thinking that it was exciting to drive over here in the summer heat as long as there was a chance to get some of Jess's poon, but all this talk about modeling and software and chaos theory is not what he had in mind. He says, "I should tell you that I have an eleven o'clock meeting back in the office."

Jess says to me, "Franklin, I think you're boring Mr. Napier. Excuse me—Ed." She gives him a winning smile. He smiles in return. She continues, "Why don't we put this in everyday terms? Let's talk about how the software can be used."

Napier nods. "Thank God for marketing people."

She laughs. "There are hundreds of possible uses for Pythia," she says. "Predicting the weather, for example. More accurately forecasting tornado zones. Even predicting earthquakes."

"I see," Napier says. I can see him doing the P&L in his head. He's thinking: The profit in predicting earthquakes is zero.

She says, "Of course, predicting earthquakes doesn't make for very compelling product demonstrations. So Peter helped us come up with this one." She nods to Peter.

Peter taps a key. The projection screen is filled with a graph of undulating green lines—a daily stock price chart.

I say, "What stock is this, Peter?"

Peter says, "Symbol HSV. Let's see, that's Home Services of America."

I say, "What does Home Services of America do, Peter?"

"No friggin' clue," Peter says.

"Okay, let's go tick-by-tick."

Peter taps a key. The chart changes to a real-time price display. The final green dot representing the latest price is continuously moving: up, down, then up again, in tiny penny increments. The motion seems random.

I say, "Okay, Peter, turn on Pythia."

He taps another key. "Done."

For a moment, nothing happens. Then, a red circle appears to the right of the screen, far from the last green tick for the stock. The circle is labeled with small text: "90% conf."

I say, "This is Pythia's projection for the stock price in the next fifteen seconds."

The actual price of the stock stutters downward, away from the circle that was just drawn. I say, "Any second now . . ."

The red circle grows darker. It changes to "93% conf." Then: "95% conf."

I say, "Pythia is telling us that she is ninety-five percent confident stock HSV will reach price twenty-two and a nickel in the next ten seconds."

Now, like magic, the stock stops descending, and starts back upward.

Pythia says, "98% conf."

The stock ticks upward again, toward the red circle that Pythia initially drew. Finally, the stock price climbs again, and the green dot reaches the center of the Pythia target circle.

The red circle brightens. Text appears: "Target reached."

"There," I say. "Pythia accurately predicted the price of HSV."

Napier is speechless. He stares at the screen, his jaw slack.

I say, "Of course, Pythia wasn't designed for financial services. It's really meant to work on complex computing tasks—as I said: weather, volcanoes, fault lines. You can see that it might even be helpful in the biotech industry, analyzing drug molecules."

"Wait a second," Napier says. He's staring at the screen. "Did it just predict how that stock would move?"

"Yes," I say. "Well, fifteen seconds out. Any more than a minute or two, and it loses accuracy."

"Can you do it again?"

"Sure," I say, but I sound uncertain. "But that's not really what the software—"

"With *any* stock?" Napier says.

"Yeah, sure. Name a stock."

"GM."

"Fine." I turn to Peter. "GM, Peter. Know how to spell that?"

He glares at me. "Got it," he says. He types something, and then the first stock chart is replaced by a chart of GM. "Here's the daily chart," Peter says. He clicks a key. "And, here's the tick-by-tick . . ."

Again, the screen changes to a magnified tick-by-tick graph of the price of GM. The movement of GM is more frenetic than the previous stock. The price flits around the seventy-dollar mark. The green dot rises and falls, dancing epileptically as thousands of shares trade hands each second. The price stutter-steps around: first up, then down, then down again.

"All right," I say, "let's run this through Pythia."

"Hang on," Peter says. A few more keystrokes, and then a red circle appears on the far right of the screen, near the 70.25 price level. It is labeled: "92% conf."

We watch the screen as the price of General Motors fluctuates wildly: back down to 69.50, then up again. The confidence level grows with each passing second: 93% confident . . . 94% confident . . .

Napier says, mostly to himself, "This is the damndest thing . . ."

The price falls further away from Pythia's red target circle. Regardless, the confidence level increases: 95% confident . . . 96% confident.

"Looks like she's wrong on this one," Napier says.

As if to bitch-slap him, the green dot reverses direction and starts shooting back up. It rockets past 69.90, then 70 dollars.

Pythia's confidence is now 97% . . . 98% . . .

The price of GM continues its rise. It lands in the red target circle: at $70.25. The screen says: "Target reached."

"You're shitting me," Napier says.

I nod to Jess. She turns on the lights. We look at Napier. He's still staring at the screen.

"Those are real-time prices?"

"Yes," I say. "You can check them yourself when you get back to your office. What time is it now?" We all look at our watches. "Okay, it's twenty after ten. When you get back, look up at where GM was at this time. It'll be seventy and a quarter."

"My God," Napier says, quietly.

"You like it?" Jess says.

"Like it?" Napier stands up. "It's amazing." He turns to me. "How many people know about this? Besides me?"

I pretend to do some counting in my head. "Let's see. There's me, Peter, and Jess. And Toby. Some of the computer guys."

"Have you talked to any other venture capitalists about this?"

"No," I say.

"Good. Let's keep it that way."

I say stupidly, "I don't understand."

"I'm willing to invest in your company. Hell, buy it from you outright. Whatever."

Jess says softly, "You see, Franklin?"

I ignore her. "But why?" I ask.

"Don't you see?" Napier says. He swivels in his chair to stare at me. "It's going to make you rich."

"But," I say, "we're talking about tiny price moves. Ten cents here. A nickel there."

Napier says: "But multiply that by ten thousand shares! By a hundred thousand shares. And if you can do that a hundred times a day . . ."

I say, "Is that legal?"

"Of course," Napier says. "Why wouldn't it be?"

I say, "It's kind of cheating."

Napier says, "It's like card counting in Vegas. You try it in my place, and we'll kick you out. But it's not against the law to *try.*"

"I see," I say. I act as if this is the first time I considered using Pythia to make money. I say, "But it wasn't really designed for that."

Napier turns to Peter Room. "You wrote the software?"

"Most of it. Me and some guys."

"Can you add something? Make it place trades at a broker, automatically?"

Peter shrugs. "With the right kind of broker . . ."

"Can you use mine?" Napier asks. "Schwab?"

Peter shakes his head. "No, we have to use something with automation hooks. FIX protocol."

I say, "I have an account at Datek."

"That'll work," Peter says.

Napier turns to Jess. His gentle, flirtatious demeanor has vanished. Now he's sharp edges—ruthless again, all business—on the hunt for money. Give men a choice between cooch and cash, they'll choose the latter every time. "Jessica," he says, "you have to keep this under wraps. You can't go around talking about this."

"All right."

Napier rises from his chair. "Gentlemen." He turns to Jess. "Jessica." He points to the screen. "I'm willing to bankroll you. We go in as equal partners. I'll shoulder the risk. You use my cash. And you can keep half of whatever we win."

"Whatever we win?" I say, stupidly. "But that's not what the software was designed for . . ."

Napier ignores me. He takes a checkbook from his suit pocket.

He leans over the table, writing with his gold pen. He tears the check from the book, hands it to me.

It's made payable to "Cash" in the amount of fifty-thousand dollars.

He says to me, "Deposit that at your broker." He turns to Peter: "On Wednesday, we'll do a little experiment. Test it with real money."

Peter looks as if he might object, but then he thinks better of it. Napier is in charge now. Which is exactly what we want him to think.

CHAPTER TWENTY

In the 1890s, enterprising telegraph operators traveled around the country ripping people off. A crook would find a mark, a rich businessman, and explain how—as a telegraph operator at Western Union—he received the results of all the horse races that were being run on any given afternoon, and how it was his job to forward those results immediately to gambling parlors, so that bets could be paid out.

The telegraph operator would have a proposition for his mark. The telegraph operator—at great personal risk—could delay telegraphing race results to a particular gambling parlor for a few minutes—just long enough to allow the mark to place a bet with certain knowledge about who won the race. Then the two partners would split the earnings.

The rip-off spread quickly, growing in complexity. At the beginning, there may have been real telegraph operators who actually delivered on their promises. But soon the con was overrun by common criminals, men with no connection to the telegraph business whatsoever. They would spin a yarn about how—with the right kind of equipment—it was possible to "intercept" telegraph messages, and how—with a few minutes' foreknowledge of race results—fortunes could be made. All that was required, explained the con man to his mark, was a modest amount of cash, enough to purchase the necessary telegraph equipment used to intercept telegraph messages. If the mark would fund the venture, the con man would buy the equipment, and the two would get rich . . .

Of course no equipment was actually purchased, and no race results were actually "intercepted." Nevertheless, the con man confidently delivered supposed "inside information" by telephone to his mark, who was standing by at a gambling parlor. The excited mark then placed a bet. If the "inside information" turned out to be correct (a one-in-seven chance), then the con man would collect additional money: his share of the lucky winning bet. Otherwise, if the "can't-lose" information turned out to lose, the con man would disappear, never to be heard from again, pocketing the cash that was intended to buy telegraph interception equipment.

This rudimentary con, in turn, evolved into something more sophisticated, in which elaborate—but entirely fictional—betting parlors were built and staffed by shills, and in which completely imaginary races were run, all for the benefit of a single mark.

Thus a fictional world was created by con men—a stage show in which the mark was the only person unaware that he was in the middle of a theatrical performance. The show was so convincing that marks believed that they had stumbled upon a surefire way to get rich. The con men would allow a mark to win a few races at their fake gambling dens, with the benefit of "inside information"—in order to whet the mark's appetite. Then, with the mark's greed fanned red-hot, the con men put the mark on the send—that is, they allowed him to return home and gather every drop of cash he could muster, perhaps by taking out a loan on his property, or withdrawing cash from his bank. The mark would then return to his new business associates loaded with cash, ready to place the single bet that would make him rich beyond his wildest dreams! Of course, the only people who got rich at this point were the con men themselves.

The mechanism for taking the cash varied. Sometimes, the con men would deliver their "inside information" in a way that could be—and of course was—misinterpreted. For example, right before the crucial race, the mark would receive a phone call from his tipster. "Place it on Shadow Dancer," the caller would whisper. The mark would hang up the phone, hurry to the betting window, and lay out a hundred thousand dollars of cash on Shadow Dancer to win the race. The bet made, the cash paid, the con man working alongside the mark would examine the betting ticket and cry in a horrified voice, "No! He said put it on Shadow Dancer *to place!* Not to win! Don't you understand the difference between win and place?" At which point, despite the pleas of the mark to the "manager" of the gambling establishment, the fake race would begin and all betting would be closed. Needless to say, Shadow Dancer would come in second, and the mark's ticket would prove worthless.

Alternately, con men would blow off their mark by having the gambling parlor raided by a swarm of blue-uniformed policemen at the critical moment before the mark was about to collect his winning bet. Fake paddy wagons would line up outside the establishment, ready to cart people off to prison. The mark would escape from the (imposter) police's grasp, but only just, and his hundred-thousand-dollar bet would be lost. But he would return home happy at least that he had evaded disgrace and prison time.

By the 1920s, the Wire con game disappeared from this country. The telegraph was superseded by more advanced communication technology, and people had grown more sophisticated.

The consensus today is that the Wire is dead, that modern technology has rendered it merely a quaint relic from a colorful age. After all, people these days are far too sophisticated to fall for it, or anything like it.

CHAPTER TWENTY-ONE

The next morning, the four of us—me, Jess, Peter, and Toby—are in the Pythia offices, playing foosball, waiting for Napier to take the next step. It's not clear what the next step is, or when it will be taken, but as we play our game we learn the answers: ten o'clock, and with a knock on the exterior glass door of our office.

I leave the game to answer it. Toby hobbles behind me on crutches. Standing in the vestibule is a large muscular man in a suit, with a crew cut and dark shades. I push open the door. "Yes?" I say.

"Mr. Napier sent me. He wants me to take the four of you to the airport."

Behind him, in the parking lot outside, I see a black stretch limo, engine idling. "I'm not really dressed for the prom," I say.

The guy with the crew cut stares at me without expression.

"Do we have a choice?" I ask.

"Not really."

I appreciate his honesty. I tell him to wait for us outside, and I return with Toby to the foosball game.

I say, "Ed Napier's courting us. He's trying to win our hearts and minds."

Jess says, whacking the foosball with a flick of her wrist: "Too bad we're heartless."

* * *

The limo takes us to the Palo Alto Airport, a postage stamp with one runway. We drive onto the tarmac and pull up alongside a Citation X private jet, which is waiting outside the hangar, engines burning.

The driver sticks the limo into park, gets out, and opens our door. We climb out. The hatch of the Citation is open, stairs unfurled to the tarmac. A man in a pilot's uniform sticks his head from the hatch. He smiles. Yelling over the roar of the jets, he says, "Welcome aboard."

On board, there's room for eight people, but we're only four. The hot blond stewardess counts as one, so that leaves room to stretch. Napier has stocked the plane with champagne, a Ridge zinfandel, and a Marlborough sauvignon blanc. In addition, there's caviar and shrimp. The stewardess is scuttling up and down the aisle, pushing drinks and hors d'oeuvres with the gusto of a peanut vendor at Pac Bell Park.

When she reaches me, I accept a glass of white wine. As she leans over, I ask her cleavage, "Are you allowed to tell us where we're going?"

"Allowed?" She looks puzzled. "Of course. We're going to Las Vegas."

"Of course," I say.

After we take off, Toby and Peter unfasten their belts and retreat to the rear of the plane. I notice Peter's face is pale and drawn, with thin lines of worry around his mouth. I wonder: Part of the con? A superb acting job? Or is he in over his head—regretful about getting involved, suddenly worried about consequences? He stares out his window sullenly, absentmindedly stroking his long red ponytail.

In contrast, Toby is beaming, nursing a glass of champagne. Either he's playing his part brilliantly, doing a convincing imitation of a feckless kid blown away by the high life, or he's really a feckless kid blown away by the high life.

Jess and I sit next to each other at the front of the plane. There may be cameras and microphones on board, and Napier may debrief the platinum blond stewardess when we touch down, so we remain quiet, each facing a different window. My solace is the feeling of the warm skin of her arm against mine. It's hardly noticeable to the stewardess—not worth a mention to Napier, if he asks—but secretly, I hope her arm remains there for the rest of the flight. For hours she doesn't move it, so maybe she feels the same way.

We touch down in Las Vegas ninety minutes later. Another stretch limousine, a white one this time, waits for us on the tarmac. We pile in and are greeted by another muscleman in a suit.

"Mr. Napier sends his greetings," the driver says over his shoulder. "He regrets that he can't meet you personally, but he will see you in The Clouds."

The Clouds is Napier's hotel. It's one of the newest on the Strip, built at a cost of two billion dollars, a colossal real estate gamble that provided plenty of fodder for Napier's critics. You can imagine the headlines in the business press: "Send in the Clouds," or "Napier's Folly," or "Clouded Vision." But Napier, as always, proved his critics wrong. The hotel was finished, and today stands fully occupied almost every day of the year.

I guess people can't get enough of bellhops dressed like angels—with tiny, vestigial wings stitched onto the back of their jackets; of harp music in the lobby; or of a white and taupe color scheme that extends from the bathrooms, to the hallways, to the casino.

The driver pulls the limo into the reception circle. The Clouds is a huge white sandstone building in flamboyant Italian Renaissance style. If Michelangelo ate a bad mushroom, this is what he'd trip about: thirty-six floors of rococo stonework and ornate cornices; of grotesque gargoyles hunched on ledges; of statues of cherubim with outstretched hands, either in welcome or in warning.

The driver gets out of the limo and opens the door for us. We climb from the car. Toby cranes his neck upward and flips down his sunglasses. "Cool," he says.

The driver leads us into the reception area. When we enter, the blast of air-conditioning is so cold that my balls shrink into cherry pits. At the far end of the hall, a young woman strums on a full-size harp, playing what sounds like a bastardized version of "Memories." Or maybe "Take Me Out to the Ballgame." Or maybe "The Star-Spangled Banner." The harp is, alas, a difficult instrument.

At the far end of the hall I see a huge banner, fifty feet across, hanging from the ceiling. It shows an artist's conception of a new hotel on the Strip. The banner says: "The *New* Tracadero, from Napier Casinos. Coming Soon!"

The driver escorts us across the lobby floor to a discreet alcove with a desk marked *VIP Check-In.* "Here you go," he says.

Toby, vaulting across the floor on his crutches, whispers to me: "VIP . . . Cool."

Behind the VIP desk sits a pretty brunette, with big blue eyes. She wears a white dress with two large angel wings on her back. I suspect that her smile is forced: Sitting in a chair all day, hunched forward because of fake angel wings, must be painful.

The driver says to her, "Clarissa, this is Mr. Napier's party."

"Thank you, Charlie," she tells the driver. He nods and leaves. The blue-eyed angel turns to us. Her smile grows even wider: "Welcome to The Clouds! Mr. Napier has asked me to make sure that your stay with us is wonderful!" She opens her desk drawer and removes four electronic card keys. "Each of you will receive a suite in our penthouse tower. They're on the thirty-sixth floor." She hands us each a key. "You'll need your key for elevator access. The entire floor is private."

Peter says, "Uh, listen, how much does this *cost*, exactly?"

The smile stays firmly planted on the blue-eyed angel's face, like a mollusk on the side of a fish tank. "This is Mr. Napier's gift to you. Everything this weekend is on the house. He's asked me to make sure you enjoy yourselves."

"Awesome," Toby says.

The angel continues, "You can use your card keys to pay for services in the gym, the spa, or any of the six restaurants here in

The Clouds. I'm aware that you came here without any clothes. You can use your card in any of the clothing shops in the atrium to outfit yourself for your stay here. Please do not be shy. It is Mr. Napier's pleasure to have you as his guests."

"That's very kind," I say.

The angel says: "Mr. Napier asks that you now go to your rooms to freshen up. And then, if you would, please meet him at one o'clock, on the thirty-fifth floor, for a caviar and champagne toast to celebrate your new business partnership."

We need to pass through the casino on the way to the elevator. All the hotels in Las Vegas are designed this way. You have to pass through the casino no matter where you want to go. Looking for the restaurant? It's back that way, past the casino. The concierge? Head through the casino and turn left. It's only a matter of time, I think, before Las Vegas designers take the next logical step: putting a casino in the middle of your hotel room, between your bed and the toilet. *Yeah, sure, I have explosive shits from the sushi last night, but let's see if I can't fit in one hand of blackjack before I take a crap.*

As we walk through the casino, Jess says softly, "If I didn't know any better, I'd think Ed was trying to butter us up."

The tones of the slots are musical, mesmerizing. The lighting here in the casino is soft, inviting. I want to stay for a while.

"You think?" I say. But I'm concentrating on Peter Room, who is walking fifteen feet ahead of the rest of us, as if to physically represent how he feels—separate. I say softly to Jess, "Peter's acting strange, isn't he?"

Jess shrugs. "Computer guys," she says, by way of explanation.

We reach the elevator bank and press the button marked "Penthouse Only." We wait for a moment, and then the elevator softly chimes, and the doors open. As if on cue, out walks Lauren Napier, stunning in a tailored white three-piece suit, with a black and white checkered clutch. Her hair is pulled back into a crisp bun. She smiles at me.

"Hello," she says.

I nod to her.

She is about to say something more, but then sees Toby, Jess, and Peter. She thinks better of it and presses her lips closed. She turns and walks away. I watch her ass as it disappears into the casino.

"Who is that?" Toby asks.

"Napier's wife," I explain.

"He's married?"

"When it suits him," I say. And for some reason, I think of Jess when I say it.

We meet at one o'clock on the thirty-fifth floor. It's one big suite, occupying the entire floor—all windows, overlooking the flashing lights of the Strip below, and the desert to the southwest. Tables with white linens have been set up, loaded with crushed ice, atop which sit oysters on the half-shell, small bowls of caviar, and shrimp. A table nearby holds flutes of champagne, pre-poured, ready to be tossed down the gullet.

When we arrive, Edward Napier is nowhere to be found. In his place are two beefy security men, with bud earpieces and wires running into their suit jackets. They stand at the side of the room, stoically.

Peter, Jess, Toby, and I mill around near the table of oysters, uncertain if we should eat. Of course Toby has no such inhibitions. He balances on his crutches and fixes himself a plate of blini, sour cream, and caviar. He places an entire blini on his tongue and swallows it, like a Eucharist wafer. "Fantastic," he says. "*Franklin,*" he says, stressing my alias so that it sounds even more ridiculous than it is, "you've got to try these."

Before I have a chance to glare at him, there's a commotion at the entrance of the suite. Napier walks into the room, accompanied by the brunette angel that checked us into the hotel. Across the room Napier sees us and smiles brightly. With his Caribbean tan, his teeth glow like Limoges porcelain. He's wearing an impeccable Armani suit, yellow tie, white shirt. His entire person glows, like a small corner of the Strip, thousands of exciting watts entering our presence. He walks to the front of the suite and then addresses us, as if we were a crowd.

"My friends," he says. He holds his hand out, vaguely in the direction of one of his beefy bodyguards, and rubs his fingers together. A bodyguard sees the signal, and scampers to the table holding champagne glasses. He grabs one, puts it in his boss's fingers.

Without acknowledging the man, Napier raises his glass. "I'd like to welcome you all here. Thank you for coming on such short notice. I hope your trip was pleasant."

There's a pause. I'm unsure if he's giving a speech, or if he expects some kind of response. Finally, I make an executive decision. "Very pleasant," I say.

"Good, good." He nods at me, as if I have done well by speaking. "Franklin, I'm excited to begin our business partnership. I want the four of you to enjoy the next day, here at my hotel. Consider this a gesture of my thanks. I'm glad to be in business with you."

He raises his glass. There's another pause. I realize he's waiting for us to make a toast with him. I take a champagne flute from the table and hand it to Jess. Then I take another and hand it to Peter. I'm about to hand a final one to Toby, but of course he already has one, half-empty.

I take the glass for myself and raise it in the air. "Hear hear," I say.

Jess says, "Hear hear."

Napier says, "Let's make some money together."

We drink the champagne. It is, I must admit, the most exquisite champagne I have ever tasted. I'm accustomed to the stuff you pick up at Safeway the day before New Year's Eve, the stuff that you don't feel bad about pouring over someone's head at the end of a big softball game. The stuff in my mouth, though, is like electric nectar, delicious. It is not meant to be used as a shampoo.

Napier says, "On Wednesday we're going to test Pythia with real money. Franklin, you've deposited my check in your brokerage account?"

"Yes," I say. "It'll clear by Wednesday."

Napier turns to Peter. "And Peter, will the software be ready to place real trades?"

"I suppose," Peter answers sullenly. He sounds like a kid being asked if he finally cleaned his room.

When Peter answers, a fleeting look of concern crosses Napier's face. Then it vanishes, and he smiles again. "Excellent! Now then . . ." He gestures at the brunette angel standing at the door of the suite. Napier says to us, "Would all of you like some chips?"

For a moment I think he's offering us tortillas and guacamole, which seems out of place after Cristal and beluga. Then I see the brunette carries four boxes, each the size of a tennis ball and covered in black velvet. The brunette hands each of us a box.

Toby opens his first. It contains a stack of black casino chips with The Clouds logo stamped on them. Blacks are worth a hundred dollars. I'm guessing there are twenty-five of them in each of our boxes. That's twenty-five hundred bucks' worth of party favors. I open mine. I've received the same.

"These are complimentary," Napier says. "Please feel free to use them in the casino and enjoy yourselves. You're all my partners now. I want to share everything with you." The unspoken part of the equation, I understand, is that he wants us to share everything with him.

As if to confirm my suspicion, Napier walks over to Jess. He smiles warmly. "Jess, why don't you come with me? I know that, as a marketing person, you'll be interested in some of the business aspects of The Clouds. Allow me to give you a private tour."

She smiles demurely. He takes her hand and leads her from the room. Over his shoulder, he calls out, "Please, enjoy!"

When he and Jess leave the room, I stare after them. Through the open door, I can see them standing at the end of the short hallway, waiting for an elevator. Finally the elevator arrives, and I watch Jess and Napier step inside and start their descent to his residence, where I'm sure he will show her many interesting "business aspects" of The Clouds, about which she was previously ignorant.

*   *   *

Four hours later, I'm downstairs in the casino at a ten-dollar blackjack table. I've already returned Napier's gift and have additionally contributed two hundred of my own dollars to the casino coffers.

For a man who makes his living ripping people off, I am a surprisingly easy mark. Unfortunately, I have the blood of a gambler—always doubling down when the odds are against me, never content to hold. I realize, too late, that I enjoy too much the rush I get when I peek at a fresh card. Each hit is enticing, full of delicious possibility.

Now I'm staring at a nine and a five in my own hand. The dealer is showing a six. The odds call for me to stand pat, but I can't resist. I flick my finger on the green felt and ask for another card. The dealer, a middle-aged Malay woman, slips me a nine. Ouch. Twenty-three. I bust.

The dealer takes my chips. I look at my remaining pile, a sad forty bucks. An old man in a ten-gallon hat sits next to me. He's smoking a big cigar. He says in a Texas twang, "Should stand on fourteen."

"Twenty-twenty hindsight," I say.

I ante two more red chips and play another hand. Now I'm looking at a five and a seven. The dealer shows a red jack. I vaguely recall I ought to hit whenever I have twelve, no matter what the dealer shows. Or is that a false memory? Am I just desperate for the rush I'll feel when I turn over another card? I feel lost, unsure of everything.

I gesture to stand pat.

The dealer flips a card from the shoe and gives the old cowboy sitting next to me an eight. He has twenty. She deals herself a nine. Cowboy wins; I lose.

The cowboy says, "Should hit when you get twelve."

"Really," I say. "Maybe I just want to give Ed Napier more of my money."

The cowboy rests his cigar on the edge of an ashtray. The mouth end is wet like a lollipop. "Lord knows he could use it."

"That right?" I ante two more red chips. The dealer flips me a king and a seven. Seventeen is a pretty good hand, isn't it? Especially when the dealer is showing a lousy five? But now I'm not so sure. Everything is hazy. Ever since I watched Jess descend in the elevator with Napier, to go on a private tour, I can't focus on the cards right in front of my face.

"From what I hear," the cowboy says. "Rumor is that building this place nearly sank him. Two billion dollars, all debt. My friend on the Gaming Commission says he doesn't even have cash for the Tracadero."

I look around the casino, at the thousands of people gathered around the slot machines, feeding quarters; at the crowds along the blackjack tables, two deep. "It doesn't look like he's hurting," I say.

"This here is an illusion," the cowboy says, simply.

Back to my hand. I'm staring at a seventeen. The dealer shows a losing five. The odds tell me I ought to stand pat. But fuck the odds. I flick my finger. The dealer hits me.

"Son," the cowboy says, "you have got to be the worst gambler I ever did run across."

The dealer flips me a four. She gives herself a ten and then another five. So there: My twenty-one beats her twenty.

The cowboy shakes his head. "Even crazy people get lucky," he explains.

My winning streak at the blackjack table lasts exactly one hand. Does that, somewhere, qualify as a streak? When my chips disappear, I leave the table and wander through the casino. I glance at my watch. I'm amazed that it is already six o'clock in the evening. Have I been playing for four hours? It seems impossible.

Across the hall I see a bar, raised above the casino floor on a platform. I decide to get hammered. I walk toward the bar until, at twenty yards, I stop in my tracks. I am frozen by what I see. It is Toby, sitting on a bar stool, his crutches balanced rakishly beside him. He is leaning forward, talking casually—perhaps even intimately—with Lauren Napier.

My first thought is that my son is purposely trying to wreck this con, perhaps out of childish rebelliousness. Could he possibly be that selfish, that foolish, to jeopardize everything I am doing . . . for *him?*

I make a beeline for the bar and climb the stairs. I head for Toby and Lauren Napier. When I'm standing directly over them, they finally look up at me. I ignore her, and drill my gaze into Toby.

"What are you *doing?*"

He smiles. "Nothing. Just talking." He says it dreamily, as if he's telling his Pops to relax; he's just having a conversation with his high school sweetheart under the bleachers.

I glance up at the ceiling, at one of the dozens of black glass half-globes—eyes in the sky—staring down at us. "You are being watched," I tell my idiot son.

Lauren smiles. She says softly, "Calm down. You're making a scene."

"Don't you understand? If your husband sees us talking . . ."

Lauren says, "He *told* me to talk to you."

"He did?"

"He told me to spend time with each of you. To learn everything I can."

"Why?" I ask. "Is he suspicious?"

"He's *careful,*" she says. For a moment, she sounds proud of him. "Anyway, I was just chatting with Toby, who is a delightful young man, by the way. I knew he was your son the moment I saw him. Very good-looking."

Toby blushes. It's unclear if the compliment was meant for me or for him. And perhaps that's the idea.

Lauren says to me, "Have a seat and calm down. I'll buy you a drink. Like old times."

I grunt and pull up a stool. I try to wedge it between Toby and Lauren, but their seats are too close, so I move it back a bit. Lauren gets the bartender's attention and orders me a beer. She turns to me. "That's what you drink, right? Beer?"

"Fine."

While she's settling the tab with the bartender, I stare at her. She's still dressed in the white three-piece suit from earlier this

morning. She looks neat and crisp, like a stack of elegant linens.
With her hair swept up in a bun, I can see the nape of her neck,
the shallow soft indentation, the wisps of loose blond hair. I forgot
how attractive she is. Now I recall that afternoon in the church,
when I first spoke to her—how for the next few hours I couldn't
get her out of my head. I remember that tight yellow T-shirt she
wore to church, those perfect breasts, and those white teeth and
their wicked smile. Now I picture her naked, and for some reason
I think of her toenails, painted red, and imagine what they will
look like as she wraps her legs around my waist.

I'm starting to have a change of plans. Instead of getting hammered, I want to get laid.

My beer comes. She says, "I was telling Toby. Ed can't stop talking about you. He says your company is the most amazing thing
he's ever seen."

"That right?" I say.

"So tell me the plan."

"It's best if we don't."

"That's what your son said."

I feel a pang of remorse that I doubted Toby. Perhaps he is more
reliable than I thought.

Lauren shrugs. "So don't tell me. As long as you intend to honor
our deal . . ."

"Of course."

"Then do whatever you want."

Out of the corner of my eye I see Toby staring at her. His in-
tensity is unnerving.

She looks at her watch. "I wonder if my husband is finished upstairs."

"Finished?" I say.

"Fucking your partner, Jessica."

I must look surprised, because she says: "Of course I know.
After all, he asked me to leave the room." She pauses. She rubs her
chin with theatrical pensiveness. "How *ever* can I get back at him?"

She lets the question hang like a piñata.

I feel the stir of an erection. But so, too, it seems, does Toby, who is staring at Lauren Napier like a dog staring at a piece of mutton.

"Toby," I say quietly, "I have an idea." I take out my wallet, hand him two one-hundred-dollar bills. "Here's some cash. Why don't you go play some slots?"

He looks at my proffered bills, but does not take them. He says, "I was kind of hoping to stick around here."

Interesting feeling, wanting to kick your own son's ass. I admit that, in the rich tapestry that is my life, this is a thread I have not yet run across.

I say gently, "Toby, son. What did we talk about?"

He looks at me quizzically.

I continue, still in a quiet gentle tone: "How you're welcome to come along, but that you need to follow my lead. How I'm in charge, since you're just learning. Right?"

Toby stares at me. I can't read his face. His lips are pressed into a slight smile, but he does not seem very mirthful.

He glances at Lauren Napier. Her face is emotionless, placid. This must happen to her all the time—being fought over by fathers and sons.

"Toby," I say again, softly.

Finally, he nods. He takes the two hundreds from my hand. He hops onto his good foot, grabs his crutches. "I'm gonna check out the casino," he says.

I want to say, "Thanks," and pat his shoulder in a comforting man-to-man gesture, but he hobbles away on his crutches so quickly that I do not have time to act.

I follow Lauren Napier through the casino to the elevator. She presses the call button, and we wait in silence for the elevator to arrive. It comes, and we allow six Japanese businessmen to exit. They ogle Lauren as they pass—she is a foot taller than them, a Nordic *gaijin*. I imagine in their country, they are quiet and polite, engineers or executives, and they would never so obviously stare at a beautiful woman. But Las Vegas lubricates us, makes us slip the bonds of our inhibitions, so that we do things we ought not.

Like this, for instance: I enter the elevator with Lauren Napier, and know that I am about to have sex with her. She presses the button marked 33. "My husband and I each have a separate floor," she explains.

"Convenient."

"For both of us," she says.

On the thirty-third floor, we walk down a short hall. She slips a card key into the door. The electronic lock tumbles, and she pushes the door open with one finger.

We enter a modest suite, decorated in a severe Asian style. The bed is a raised futon on a tatami mat. Near the bed is a lacquered Chinese cabinet, black with red trim. There's a black bureau with a single orchid in a pot: The flower has white petals with red speckles, like splattered blood. A plasma television hangs on the wall.

She closes the door and, without a word, kisses me. I have not kissed a woman in six years—not since before I went to prison. It is a strange feeling, to have her tongue in my mouth, and I am surprised by her aggressiveness, the way she probes my mouth and grips firmly the back of my head.

She unbuttons my shirt and scratches her nails through my chest hair. She leads me to the bed. We undress each other. We make love.

I was right about her toenails. They are painted red, like the shiny Red Hots you buy at the movies.

An hour later, when we are finished with each other, and our curiosity and boredom have been sated, I leave the thirty-third floor, and head back, alone, to my own suite.

As the elevator ascends, I think about Jess and Napier, and wonder how many times they have made love, and whether Jess truly enjoyed it, or if she was just playing her part in the con, doing me a favor.

*   *   *

In my bedroom, I stare at myself in the mirror, and I think about Jess. I am comforted by the thought that, in a con, it is sometimes necessary to give the mark some pussy, to rattle his brain and keep him off balance.

The next morning, we are driven back to the airport in our prom limo by one of Napier's goons. We board Napier's Citation, and take off back to Palo Alto.

The same platinum blond stewardess who brought us here is serving us again, offering more champagne and wine. None of us—not even Toby, amazingly—accepts her offer.

It is a quiet plane ride. Toby does not speak to me. I do not speak to Jess. Peter does not speak to anyone. Each of us sits in our own private row, staring out the window. By the time we touch down, it is a relief to get away from my team, if only for an hour, because the quiet was painful.

This is the problem with a Big Con, if you must know. It requires months of preparation. A Big Con cannot be run alone, and so it requires that you build a team of capable people. It requires that you work together, know each member of your team intimately, that you are able to predict each other's every move. It requires, in short, that you trust each other.

But what kind of people can you ask to run a con with you? Quite simply, dishonest people. Which is the problem. How can you trust someone to watch your back, when you're secretly afraid of what they do behind it?

CHAPTER TWENTY-TWO

When I get back to my apartment, I have two messages on my answering machine from Celia. She left the first one at three o'clock yesterday afternoon. "Call me," the message says. The second message was left an hour ago—at eleven o'clock in the morning. On this one she sounds more concerned. "Kip, where are you? It's Celia. Please call me."

I pick up the phone and dial her number. She answers first ring.

"It's me," I say, "Kip."

"Where've you been?" It sounds like an accusation.

"We're divorced, Celia," I say. "Remember?"

"I was worried. Where's Toby?"

When the limo dropped us off at the apartment, Toby decided not to get out of the car with me, but instead wanted to spend time alone in Palo Alto. He asked the driver to take him downtown. He did not tell me when he would return to my apartment. Or if.

I decide not to go into these details. I say, "He's in town. Just hanging out."

"Is everything okay?"

"Fine," I say. "What's wrong?"

"I need to talk to you. Some men came by yesterday."

"Men?"

"Two of them. They said they were police, and they flashed a badge, but now I'm not so sure."

"What were their names?"

She hesitates. Then she admits: "I don't remember." She pauses. "I'm sorry, Kip."

"It's okay. What'd they want?"

"It was strange. They were asking about you. Lots of questions."

I feel a chill. I try to keep my voice neutral. "What kind of questions?"

"Who you are, where you live, how you earn money. Very vague. That's when I got suspicious."

"So what'd you tell them?"

"Nothing. I swear. That we're divorced. That I haven't spoken to you in years. They didn't seem to believe me."

"That's fine," I say. "You did good. Thank you, Celia."

"Kip, what's going on? Is everything okay?"

"Everything's fine."

"Are you doing . . ." She stops, backs up. "Are you still working at the cleaners?"

"No," I say.

"I see." She sounds disappointed. "I thought you liked that kind of job."

"Yeah," I say. "I just needed to do something else. For a little while."

"Is Toby involved?"

"No, of course not," I lie.

"Kip," she says, "be careful. Toby's glad to have you back. He likes that you're a regular guy again. So don't . . . go anywhere."

She means: Don't get caught and get sent to Lompoc, idiot. I say, "I promise. Everything will be fine."

"When he gets back, have him call."

"I will," I say.

We hang up.

I wander around my apartment, looking for signs that someone broke in and searched. Everything seems orderly, nothing out of place. I walk to the bedroom. I open a bureau drawer. My underwear sits in neat piles, undisturbed.

The apartment appears the way I left it. But searching an apartment without leaving a trace is not hard: most police—or crimi-nals—know how to do it.

I wonder who visited Celia. The likely scenario is: Napier's men. But it could also have been Sustevich, checking up on me. I have six million of his dollars, after all. Perhaps he saw me board a mysterious flight at the Palo Alto Airport and got nervous. Maybe his men have been watching me this whole time, keeping tabs on their investment like hawk-eyed venture capitalists. Maybe they're watching me right now.

I walk to the living room, wrench open my curtain. I look out-side, past the rosebushes, and try to peer over the fence to the street. I see no cars idling, no stakeout teams hunched over their dashboard, no glint of binoculars from a nearby rooftop.

Maybe the people who questioned Celia really were police. Maybe they were checking up on me, because a little birdie told them that I am up to no good.

Which of course leads me to wonder: Who is the little birdie? And what is it singing?

It's Wednesday, and time to let Ed Napier beat the stock market.

Toby came back last night, after vanishing for two days. He hobbled into my apartment at nine P.M., while I was trying to drink myself to sleep at the kitchen table, and he acted as if nothing had happened between us. "Hey, Dad," he said. "Drinking alone is a warning sign." He leaned his crutches on the wall and plopped down across from me. "So let me help you." And so he did, and we polished off a bottle of Jack Daniel's, another exemplary instance of father-son bonding. Who said I'm not a good dad?

When I asked Toby where he went for two days, he said vaguely, "The hotel, downtown. I just needed some time away." I suppose I could have probed further, asking the name of the hotel so I could double-check his story, but what would be the point? What would I hope to discover? The main thing is that Toby is back, and he's in good spirits, and whatever happened in Vegas is in the past, forgotten.

So he's in the office this morning when Napier comes by. Napier arrives in his cherry-red Mercedes, maybe from a breakfast at Buck's, or maybe having just rolled out of his goose-down-duvet-covered bed. He knocks on our glass door with unusual vigor.

When I answer, he says, "Good morning, Franklin. Ready to make some money?"

He's in good spirits. Most people are, when they think they're about to get something for nothing.

I lead him to the conference room. Jess has already set everything up: The screen is unfurled from the ceiling; the lights are dim; the projector on. The only thing Jess has not done is acknowledge me. We haven't spoken since Vegas.

Peter has been working on the software for the last forty-eight hours. Ed Napier is in for quite a show.

I pull out a chair for Napier, and he sits facing the screen. I say, "Your check for fifty thousand dollars has cleared and is now deposited in my brokerage account at Datek. As you suggested, we'll use the money to buy stocks based on Pythia's predictions. Peter, why don't you explain what's on the screen?"

Peter walks to the front of the room. He points to the projection screen. "Fine. It's simple, actually. What we'll do is scan the stock market for five stocks that Pythia can predict with a high confidence level. I have no idea which stocks she'll choose; it depends on the market at the time we start. We're only going long, to avoid restrictions on short sales. Nothing greedy. Just five stocks, ten thousand dollars apiece. We can use margin, so we'll effectively buy $20,000 worth of each stock. Any questions?"

Napier shakes his head. "Go," he says.

"Okay." Peter returns to the keyboard, types something. On the projection screen, five stock charts cascade into view. The charts are composed of thin green lines—the random fluctuation of each stock's price at one-minute intervals. On the right of each chart is a red circle—Pythia's prediction for where the stock is heading.

Peter says, "The projection time frame is about thirty seconds. Pythia is placing the trades now."

As if on cue, a dollar amount appears next to each stock chart: "$10,000/ 1101 shares long" and "$10,000 / 784 shares long" . . .

Peter says, "You can see that Pythia just bought eleven hundred shares of Apple Computer and seven hundred or so shares of US Steel."

We watch as Pythia places three more stock trades. "Okay," Peter says. "We're now fully invested in the market and are using fifty thousand dollars to gamble. Fifty thousand of Mr. Napier's dollars. Now let's see if Pythia's predictions pan out."

"They *better* pan out," Napier says, but from his friendly tone, he has no doubt.

Confidence levels appear next to each of the red target circles. 92% confident . . . 95% confident . . . 93% confident . . .

The seconds pass, and the confidence levels increase. Now they are 95% . . . 96% . . . 98% . . .

The five stocks rise toward the red target circles.

Another ten seconds pass.

In each of the five charts, the stock prices flutter, but inexorably rise. They approach their red targets.

"Here we go," Peter says. In a rapid sequence, like dominoes dropping, the stock price lands inside each target, and—one after another—each red circle brightens and says, "Target reached."

"Let's see how we did," Peter says. He types something into the keyboard. The stock charts disappear from the screen, and are replaced by five rows of numbers:

	Entry price	# shares	$ Gain	P/L	Net P/L
CELG	$ 28.34	706	$ 0.22	$ 152.86	$ 151.81
X	$ 25.50	784	$ 1.60	$1,254.90	$1,253.73
ATML	$ 3.36	5,952	$ 0.09	$ 535.68	$ 526.75
RFMD	$ 5.73	3,490	$ 0.05	$ 189.51	$ 184.27
AAPL	$ 18.16	1,101	$ 0.80	$ 881.06	$ 879.41
				$3,014.01	$2,995.96

Peter says, "It looks like we made about three thousand dollars. Actually, a little less, after commissions."

Toby pipes up, "That's it? Only three thousand?"

I say, "Not bad for thirty seconds' worth of work. That's a return of what?"

Jess says: "Nearly six percent."

I say, "Right. Six percent in thirty seconds. Imagine if we did that again and again. It's possible to reinvest our winnings, every half-minute. We could program the computer to do it automatically. If we kept doing it, over and over, our returns would be . . ." I let my voice trail off. "Quite large," I say, finally.

"Astronomical," Napier says. He's still staring at the screen. He can't tear his eyes off it.

The room is silent. We stare at Napier, who is still staring at the screen. Finally he turns to Peter.

"Can you do it? Today? Right now?"

"What?" Peter says.

"Make it repeat itself. Keep picking stocks over and over."

"No," Peter says. "Not today. It'll take some work. Not much . . ."

"How about tomorrow?"

Peter says, "I suppose . . ."

He turns to me. "What do you say, Franklin?"

I shrug.

Napier says, "Let's say I wired you two hundred grand. Right now. This morning. You'd have it in your account by tomorrow. Could we try this again?"

"Yes," I say.

He turns to Peter. "Tomorrow, okay? We'll do it enough times to double our money. As an experiment. All right?"

Peter hesitates. He looks to me. I nod. Finally Peter says, "Yeah, okay."

Napier stands. He straightens his tie. He nods to the others. "Very good." He crooks his finger at me. "Franklin, come with me."

I follow him from the conference room and close the door behind me. He says, "What's wrong with him?"

"Who?"

"Peter."

I shrug. "He thinks we're doing something illegal."

Napier drills his eyes into me. "Are you?"

"No."

"Then he has nothing to worry about."

I nod.

"Give me your wiring information. I'll deposit two hundred grand in your account. Tomorrow we'll see if Pythia can double it."

After Napier leaves, I return to the conference room. Instead of smiles and cheers, I am met by quiet. The four of us watch through the window as Napier pulls his Mercedes out of the parking lot.

Finally, when he is gone, Jess says, "Well that was easy."

"Yes," I say.

But I feel little triumph. I know that we are about to reach the point of no return. Edward Napier will test us one final time, by wiring nearly a quarter of a million dollars into our bank account.

Most small-time con men would quit here. They'd divide the two hundred grand, split it four ways, and skip town.

But for us, this is only the beginning. Soon we'll put Napier on the send, and a quarter-million dollars—rather than seeming large—will become small and insignificant, a rounding error.

That's the difference between small-time crooks and people like me. Ambition. A can-do attitude. The desire to change the world. My feeling is: If you're going to gamble, you might as well do it big. If you're going to risk prison or death or dismemberment, score as huge as you can. You may not have another chance.

But I get a strange feeling as I sit at the conference table, staring out the window at the cars speeding down Bayfront. I remember the afternoon I recently spent at the blackjack table, how I insisted on hitting when I should have stood pat. And how that—

inevitably, predictably—led me to bust, and, finally, to lose everything I had.

Yeah, I know what you're thinking.

But not everything turns out the way you think. Sometimes,
in real life, a premonition turns out to be empty, extraneous, a
loose end.

CHAPTER TWENTY-THREE

I'm driving home with Toby, who sits in the back seat of my Honda and stretches his leg cast into the front, using the gearbox like an ottoman.

"So Dad," he says, "tell me the plan."

I look at him in the rearview. "You know the plan," I say.

"Only the broad strokes," he says. "So tell me if I'm right. Tomorrow Napier gives us money. And we let him win. Then we put him on the send, for one more big bet. Is that right?"

I'm speeding along the Bay, past the salt ponds. Cargill owns twenty-five thousand acres of estuaries on the shore. Since the Gold Rush over a century ago, they've been harvesting salt here, by pumping bay water through dikes and levees and letting it evaporate in the sun. In the dry autumn, they harvest the white cake left behind. It's a disgusting process that leaves the shoreline—now pockmarked with stalagmites—poorer, but which, I suppose, leaves the American Potato Chip Industry infinitely richer.

"Something like that," I say.

"How does it end?"

"How do you *think* it ends?"

"I don't know. You blow him off, right? Make him think we've *all* lost—that we're ruined—so he doesn't come after us."

I am surprised at Toby's sudden interest in my line of work. "Why so curious?" I ask.

"Because I want to learn."

"Plan on following me into the business?"

"No," he says. He's staring at my cross-sectioned eyes in the rectangle of the rearview mirror. He's searching them, trying to determine if I am making fun. "Just curious," he says, but he looks away and drops it.

I want to apologize, but I don't have the chance. I notice something strange in the mirror. A black Lincoln Town Car. The windshield is tinted, so that I can barely discern the outline of two men behind the glass. The car is tailing me.

"Don't look," I say to Toby. "But we're being followed."

Toby immediately turns around in his seat and cranes his neck to see. Ever since he was five, he has been a poor listener.

"Who are they?" he says.

"I don't know. You ever see that car before?"

"No."

I step on the gas and watch the speedometer bump up against seventy. I lurch into the left lane, rocketing past a slow Volvo driven by a nun wearing a habit. As I pass, she shakes her head at me and gives me a dirty look. Ashamed, I look away.

Toby says, "Hey, Dad, I think that nun's giving you the finger."

I do a double take. Sure enough, in my rearview, I see the nun flipping me the bird through her windshield.

"You don't see *that* very often," Toby remarks.

True enough. I glance back to see the Lincoln still following me, a steady four car lengths behind. I note the license plate number: C5K-885.

"Write this down," I say to Toby. "C5K-885."

"Okay," Toby says. There's a pause. "Uh . . . You have a pen?"

I shake my head. The kid has always been a disappointment to me. I lean across the center console, my elbow knocking into his cast.

"Ouch," he says.

"Maybe you should put your foot down."

"Ouch, I can't."

I pop the glove compartment. I find a Bic, toss it over my shoulder to him.

I say, "C5K-885."

He says, "Okay, hold on, hold on . . ."

"C5K-885," I repeat.

"What is it?"

"C5K-885."

"Slower."

"C . . . 5 . . . K—"

"Dad, look out!"

I slam on the brakes. Ahead of me: an unfortunately placed traffic light, now a surprising shade of red. Between me and the traffic light: four civilian automobiles, all stopped obediently at the light.

My Honda shudders and screeches, and is sent into a skid. We start to fishtail, and I lose control. I try turning left, into the skid, just like they tell you to do.

Who came up with the idea that you should turn *into* the skid? I must find him to discuss this further. The sudden jerk sends the front of the car careering into the concrete divider between the highway's east and west lanes. We slam into the wall, and I feel the seat belt go taut, as my chest snaps against it.

Even as it's happening, I'm thinking about Toby. I hear myself say it, which is impossible, since the whole crash takes less than a second. I say: *O please God, let him be wearing his seat belt. Please, for once, Toby, do the right thing.*

There's a sound like a gunshot, as my airbag pops open. The canvas slaps me across the face like a woman's hand. Then it deflates and drapes over the steering wheel like an embarrassing reminder of spent passion.

We've stopped in the middle of the highway, facing the wrong direction. I see the Lincoln flash its blinker, pull into the right lane, and continue past us.

Next I see the Volvo hurtling directly toward us. The nun slams her brakes. Her tires start smoking and there's another screech. Her arms grip the steering wheel, locked ramrod straight, and her teeth are clenched in rigor mortis.

Her Volvo slows just enough that the impact with my Honda is a gentle thud. I'm knocked backward an inch. I hear her headlights shatter. I see her through the windshield: She's okay— must be, since she's cursing at me, though her words are muted through the two layers of glass.

I turn slowly in my seat to look at Toby. I dread what I am about to see: that he is dead, his neck snapped, blood dribbling from the corner of his mouth; or that he is missing completely— shot out of the car so fast that I missed him—splattered fifty feet away on the asphalt.

But when I turn around, he is looking at me, smiling, holding the Bic pen near his ear, as if—the moment things settle down—he will finish recording the license plate I have repeated to him three times.

"Jesus, Dad," he says, "are you trying to kill me?"

I laugh. "I'm trying to *save* you," I say, although, I must admit, all evidence points to the contrary.

A Menlo Park cop comes and takes our statements, snapping enough Polaroids of the accident scene to fill a scrapbook.

I don't mention the Lincoln that was following us, and I don't make excuses. I tell the officer the truth—that I was looking in my glove compartment instead of at the road. I leave out the part about how it was really all my son's fault, even though this is what I secretly believe.

The cop gives me a Breathalyzer and I pass. We're on our way, in a taxi, in less than thirty minutes. As we go, I watch my Honda, its hood crumpled like an accordion, departing on a tow truck in the other direction, to Hank's Service Station on Willow. Goodbye, Honda.

The taxi takes us to Palo Alto, and drops me and Toby at my apartment. My octogenarian landlord, Mr. Santullo, waits for us in the driveway. He wears his undershirt, with tufts of white chest hair poking through, and the blue terry-cloth robe. I wonder: How does he know when I will come home? Does he stand in the driveway for hours, waiting, until I appear? Is that what old age is destined to bring me—lonely days, hours of standing in the driveway waiting for someone to return? Will there even be anyone in my life who returns to me?

"Kip," he says, "I need your help."

"Okay, Mr. Santullo," I say. I gesture to Toby. "Have you met my son, Toby?"

"My grandson isn't here," he says, answering a different question.

I say, "Okay, Mr. Santullo." To Toby: "I'll be right there." I toss him my keys. They jingle as they fly. He plucks them from the air and heads to my apartment.

I follow Mr. Santullo upstairs to the second floor. We pause at the door to his apartment while he searches for the right key. He finds it, finally.

Inside, his apartment is a museum of 1950s decor, with an olive broadcloth sofa, brown carpet the color of old shoes, and a Kitchen of the Future, as envisioned when the Future surely included coffee percolators and electric stovetops.

Mr. Santullo waves at the couch. "Sit down. You want a highball?"

I have been inside Mr. Santullo's apartment exactly five times, and each time he has offered me a highball. I look around the room. On the bookshelves, above the television, and on the kitchen counter—on every available space—I see old photographs of his wife—now long dead—and of Mr. Santullo as a young man—wealthy, happy, full of strength, flushed with cash and success—ready to take on the world. I picture him and his wife in this apartment, forty years ago, entertaining friends, passing out highballs sloshing in beaded glasses to guests milling in the dining room and on the balcony. I imagine boisterous laughter, ribald jokes, women cackling. There were probably children, too, scampering through the apartment, banging into the knees of adults, being corraled for photos and kisses.

Now I look at Mr. Santullo. He is a shrunken man, in every sense of the word—his frame collapsed into a bell-shaped hump, his hair white, his face thin, his teeth mere yellow and black stumps. His wife died twenty years ago. His daughter died recently. He is alone. His world has shrunk to the mere space in this apartment, and to the five yards of concrete leading up to the sidewalk outside.

At what age does it happen? At what age does the world—which you are so accustomed to commanding—collapse to a keyhole? Does it happen suddenly? Do you wake one morning and realize that it is, practically speaking, over—that your connections to the living have vanished? Or is it more gradual—a slow descent into darkness? Until this moment, I have felt sorry for Mr. Santullo, saddened about his growing dementia. Now I wonder: Is it, in fact, a mercy?

And how different am I? I am a fifty-four-year-old ex-con. My wife left me. Until three weeks ago, I barely spoke to my son. I have nothing: no family, no job, no lover. I wake up alone. I sleep alone. I will, I am certain, die alone. So maybe this is how it happens. While you try to fix all your mistakes, while you wait for your life to get better, it simply runs out.

"Yeah," I say to Mr. Santullo. "I think I'll have that highball."

A highball is: whiskey, ice, and ginger ale, served in a tall glass. Although I fancy myself a talented drinker, one facile with all aspects of the hobby, I must shamefully admit: I had no idea what a highball was. Nor that it was so delicious. But then again, how could I know? I am drinking the first highball to appear in North America since 1962.

Mr. Santullo sits down on the couch beside me, leaving the bottle of Wild Turkey and the can of ginger ale open, on the bar, like a tantalizing promise.

"Kip," he says, "I need help."

I sip the highball. "What can I do for you, Mr. Santullo?"

"My bills," he says. He points to the buffet at the side of the room. On it I see a stack of papers, two fingers deep, and a checkbook. "You pay them for me, all right?"

"You sure? You trust me to do that?"

He chuckles. Maybe that means yes. Or maybe he didn't hear the question.

I rise from the sofa, finish the drink in my glass, shake the ice. I approach the side table, look through the bills. Three months' worth of paperwork: cable TV, electricity, phone service, water. The most recent bills are stamped with ominous "Final Notice" warnings.

Mr. Santullo says, "I can't see the damn things! Too small!"

I say, "Where's your grandson?" What I mean is: Why not ask him?

Mr. Santullo nods. "My grandson is Arabian," he says.

"Yeah," I say. "Understood."

I think that Mr. Santullo's non sequitur will be the end of our conversation, and that I will now retire with his pile of paperwork to my apartment, where I will spend an hour sorting and paying his bills. "All right, Mr. Santullo," I say. "I'll take care of this for you. No problem. And thanks for that highball."

Mr. Santullo nods and says, "He wants me to change the will."

"What's that?"

"My grandson. But I told him. I know what he's up to." He wags his index finger at me. "I know."

"That right?"

"I know what he's up to," he says again.

I lay my empty highball glass gently on the buffet and gather the bills. I take his checkbook. "I'll pay all these and stick them in the mail for you."

"Thanks, Kip."

I nod. On my way out of the apartment, Mr. Santullo says, "My grandson is Arabian."

"Yup," I say, and close the door gently behind me.

So that's what it comes down to.

Everyone cheats. Some people are so lousy, they try to steal from their own family. Some people are so low, they rip off the frail and the elderly.

So, all things considered, how bad am I? Everyone's conning everyone. I'm the only one scrupulous enough to make an honest living at it.

CHAPTER TWENTY-FOUR

This morning I wake early and stumble from the couch. Toby is still sleeping in my bedroom. I grab the phone from the kitchen wall and dial Jess.

"Good morning," I say. "Are you sleeping?"

"Hmm," she says. I picture her in bed, arching her back, wearing a tight T-shirt, her nipples poking through the waffled cotton like pinkie fingers. "What's wrong?"

"Nothing." I try to keep my voice quiet. "I haven't spoken to you since Vegas. You alone?"

"Of course."

"Everything okay? With Napier?"

"Hmm." She's still groggy. Maybe she's rubbing her eyes, looking at the clock. She takes a breath, yawns. Finally, she says: "He wants to see me tonight. He told his wife he's having a business dinner."

"I see." I try to keep my voice neutral.

"That's what you want, right?"

"Yeah."

"I'm doing it for you. You want me to stay close to him. That's what you said."

"Yeah, fine. That's what I said." Although, now that I repeat it out loud, I'm not so sure.

"You know what's funny?"

I grunt.

"He hasn't hit me."

"Who?"

"Ed," she says.

Her first-name familiarity with our mark is momentarily disconcerting. "Meaning?"

"When we started, you told me he hits his wife. Knowing that made it easier. You know, to steal from him. So I was sort of expecting . . . *something*. If not a punch, maybe a threat. But so far, nothing. He's been a gentleman."

"Maybe you don't know him well enough."

"Umm . . ." She thinks about it. "I know him pretty well," she says finally. Which kills me a little inside.

"I see."

"And there's something else."

"Something else?"

"It's like there's something wrong with him. Something I can't put my finger on. Something doesn't ring true."

I say: "You think he's on to us?"

"Ed?" Again with the first name. *Yeah, Ed,* I want to say. *Schnookums.*

"I think . . ." She pauses, considers her words. "I think he's . . . suspicious."

"Which is what we want," I say.

"Which is what we want," she repeats. I hear the sound of rustling sheets. I picture her sitting up, pushing herself back against the headboard. "The thing is, he didn't get to be a billionaire for nothing. He wasn't born with the money. He earned it."

"You sound smitten."

For the first time she is annoyed. "I'm not smitten. I'm just pointing something out. That there's something strange about him and you should be careful."

"*You* should be careful," I retort.

"We should all be careful," she says.

After we hang up, I wonder: Will Jess ever forgive me, for what I am about to do?

*   *   *

My Honda is still in the shop, so Toby and I take a taxi to work. Napier shows up at 10:02 A.M. This time he brings a guest: a well-muscled goon in a suit I have never seen before. The goon follows a foot behind as Napier strides down our hall into the conference room. I think I see a lump under the goon's jacket; he's packing heat.

Napier doesn't bother introducing him. His message is clear. I'm in charge of the company now, and please meet your new H.R. Director, Mr. Muscles, and his assistant, Mr. Glock. They will ensure your employment at Pythia is a productive one.

The conference room is set up as yesterday: screen down, lights dimmed, computer humming.

Napier says to me: "The money is in your account?"

"Two hundred thousand dollars," I say.

"Let's double it," Napier says, as if he's asking a gas station attendant to fill 'er up. *Sure,* I think, *let's just double that two hundred Gs. You want me to check your oil while I'm at it?*

Peter says, "I spent all night working on the software."

He waits for some kind of praise. When none comes, he says, "Anyway, here's what it'll do. Every thirty seconds, Pythia will scan the entire market for high-probability stock movements. She picks the ten most likely winners each time and invests ten percent of the account in each stock. At the end of each cycle, she'll try again, using any additional funds she won. Assuming a conservative win rate of plus four percent every thirty seconds, we'll double our money in—"

"Ten minutes," Napier says.

Peter says, "Right."

I glance to Jess. She's looking at me, as if to say: *See? He's smart.*

"I'm ready," Napier says.

Peter looks to me. It's becoming increasingly preposterous to pretend that I am in charge. But I nod and wave my hand for him to go ahead.

Peter walks to the keyboard, types a command. The screen is filled with ten small stock charts. Pythia draws ten red target circles. In thirty seconds, nine of the targets are hit.

Immediately ten new stock charts appear. Another ten red target circles. Thirty seconds pass. Ten winners.

The cycle repeats itself nine more times. Ten winners . . . nine winners . . . ten winners . . . eight winners . . .

We stare at the screen, without speaking. It's hypnotic. We feel little pinpricks of endorphin each time a chart appears. We make three thousand dollars here, four thousand dollars there. Soon I lose track of the money we're winning, but I know it must be large.

"Jesus," I hear Toby say.

Ten minutes later, like addicts, we're sitting slack in our chairs, spent, looking at the screen, even though the trading is done.

Finally, Peter says, "That's it."

He types something into the keyboard. A chart appears, itemizing our profit for the day. At the bottom it says: "Account balance = $485,163.30." In ten minutes, we have doubled Ed Napier's money.

I walk to the front of the room, pull the speakerphone toward me. I dial a telephone number. A pleasant woman comes on the line. "Thank you for calling Datek Online," she says. "This is Bonnie speaking. Can I please have your account number."

I call out my account number.

Bonnie says, "Hello, sir. How may I help you?"

"Bonnie, could you kindly tell me my exact account balance, in cash, at this moment?"

"Hold on, sir," she says. We hear the muted sound of a keyboard clicking somewhere in the American Midwest. "Here we go," Bonnie says. "Your account balance is $485,163. And thirty cents."

"Thank you," I say. I hang up the phone.

I nod at Toby, who is standing at the side of the room, leaning on his crutches. He flips on the lights.

The six of us blink at each other in the sudden glare.

Napier says, "I'd like that money wired back into my account, immediately."

I nod. "I'll do that right now."

Napier adds, "Not that I don't trust you, partner. Just want to make sure everything's on the up-and-up." He turns to our new heat-packing H.R. Director, and says, "You can't be too careful. Now that we're talking about real money."

CHAPTER TWENTY-FIVE

Dinner tonight is steaks on the grill. I keep a rusty old Weber kettle in Mr. Santullo's backyard, tucked under the stairs. Toby and I wheel it out. Then we sit on cheap lawn chairs, sipping Buds from the can, watching the charcoal burn.

It's a warm August night, and I'm wearing a T-shirt and jeans, and my son is sitting beside me, and I feel the exact opposite of déjà vu. That is: I feel like I've *never* lived this perfect moment before, to my eternal regret and shame.

There's something hypnotic about the coals, and the smell of lighter fluid, and the fireflies that flare near Mr. Santullo's rosemary bush. There's no need to talk. Just sitting here is fine—perfect.

In a few weeks, the con will be over, and I will leave this place—disappear for several months, maybe years. I will rent a house somewhere, maybe a house on stilts, with a thatched roof, near the sea. I'll bring my son with me. Or perhaps I'll bring Jessica Smith.

Can I bring them both? That's a question I try not to think about. Because I know the answer. The answer is no.

After I throw the steaks on the hot metal, Toby says, "I want to talk about the con."

"Shoot."

"I'm going to guess what happens. You tell me if I'm right."

I turn the steaks with a fork, purse my lips, neither agree nor disagree.

Toby says: "So Ed Napier thinks he has a foolproof way to make money in the stock market. And he needs the cash, because of that hotel he's trying to buy."

I feel Toby looking at me for encouragement. I pretend not to notice, and I poke a fork into a steak.

"Anyway," he continues, "we let Napier make bigger and bigger bets, and we pay him with the Professor's money to make it look real. Then we let Napier make one last big bet. But something goes wrong, and he loses, and we keep his money."

I say, "How do you like your steak?"

"Rare."

"Then I should have asked you five minutes ago. How does well-done sound?"

"Fine."

I remove the steaks to a plate, cover the grill. Again, I feel Toby staring at me.

"Well?" he says.

"Well what?"

"Is that the way the con's going to work?"

"Yeah," I say. "That's the way it's going to work. More or less."

"More or less?"

"Let's eat," I say. And that is that.

CHAPTER TWENTY-SIX

The next morning I am woken by the telephone ringing in the kitchen. "Hello?" I say. I think it will be Jess, telling me how her date went last night with Napier.

But it is Ed Napier himself. I'm still groggy, but somewhere in the back of my mind, I wonder how he found my home telephone number. I have shared with him only my cell phone.

"Franklin?" he says. "It's Ed Napier." His voice is as loud on the phone as in person—booming, take-charge, ready to change the world.

"Hi," I say.

"I checked with my bank. The money you wired is there. All four hundred thousand dollars. Looks like you're for real."

"Did you ever doubt me?" I say.

"I want you and Toby to join me for breakfast. Come over to my place, in Woodside. We need to talk."

"Yeah, okay," I say.

He gives me his address. I hang up.

I go to the bedroom, where Toby is asleep, as usual. I wake him. I want him to join me.

The taxi drops me and Toby at the front gate of Napier's estate. We are met by a middle-aged security man who looks curiously after our taxi as it pulls away. I doubt if many of Napier's venture capital associates arrive at his mansion in a Yellow cab.

I tell the security man that I am Franklin Edison, to see Mr. Napier.

"Yes," he says. He checks his clipboard. "Mr. Napier called down and said you would be coming. This way."

He closes the gate behind us and leads us up a flagstone path. We approach the mansion, which is set above us on a hill. It is Spanish-Moorish in style, made of white limestone, with a roof of curved red clay tiles.

"Wow," Toby says. "Cool house."

The walkway spills into an arcaded loggia. We pass through the loggia, which is filled with rattan furniture and potted red bougainvillea plants. The house looks curiously like a Ralph Lauren showroom. I am half-expecting to be met by a perky blond salesgirl in a floral sundress. Imagine my disappointment when we are met by two toughs in suits.

The older security guard says, "These gentlemen will take you back." He nods at the bruisers.

"Will you come this way?" a bruiser says to me, grabbing my elbow.

The other bruiser takes Toby's arm. "Hey," Toby says. He tries to pull away from the bruiser, but the man's grip is firm, implacable. Toby was expecting a delightful breakfast on the veranda, perhaps poached eggs and mimosas, but it seems Napier has other plans.

The bruisers guide us through the arcade and into the house. We pass through a sitting room, beautifully decorated in 1930s Hacienda style, with a brown leather couch and a billiards table. I hope briefly that the bruisers will deposit us in this charming room, where I will be able to brush up on my pool while I wait for Ed Napier to appear. Alas, this possibility looks increasingly remote. The goons lead us out of the room and down a long hallway. In contrast to the loggia and the sitting room, there has been little effort to decorate this corridor. It is plain brown wood. I am beginning to get a bad feeling.

At the end of the corridor we come to a steel door. One goon releases my elbow and reaches into his pocket. He retrieves a ring of keys. He unlocks the door, swings it open.

All pretense of politeness now vanishes. Toby and I are shoved through the steel door, into a cold concrete room, lit with industrial fluorescents. There is a table pushed up against the far wall, and two metal folding chairs. Peter and Jess stand beside the table. They look pale. Peter's hands are shaking.

"Hi, guys," I say. To Jess: "How was your date last night?"

One goon shuts the door behind us, and uses the key to lock the six of us inside. The other goon reaches into his pocket and pulls out a gun.

I say, "Won't Mr. Napier be joining us for breakfast?"

"Not quite yet," the one with the gun says.

"Something we need to do first?" I ask.

The other goon smiles. He walks up to me. "Yeah," he says. "Something *I* need to do." Without warning, he swings his fist into my abdomen.

"Oof," I say, and drop to my knees. The other man—the one with the gun—stands guard at the door, looking at me without expression.

"Hey—" Toby says. He takes a step toward me.

The man with the gun turns and aims at Toby's head. My son now has second thoughts. He freezes, raises his palms in peace. "No problem," Toby says. "No problem."

The goon with the good right jab winds back his foot, as if to kick a soccer ball. Unfortunately, in this case, the soccer ball is me. His Cole Haan nails my chest, knocking the wind from me and sending me, arms flailing, backward. I hear Jess scream. I land on the concrete, trying to keep my chin tucked so I won't slam my skull on the floor. I'm off balance. I raise my arm feebly over my head to protect myself.

The goon apparently possesses the can-do attitude that Ed Napier so admires. I know this because he is not content merely to use his fist and shoe to strike me. He walks across the room and grabs the metal chair. He folds it like a dainty umbrella, returns to where I am curled on the floor, and raises it high over his head. He smashes it down across my back.

Jess yells, "Please, stop!"

I try to say, "Wait," but I'm not sure if any words come out. My head is throbbing. I cough and feel liquid in my throat. I'm not sure if it is phlegm or blood.

I'm curled in a fetal position, rocking pathetically on the concrete. I keep my hands over my head and face, to protect against another blow, which I am sure is about to come. But it never does. I hear one of the goons clearing his throat. Then another sound: of a door unlocking, creaking open.

I look up. Ed Napier has joined us in the room. He shuts the door.

"Hello, Franklin Edison," he says. He smiles, repeats the name. *"Franklin Edison,* is it? Or do you mind if I call you Kip Largo?"

I scrabble on the concrete, to a kneeling position. "Either is fine," I say, agreeably.

"I know who you are, Mr. Largo," Ed Napier says. "You're a con man. You just got out of prison. You served five years in a federal penitentiary for ripping off fat people."

"That's not true," I say. I mean the part about ripping off fat people. Since Toby and Jess are here, I want to explain that the Diet Deck was a real product, and that it may have even helped a few of the fatties; but that it was securities fraud that did me in. But I taste blood in my mouth, and I'm having a hard time breathing. I skip the details.

Napier says, "Did you think that you would be able to con *me?* Do you know who I *am?"*

I nod.

Napier turns to a goon. "Tell him."

The goon walks up to me and kicks me in the chest, sending me backward onto the floor. "He's Ed Napier," the goon says, loudly.

I try to roll away from my tormentors, across the concrete floor. I notice I'm leaving a trail of blood. "Okay," I say, "now I understand."

"What's the con, Kip?" Napier asks. "There is no Pythia, is there?"

"Stop hurting me," I say.

Napier says to a goon, "I don't think he heard me."

The goon strides over, pulls back his shoe, and kicks me in the face. My neck snaps. I look down and see two of my teeth skittering across the concrete floor like Chiclets. The goon says, "Mr. Napier asked you a question."

"Please," Jess says again. "You're going to kill him."

"Interesting prediction," Napier says. "I have a ninety-percent confidence level you may be right."

I say, "Stop. Please." I touch a finger to my mouth, look at it. It is red with blood. "Okay," I say. "You're right. There is no Pythia."

"What are you trying to do?" Napier asks. "Are you trying to con me? What the *fuck* are you thinking? Don't you know who my friends are? Don't you know who my business partners are?"

I cough. I think I might pass out. Passing out is not part of the plan. Neither was the kick in the face. Napier's men are a bit overzealous. I say, "It's not what you think."

"Tell me what to think," Napier says.

I cough again. I groan.

Napier says to his goon, "I guess he didn't hear me."

The goon walks over to me, lifts his shoe for another kick.

"Wait," I say. "I'll tell you."

Napier holds up two fingers. The goon freezes with his shoe raised, as if he's a dancer in a boy band, about to bust a move.

I say, "It *is* a con. That part's true. But the money is real. The profits are real."

The goon looks to Napier, as if to ask: May I kick him now?

"You have thirty seconds," Napier says to me, "to tell me everything."

The goon's face registers discomfort. *Thirty seconds? I can't stand with my foot up for a half a minute!* He lowers his shoe to the ground.

I say, "We need your money to make it work. We're not trying to steal from you. We'll pay you back. The money we made this morning—it was real."

"Bullshit."

"The software—it's not predicting anything. There's no genetic algorithms. No neural networks. It's low-tech. We intercept orders at the brokers. We change the IP routing. All the online brokers—Datek, Ameritrade, E-Trade. We intercept all their orders. The orders come to us first. We hold them for twenty seconds, thirty seconds max. Our software analyzes them. We put our order in first, then release the others."

"Slow down," Napier says. "Say it again."

I take a breath. I cough. I look at my hand. It's speckled with blood. "It's simple," I say. "When someone enters an order on the Internet to buy a stock, we intercept it. It goes to us first, not the broker. We collect thousands of orders—hundreds of thousands—see which stocks people are going to buy. If we see a thousand people are buying a stock, we put an order in to buy it first. Then we release the other orders, after we've bought the stock. The stock price goes up because everyone's trying to buy. We make money and sell the stock."

"You're front-running . . ."

"Intercepting stock information before it gets traded. It doesn't hurt anyone."

"It's illegal," Napier says.

I shrug.

"Why the big act? The Pythia company? Why do you need me?"

"Money. I need capital."

"Explain."

"We have a month—maybe two—before they catch on. That's why I need you. We need to make as much money as we can in one month, before they figure it out. If we can only gamble a few times, let's gamble big."

"You were going to rip me off," he says, although now he doesn't sound sure.

"No," I say. "I swear. The money's real. I'm splitting it with you, fifty-fifty, just like we agreed. Look, you checked your bank account. There's four hundred thousand dollars in there. I'm not trying to rip you off."

"If you're lying to me, I'm going to kill you."

"I'm not lying to you."

"I may kill you anyway," Napier says. He stares at me. He's weighing the evidence. I'm a con man, but then again, I just wired four hundred thousand dollars of cash into his bank account. That's not the kind of cash most people have lying around. I must be on to *something*.

"So there really is software," Napier says.

"It's not rocket science. It just looks at what everyone else is about to do. And we do it first. The hard part is intercepting the orders."

"How do you do it?"

"I can show you," I say.

Now I'm on Napier's Citation jet, twenty thousand feet above the ground, with Peter sitting beside me. Toby and Jess sit in the back of the plane. Napier is asleep, snoring in the front seat, dreaming about his next weekend in St. Croix, or maybe an upcoming lobster dinner at the Palm. The goon with the blood-stained Cole Haan shoes sits in the chair across from us, wide awake and staring.

Last time I was on this plane, I was being served caviar and champagne by a platinum blonde with great tits. Now I'm being stared at by a well-muscled Italian guy with big pores and a good corner kick. Times change.

Before they took us to the airport, they let me clean up. By clean up, I mean: I was allowed to collect my two loose teeth from the floor and put them in my slacks pocket, and to wipe the blood off my face with cold water. Despite my efforts I'm sure that when we touch down in New York, I won't be discovered by Wilhelmina on a busy sidewalk and asked to do some modeling work.

After six hours, we touch down at La Guardia. At the gate,

we're met by two fat guys in suits. They shake Napier's hand and bow their heads respectfully. They lead us from the terminal into the parking lot. I'm expecting a limo at a minimum, maybe a Rolls. But they show us to a van painted blue and white, with a yellow siren light on the roof and a Consolidated Edison logo on each side.

"Like you asked, Mr. Napier," one of the fat guys says.

My crew of four pile into the back of the utility company van, stepping over coils of copper cable, wire cutters, and leather utility belts. Napier and his muscle sit in the back seat of the van, the two New York goons up front.

When we pull out of the La Guardia parking lot, the driver says, "Where to, Mr. Napier?"

Napier turns around in his seat to look at me. "Where is it?"

"Downtown," I say. "Fourteenth and Fifth."

We speed through Queens and take the Midtown Tunnel into Manhattan. A half-hour after we start, we pull in front of an art deco building, five stories high. An engraved steel sign near the front door says: "Datek Securities."

"This is it," I say.

We double-park on Fourteenth Street. Napier's muscle climbs out of the van and circles around the back to let us out.

We jump down to the pavement. One of the New York goons hands each of us a white hard hat with the Con Ed logo. Although each of us looks ridiculous in his own way, I'm certain Ed Napier looks the most absurd: St. Bart's tan, Hermès tie, Armani suit—and a white plastic hard hat. But then again, I'm missing my two front teeth and have a swastika-shaped gash on my forehead like Charles Manson. Maybe Napier's laughing at *me*.

Napier says, "Show me."

Peter leads the way down the block. At the corner of Fifth, he points down to the asphalt of the street, at a manhole cover. "This is it."

The New York goons try lifting the manhole cover, with their fingers, unsuccessfully. One of them shakes his head and then goes back to the van. He returns, moments later, with a crowbar and a flashlight. He pries open the manhole cover and slides it across the asphalt.

"Down there," Peter says.

Peter crouches, grabs a rung of the ladder, lowers himself into the manhole. I look to Napier for permission to follow. He nods.

I say to Toby, "Stand watch."

He points to the cast on his leg. "Not going anywhere."

I follow Peter down under the street. We descend twelve feet into a tunnel. It's dark and cool. The wall, for as far as we can see into the blackness, is snaked with thick wires and PVC pipes. I stand clear of the ladder to let Napier descend. He jumps off beside me. Jess follows.

Napier calls up to his man, "Give me the light."

Napier's muscle tosses the flashlight down the hole. Napier catches it. He swings the beam to Peter's face.

"This is where I did it," Peter says. "There."

Peter points to the wall. Napier tilts the flashlight beam to illuminate a black plastic cube, the size of a cigar box. On the face of the box, two green LEDs blink spasmodically.

Peter says, "Datek has one T-3 line running to its office through here." He points to a black wire, pinkie-width, that has been spliced to the rear panel of the plastic box. "And here's the line out." He points to a second black cable coming out of the box. "Think of this as a router. We installed it six weeks ago. Every packet coming into Datek hits this box first."

"And you intercept everything coming in?" Napier says.

"Exactly. When a packet comes into this box, it's relayed back to California, to our office. We decide whether to forward it right away to Datek, or to hold it."

"If it's a stock order, you hold it," Napier says. He's starting to understand the con.

"That's right," Peter says. "We can queue up tens of thousands of orders at a time. We'll look at ten thousand orders and decide who's buying which stocks. If we see that a lot of people are buying one particular stock, we send our order from California to buy the stock first. As soon as we're filled, we release all the other orders that have been queued. It sounds like a big deal, but the process is fast. The extra bounce to California and back takes about a tenth of a second. Plus however long we hold the orders."

"And no one notices?" Napier says.

"Not yet. They probably will, eventually. But we never hold orders for very long. Thirty seconds at the most. And not all the time. Just for a few minutes each day. So it's going to be a while before people catch on."

"What makes you think you'll *ever* get caught?"

I answer for Peter. "Because you always get caught. That's the rule. That's how life works."

Napier nods. He understands that rule. His entire life—his purchase of his first casino with mob money, his kickbacks to the Genovese family, his payoffs to the Nevada Gaming Commission—has been one example after another of *not* getting caught, *just*. He knows that he is due.

Peter continues. "We have one box here, near Datek, one box in Omaha near Ameritrade, and a box uptown near E-Trade. Between the three of them, we can look at around forty percent of daily Nasdaq volume. That may not sound like a lot, but it's enough to practically guarantee that we can call when a stock's going to move."

"Amazing," Napier says. He thinks about it. "Is there anything linking the box to you? Let's say someone comes down here, finds the thing."

Peter says, "Every forty-eight hours the boxes contact our servers in California. If the servers don't respond with the correct security code, the boxes are programmed to erase their own memory. They just stop doing any funny stuff. Like they're not even here. If someone comes down here and finds the box, there's nothing pointing to us. A few off-the-shelf components you can buy at Radio Shack."

"Good," Napier says.

I rub my tongue across my top gum, feeling the sockets where my two front teeth are missing. I say to Napier, "What do you think?"

He nods. "For a bunch of shitheads," he says, "you did pretty good."

At eleven o'clock at night, we touch down in Palo Alto. Napier takes us back to his mansion.

We walk across the arcaded loggia, through the warm night and the sound of crickets. I smell jasmine and rosemary. It has been twelve hours since I was beaten to a pulp by Napier's men, and I could use a drink.

Napier leads us through the sitting room, into his dining hall. The table is set formally with white linens and tapered candlesticks.

Napier says, "Sit down."

We take our seats at the table. A man in a suit appears, carrying a bottle of wine on a silver coaster. He pours us each a glass.

"Now," Napier says, "let's drink to our new agreement."

"What new agreement?" I say.

"I'll lend you money. You keep doing what you're doing. Make money in the stock market. We split everything eighty-twenty."

"That wasn't our agreement," I say.

"Like I said," Napier explains. "Our *new* agreement."

"And if I refuse?" I ask, even though I know the answer.

"Then I turn you in. I make a phone call to the FBI, and I describe how you're manipulating stocks. You'll go back to prison, Kip, for a long time. Understand?"

I nod.

"There's one more thing," Napier says. "If I find out you're ripping me off, in any way, or lying to me, even the slightest bit, I'll have you all killed. Every one of you."

He looks at each of us, slowly—perhaps in the order he will have us killed?—to make sure we understand.

"Now," he says. He takes a glass from the table and lifts it high in the air. "I'd like to propose a toast. To our new partnership."

My own team turns to me, looking for guidance. I shrug, as if to say: What the hell. I raise my own glass. "To our new partner-ship," I say. "And to complete and total honesty."

Everyone raises their glass in a toast.

I can't help but notice that Napier is smiling, as if I've said something funny.

CHAPTER TWENTY-SEVEN

Of course the box that we installed beneath Fourteenth Street in Manhattan contains merely this: a nine-volt battery and two blinking green LEDs. Despite Peter's intricate explanation about how the box intercepts Internet packets, and routes them back to California, and how we analyze tens of thousands of stock market orders, the reality is more prosaic. The box does nothing, except blink green lights. We intercept nothing. We analyze nothing.

What we do is: We blink green lights.

Did you believe otherwise? You must keep in mind: This is a story about a con. In a con, everyone takes part in a play. And everyone knows it is a play, except for one man. The thing you want to make sure, when you're running a con, is that the man is not you.

CHAPTER TWENTY-EIGHT

When I wake the next morning, I have mysteriously been transported to the cathedral at Chartres, France; and my head is firmly planted inside the huge brass bell at the top of the steeple. Below me, a monk plays a sprightly version of "Yankee Doodle Dandy" on the carillon.

At least, that is how my skull feels. It takes a moment to realize that I am not in Chartres, but rather—less interestingly—am lying on my Naugahyde couch, in my Palo Alto living room, in a puddle of drool, with a bruised sternum, two missing front teeth, and a headache that burns bright like a magnesium flare on a rain-slicked road.

I sit up, peeling my face from the Naugahyde. I rub my cheek and feel the couch imprint in my skin, like cheesecloth. I try to remember what happened last night: the long flight back from New York, the dinner at Napier's, the threat-inspired business partnership, the several glasses of wine, and then the quiet ride back to my apartment in Jess's car.

I look at my watch. It is ten o'clock on a Saturday morning. I stumble across my living room, and am surprised to see that—last night, while I was being beaten up by mob thugs—MrVitamin.com rang up $983 worth of vitamin sales. It seems impossible, so I sit down at the computer and pull up the transaction records to double-check. Sure enough, the sales are real—from all over the country—a box of vitamins here, a box of fish oil tablets there. The reason for the sudden interest in my Web site is a mystery: Maybe I got some good press in a newspaper, or maybe it's just a fluke. But it's a good feeling to know that, if the Big Con business doesn't work out, and I survive this fiasco, I may have a future in online retail.

I spend thirty minutes flipping through the Yellow Pages, calling dentists, trying to find a nearby office with emergency Saturday hours.

I wind up taking a taxi to San Jose, to a dentist with an exotic foreign name full of surprising consonants, and a suspiciously empty appointment book.

But Dr. Chatchadabenjakalani, if indeed he really is a doctor, is pleasant and efficient. His office, on the second floor, above a Vietnamese restaurant, is clean, although it does smell vaguely like nam pla, Thai fish sauce. Before I recline in his dental chair, I reach into my pocket and offer the doctor my two front teeth, which I have been carrying for the past day like lucky charms. I notice that the root side of the teeth have turned black.

Dr. Chatchadabenjakalani holds out his hand and graciously accepts my teeth. He lifts his eyeglasses to his forehead and looks at my incisors, carefully, like an Amsterdam diamond merchant. Finally he pronounces, "I think these are no good." He hands them back to me, in case I want them.

I say, "It's okay. You keep them."

Two hours later, I'm back in Palo Alto, with two shiny white choppers in the front of my mouth, good as new. I'm not agitated by the five-hundred-dollar bill the good doctor handed me on the way out. I consider it a business expense, the same way that regular people treat legal bills, or photocopying costs. Having your front teeth replaced, after you're kicked in the face by your mark's thugs? In my line of work, that's just the cost of doing business.

When I get back to my apartment, Toby is sitting on the couch, talking softly into his cell phone. As I enter the room he says into the phone, "I better go. That's Dad."

I close the door behind me. He says goodbye into the phone, snaps the clamshell shut, tosses it onto the couch beside him.

"Who's that?" I ask.

"Mom."

"What did she want?"

"Just checking up on me. Making sure I'm not dead."

I put my keys down on the table near the entry, join Toby in the living room. He stares at my mouth.

"Your teeth look good," he says.

"Dr. Chatchadabenjakalani."

"You're kidding."

"He's Thai."

"You think that's why they're so backward over there, eating with chopsticks? They spend too much time saying each other's names, not enough time inventing things, like the fork?"

I sit down next to him. "I think that's a very racist thing to say."

"But true, right?"

"Probably."

"You mind if I ask you a question?"

I shrug.

"You wanted Napier to find out about you, right? You let him figure out who you were, that you're a con man. That's also part of the con, isn't it?"

"Your never-ending quest for a con education."

"Don't you want to teach me?"

"I don't want you to do what I do. I want you to be a doctor. Or an engineer. Or a dentist. You know what I learned today? They do very well."

"It's a little late for that," he says. "I am what I am."

I want to say: And *what* is that? But I manage to shut up and not insult my own son. Instead, I say, "It's never too late to change."

He smirks. "You mean, like you?"

I sigh. Sometimes he can be mean. Whose gene is that? Mine or Celia's? Then I realize: my own father's. Mean old asshole.

I answer another question. "Yes," I say, "I expected Napier to find out about me. It's the only way the thing's going to work. He needs to believe he's doing something illegal."

Toby nods. "So that we can blow him off at the end of the con. Pretend to get arrested, or whatever. Right?"

I don't answer. I rise from the couch. "I'm starving. You want to grab some lunch?"

"Just ate."

"Fine. I'll be back."

I walk into town.

It's Saturday, late August, and Stanford is in summer session. University Avenue, which during the autumn bustles with college kids and skateboarders, is quiet. The entire town seems empty and provisional, a movie set about to be struck. As I walk along the sidewalk, I take out my cell phone, dial a number.

After two rings, Celia picks up. "Hello?"

"Hi, it's Kip."

"Hi, Kip." I hear her say something to whoever is in the room with her—something that sounds like "my husband . . ." Then I hear a man's voice, and the sound of rustling sheets. Finally, she comes back on the line. "What's the matter?"

"Toby asked me to call you. He wanted to apologize for hanging up so suddenly."

"I'm sorry?"

"When you just spoke to him. He felt bad that he ended the call so quickly. He asked me to tell you he's sorry."

"I don't . . . I didn't talk to Toby . . ." She sounds puzzled.

"That's funny," I say. "Must have misunderstood. Anyway, how are things?"

"Are you calling to shoot the breeze?"

"Yeah," I say, "sure. How's Carl? Everything good?"

"Everything's fine." Icy now. Oh well.

"All right," I say. "Sounds like this is a bad time."

"No . . . it's just . . ."

"I understand. We'll catch up later. Bye, Celia."

"Bye."

I hang up, drop the phone in my pocket.

So it turns out: Toby is a pretty decent liar. He wasn't on the phone with his mother. Maybe I was wrong about those genes. Maybe they're mine after all.

I decide to skip breakfast and go directly to lunch.

On my way, I stick two quarters in a newspaper vending machine, grab a *San Jose Merc*. Then I head over to El Pollo Loco and order a fish taco and a Coke. The counter clerk hands me a receipt. "You're number thirteen," he says. "We'll call you when it's ready."

I have a seat at a table and start to read the paper. As if I'm an actor in a giant, universe-wide karmic joke, I turn to the business section and see, above the fold, a photo of Ed Napier in a tuxedo, standing behind a roulette table. It seems I can't escape Ed Napier, even when all I want is a fish taco. The article is about Napier's battle to purchase the old Tracadero. What used to be a real estate story of limited interest has now apparently become a mainstream soap opera. Broad outline: The old Tracadero casino goes bankrupt. Ed Napier comes along as a white knight, and offers to buy the Tracadero, tear it down, and redevelop the site. On it, he will build the largest casino in Las Vegas, four times as large as The Clouds! (This is how the newspapers quote Napier—with exclamation marks after his excited pronouncements! The hotel will be big! The biggest in Las Vegas!)

The bondholders of the old Tracadero, who just weeks earlier thought they would see only cents on every dollar of investment, agree to the deal. Unfortunately for Napier, at the last moment, another investor group swoops in and makes a competing bid. This bid comes from a little-known consortium of European and Japanese investors. So Napier raises his bid, and changes it from an all-equity offer to equity plus cash. The Tracadero bondholders agree to Napier's new terms. But then the Europeans and Japanese raise their bid to include more cash. Napier matches their bid yet again. Now that we have a bidding war, the newspapers smell a story.

Some report that maybe Napier doesn't have the cash he claims, after all. Because his company is private, almost no one knows its financial position, but rumors circulate that it is precarious. Building The Clouds nearly bankrupted Napier, some say. Some politicians begin to rumble about Napier's ties to organized crime. Still other politicians begin to rumble that the Tracadero—the last potential development site along the Strip—shouldn't be sold to European and Japanese foreigners.

What is clear, behind all the smoke screens and payoffs to newspapermen and politicians, is that two companies are locked in a mortal battle for a billion-dollar payday. Ed Napier is running low on cash, and he needs more of it, and fast, to claim the prize.

That, of course, is where I come in.

As I digest this, I notice a figure slide into the chair across from me. I put down the newspaper and see Dmitri, Professor Sustevich's employee.

"Hello, Dmitri," I say. "How's the evil henchman business?"

"Please come with me," Dmitri says.

"Sorry, Dmitri," I say. I reach into my shirt pocket, pull out my Pollo Loco receipt, show it to him. "I'm number thirteen. I'm waiting for a fish taco."

"Professor Sustevich wants to see you."

"And I want to see him," I say. "After I eat my fish taco."

The public address system crackles and a voice announces, "Number thirteen. Number thirteen."

"See?" I say.

I rise from my seat. I am surprised to feel a hand on my shoulder. I turn to see Hovsep, Sustevich's match-head specialist, standing behind me. Where did he come from? I feel a long cold finger in my back, poking my kidney. It takes me a moment to realize that it is not a finger.

"What are you going to do?" I say. "Shoot me in the middle of El Pollo Loco?"

Dmitri looks puzzled. "What is that?"

It takes me a moment to realize: He thinks I'm talking about a body part he's never heard of. "No," I say. "I mean: You're going to shoot me in the middle of a restaurant?"

"Yes," Dmitri says, simply.

"The Professor told you to do that? Shoot me in public?"

"Yes," Dmitri says again. He stares at me without expression.

"Okay," I say. "I can eat later. Your car outside?"

I'm led to a black Lincoln Town Car. We drive north on I-280 into the city.

Thirty minutes later, we pull up to the gate of Sustevich's Pacific Heights mansion. A burly man walks out of the security booth, leans over the car door. Dmitri rolls down his window and says something in Russian. The two men laugh. Maybe they're exchanging Moscow League hockey scores, or reminiscing about that night they so enjoyed in the strip club. Or maybe they're laughing about what is going to happen to me next.

The security guard returns to his booth, and the wrought iron gate swings open. The Town Car pulls in and the gate closes behind us with a solid clang.

On the portico outside the mansion, I am met by the same beefy blond man who—many weeks ago—felt up my testicles while patting me down for weapons. "You again," I say. "After last time, I was hoping for at least a phone call."

"Cell phone please," he says, and holds out his open palm. I reach into my pocket, pull out my Motorola. I slap it into his hand.

"Please lift your arms," the blond beefcake says.

I lift my arms. The Russian man pats me down: along my arms, then down my rib cage. He squats, pats from my ankles to my inner thigh, then swings over for a quick squeeze of testicles. He stands. "Come with me," he says.

He leads me to the foyer, the big room with the expensive black and white marble floor and the sweeping circular staircase. On the center table is a spray of gladiolas, like a funeral arrangement. Professor Sustevich is walking down the stairs as I enter. "Ah, Mr. Largo," he calls down to me. "Thank you for coming."

"Wouldn't miss it for the world."

Sustevich says, "Please, come with me." He walks across the foyer into the living room. I follow.

He says, "You want something to eat?"

"Fish taco," I say.

"Fish taco?" He looks puzzled. "I don't know what that is."

"Just an expression. Whenever you're happy, shout out, 'Fish taco!'"

"I see."

"It's what all the kids are saying nowadays. The MTV Generation."

"Hmm." He regards me carefully. "A drink?"

"Fish taco, yes!"

He nods. "I understand." He walks to the side table, unscrews a bottle of JW Blue Label. "You drink scotch?"

"I do today," I say. I point to my teeth. "Just had some dental work."

"Really?"

"Two goons knocked out my front teeth."

He looks at my teeth. "I can't tell."

"Dr. Chatchadabenjakalani," I say. "Not really the kind of name you want to say missing two front teeth. But he's a master. Only five hundred bucks."

"I see." He pours two glasses of scotch, hands me one. "Do you know why I asked you here today?"

I down my scotch in three swallows. I figure I'm going to need it. "I'm guessing you're going to threaten me, tell me to repay the money I borrowed. Or else."

"Yes," the Professor says. "That's exactly right."

"No offense, but couldn't you have called? Did I have to come all the way up to the city?"

"But I mean to demonstrate."

"I don't like the sound of that," I say.

Sustevich turns to his right and speaks to the empty room. "Dmitri," he says. He says the name quietly, as if Dmitri is standing beside him. For exactly one second, Sustevich appears insane, talking to an invisible friend. Then, like magic, Dmitri appears

from around the corner and walks into the exact spot where Sustevich stares.

"Yes, Professor?"

"How much more time does Mr. Largo have? To repay our
twelve million dollars?"

"Eight days."

The Professor nods. "Eight days. Not much time. Will you be
able to repay me?"

"I think so. But let's say—just for the sake of discussion—I
asked for a few more days. Is it negotiable?"

"Yes," Sustevich says.

"Well, then," I say, thinking the Professor is reasonable, after all.

"But I will cut off one of your fingers for each day you request."

I nod. "I see. So ten days is really the upper limit."

"Not necessarily."

"I think I'll try to meet that original deadline."

"Very wise. Dmitri, please take Mr. Largo to the basement and
demonstrate the importance of timely repayment of debts."

"You know," I say, "that's not really necessary."

Dmitri pulls a pistol from his pocket and smiles at me. "Please,"
Dmitri says, "come with me."

"Listen," I say to Sustevich. "We're business partners. There's no
need for violence."

"I understand the other day you went to the Palo Alto Airport.
You boarded a jet plane. Twice in two days. I hope you don't try to
leave without repaying your debt to me. That would be unwise."

"Agreed," I say.

"Please," Dmitri says, "come with me."

"I'm not coming with you," I say.

Dmitri pushes the barrel of the pistol against my forehead. He
cocks the trigger sloppily with his meaty thumb.

"Whoa whoa whoa," I say. I lift my hands slowly into the air.
"Let's calm down with that trigger. Looks cool in the movies, but
not a smart thing to do, pulling it back with your thumb like that,
safety off. Where the hell did you learn that?"

"Russian army," Dmitri says.

"Oh," I say.

"Dmitri is very jumpy," Sustevich says. "You should go with him."

"Fine."

Dmitri raises the barrel of the pistol, away from my forehead.

The Professor says, "I'll see you in eight days. You'll be here?"

"With bells on."

"Fish tacos, then, Mr. Largo," Sustevich says, tipping his fingers in a rakish salute. He turns and leaves the room.

"Yeah, fish tacos to you, too."

Dmitri leads me down a dark flight of stairs into a basement. It's a bare concrete room, forty feet square, with a single light bulb in an enamel socket and a pull string switch. I suspect this room is the last thing many men see.

"All right, Dmitri," I say. "What's the plan? You're going to beat me up?"

"Yes."

"There's no need for that. I'm partners with your boss. I'm making money for him. I'm working for him."

"Yes," he says.

"Dmitri," I say, "maybe punching employees is how you handle things in Russia, but this is Silicon Valley. This is the New Economy. Everyone's a freelance employee here. The Internet changes everything. We're all working on 'Project Me.'"

"Yes," he says. With this as a warning, he delivers a right hook into my jaw. I fly backward and land on the concrete floor. I feel a bolt of pain shoot from my coccyx to my neck. Perhaps I've broken my hip?

"Goddamn it," I say. "I just paid five hundred bucks for fucking dental work. Are you crazy?"

I immediately regret the question, because apparently Dmitri takes it as a kind of workplace suggestion. He delivers a solid kick into my teeth. If it wasn't so painful, I would laugh, because there

goes Dr. Chatchadabenjakalani's work, skittering across the concrete floor: a front tooth rattling into the far wall like a ball into a
roulette wheel.

"Oh," I say, sadly, as I touch my index finger to the new gap in
my mouth.

"Okay," Dmitri says. "That's it. You have eight days. Next time
I make you drink acid."

"Drink acid?" I say. I shake my head. "You Russians are out of
your mind."

"Yes," Dmitri says. He bends down, offers his hand. Now that
he has punched me and knocked out my front tooth, he's my
buddy. He pulls me to a standing position, pats me on the back.
"Eight days," he says again. "You need to pay us twelve million dollars."

"I know," I say. "Or else you'll kill me with acid."

"And your son," Dmitri says, raising his index finger. "Don't forget your son."

The taxi ride home costs a hundred twenty dollars, which is, I
decide as I leave the cab and slam the door shut, ridiculous. Since
the car accident I've spent more on taxis than I paid originally for
my used Honda.

When I get back to the apartment I make two quick phone
calls: the first to Hank's Service Station to ask about my car ("three
more days"). The second, to Dr. Chatchadabenjakalani ("come
right over"). One more taxi ride to San Jose (twenty-three dollars)
and two novocaine injections later, I have a new *new* front tooth,
which is—unfortunately—only an approximate color match to my
old new front tooth. After the cap is bonded into my gums, Dr.
Chatchadabenjakalani holds a mirror to my face, like a barber
showing off a new flattop.

"Okay?" he asks.

I stare at my new two-tone smile, a taupe and white color
scheme like an Ed Napier hotel lobby. What the hell, I think. My
days of seducing women are long past. "Good job, doc," I say.

The doctor escorts me to the reception desk and rings the

charges on his computer terminal. I'm expecting some kind of bulk discount—I've bought three teeth in twelve hours, after all—but Dr. Chatchadabenjakalani hands me an invoice of $250 for the single tooth, which is exactly half what he charged me for the original two.

I must admit that the "it's-a-business-expense" equanimity I felt when leaving the office for the first time has rapidly dissipated. When Dr. Chatchadabenjakalani joyfully calls after me as I leave the office, "See you later tonight perhaps!"—I wave my hand over my shoulder and grunt goodbye.

That night, Toby and I watch wrestling on television. I have a newfound appreciation for the sport. It occurs to me, as I watch the two long-haired muscular men prancing around the ring, their chests glistening with oil, that I have a lot in common with Killer Eight Ball and Frankie the Fist. The men are actors, of course, following a script; and much of the cartoonish violence is fake—mere choreography. But every now and then something unexpected happens: a punch thrown too far to the right, a slip on the canvas, a mistimed jump or forgotten roll. Muscles are bruised, bones broken. There even have been times, I know, when men have died.

I rub my tongue over my two-toned front teeth. The only difference between my kind of con and theirs, I think, is the amount of money at stake. And, of course, the part about the drinking of acid. That hasn't happened to a wrestler yet, as far as I know.

While we're watching TV, the phone rings. I pick up. It's Ed Napier.

"Tomorrow morning," he says, "I'm wiring money into your account. Three million dollars."

"Three million dollars," I repeat. "Okay."

"Remember our agreement?"

"Sure," I say.

"Don't do anything stupid."

"I won't."

"Call me when the funds clear."

He hangs up.

Toby turns to me. "Who was that?"

"Ed Napier."

"And?"

"He's going to wire three million dollars into my account to-morrow."

"Three million dollars," he says. "You only owe Sustevich twelve. Almost there."

"Almost," I agree.

Toby smiles and nods. For the first time in my life, he is impressed with his father.

Chapter Twenty-Nine

It's Monday morning at ten o'clock, and Toby, Jess, and I are playing foosball.

Foosball is a game of miniaturized violence. We twirl our wrists, slam rows of four-inch-tall celluloid soccer players against a yellow Ping-Pong ball. The table shakes and thumps. The ball flies, crashes against the wall, ricochets back.

I flick my wrist. My plastic man knocks the ball home. Jess yells, "No!"

The ball blurs past Jess's defender and into the net. "Shit," she says. "Where the hell is Peter?"

It's two against one: me and Toby on one side, Jess on the other. Peter has been missing all morning. We can get by without his programming skills for a morning, but we need him for foosball, desperately.

"Toby," I say, "call him."

"I just did."

"Call again."

Toby leaves the table, grabs his crutches, hobbles to a phone. He dials Peter's number, listens to the message, hangs up. "Not answering his cell," he says.

"You try his home number?"

Toby nods.

"Where is he?" Jess says again.

"He'll be here," I say. I take the foosball out of the net, toss it onto the table. "Five serving two," I say, and knock the ball into Jess's little plastic man.

Peter arrives a little past eleven, pale and out of breath.

"We have to talk," he says as he walks into the room.

Toby, Jess, and I are still playing foosball. She is losing, badly. "Take your position," she says. Without looking up, she points to the spot beside her.

Toby tosses the ball onto the table. Jess whips her man around, sending the ball shooting toward our goal. Toby wrenches his defenders to the left, rattling the table. He stops the ball with a *thwack*.

"We have to talk," Peter Room says again.

He reaches down to the table, grabs the ball, pockets it.

"Hey!" Toby says.

"This is important," Peter says.

I look up. "What's the matter?"

"I quit."

"You what?"

"I quit."

"You can't quit," I say. "We're in the middle of . . . of what we're doing. We need you."

"Something's going on," he says.

"Meaning what?"

"I'm being followed."

"So you're being followed," I say. "Big deal. Me and Toby are being followed, too. Isn't that right, Toby?"

"It's true. Freaked my dad out so much, he got in a car accident. Nearly killed a nun."

I say to Peter, "It's probably Napier's men. Maybe Sustevich's."

"I don't think so," he says. "There are too many of them. There's like five teams of them. They're in my parking lot when I get home at night. Another team tails me on 101. I saw a third team in Mountain View yesterday. And then there are faces. They seem so familiar, but I can't place them. I see the same people all the time on the street, or in a restaurant. I'm telling you: I'm being followed."

"By who?" I say.

"The police."

I say, "The Palo Alto police don't run twenty-man stakeout teams. They rescue cats from trees."

"The FBI, then," Peter says.

"You're imagining it," I say.

"Maybe. But I quit."

"Peter," I say, "calm down. You're not quitting."

"I am not going to prison, Kip. I know, for you, it's old hat—no big deal. But I'm sorry. I am not playing this game. It's not worth it."

"First of all," I say calmly, "it's not a game. Not anymore. Now people's lives are at stake." Just in case he's not clear about what I mean, I add, "Me and Toby's, for example."

"But—"

I interrupt him. "Second of all, it *is* worth it. We're talking about a lot of money."

"You promised me," Peter says. "You promised I wouldn't get in trouble."

"You're not in trouble."

"Then why are the police following me?"

"Peter, will you calm down?" I turn to Jess. "Jess, have you noticed anyone following you?"

"I don't know. Maybe once or twice. But I'm not sure."

"Peter," I say, "we need you. It'll be over in seven days. You're going to be a million dollars richer. For seven days work."

"Kip, don't you see? This thing is out of control." He shakes his head. He points at me. "I mean, look at your teeth."

"What's wrong with my teeth?" I say, suddenly embarrassed. I curl my upper lip over my two front choppers.

"They're two different colors, man."

"You can tell?"

"Yes, I can tell."

I look to Jess. She shrugs, to say she can tell, too.

"Look," Peter says, "this is getting scary. Big Italian guys in suits are beating you up. Russian guys with guns."

"Dmitri's a friend of mine," I say. I think about how he helped me up from the floor after knocking out my tooth.

"I'm sorry. I don't want to get killed. I'm happy making a hundred grand a year writing Java code. I don't need this shit."

"Peter," I say, "remember what I told you? When you asked to join?" I repeat the words, stressing them. *"When you asked to join."*

"What?"

"'Once you're in, you're in.'"

"Are you threatening me, Kip?"

"No," I say. I raise my palms. "I would never hurt you."

"Hurt me? Now we're talking about violence? Against me?"

"I said: *I would never hurt you.* Relax."

He shakes his head.

Jess says, "Peter, Kip didn't threaten you. Calm down. We need you for seven more days. Then you can take a vacation."

"Come on, Peter," Toby says.

"Seven more days?" Peter says.

"Seven more days," I say. "Please."

Peter shakes his head again, walks out of the room. But he doesn't storm from the office in a huff, so it looks to everyone in the room that we have Peter's services for at least another seven days. Which is how I want it to look.

CHAPTER THIRTY

When a con goes well, you feel like Jesus Christ, turning water into wine, feeding the multitudes, raising the dead.

This morning, Napier visits my office for a taste of my own personal Jesus. He has wired three million dollars into my brokerage account. Moments from now, I will turn his three million dollars into six, and then wire it back to him. This is the beginning of the end. After today, Napier will become mad with greed. He will see the opportunity to multiply his loaves, and he will grasp it. Then he will learn, too late, that money is like salvation: It's not given easily; and when it comes, you can't hold it for long.

In the conference room, we dim the lights, flip the projector, and watch as Pythia plasters the screen with ten stock charts, and ten predictions. The red prediction circles splatter on the screen like raindrops in a puddle, one after another, and stock prices rise and fall, and land in the circles where Pythia says they will. We make ten thousand dollars here. Nine thousand there. We watch as Pythia repeats the process, ten charts at a time, one hundred thousand dollars gambled each thirty seconds, until our winnings build to five hundred thousand dollars, then seven hundred thousand, and then, finally, a million.

In four minutes, we've made two million dollars. In six minutes, three million dollars.

Finally, Peter walks to the keyboard, types something. We look at a table filled with numbers. He turns to Ed Napier. "You just turned three million dollars into six million."

"Did I?" Napier says. "Never worked so little in my life. And that's saying something."

On the speakerphone, in front of Napier and my team, I call my broker and give wiring instructions: I will now wire six million dollars from my account to Napier's. Of course I cannot really predict the stock market, and of course Pythia did not place real stock trades, and of course the entire Pythia company, and the software, and the science behind it, are completely and utterly false. However, to make the con work, the money must be real. So the six million dollars I now deposit into Napier's account is no illusion. It's the money that Sustevich lent us. It was his investment in our con, his venture capital.

Thirty seconds after I replace the phone receiver, there is a knock on our office door. I walk down the hall to answer it. Toby and Jess follow.

I pull open the door. Two men—one white, one black—both in identical suits and stylish aviator sunglasses—stare at me.

"Kip Largo?" the white man says.

"Yes?"

He flashes a badge. "My name is Agent Farrell. This is Agent Crosby. We're from the FBI. May we come in? We have a few questions."

PART THREE

CACKLEBLADDER

CHAPTER THIRTY-ONE

I lead the FBI agents down the hall, past the Ms. Pac-Man machine, past our Potemkin village server room, and into our conference room. Peter at least had the good sense to shut down the projector and hide from the agents the evidence of our massive stock fraud, which was being projected in bright colors across a five-foot-wide screen.

"So, what is this about, gentlemen?" I say. I hear my own voice. I sound friendly, but nervous. I wave my hand, offer the agents seats at our conference table. They neither accept nor decline my offer, but instead continue standing, perfectly still.

Agent Crosby says to me, "Are you in charge here?"

"Sometimes," I say. "When things are going well."

My attempt at humor falls flat. Crosby stares at me. He's a big man, dark-skinned, with a head that was stylishly shaved a week ago, but now simply looks untended, like a remote patch of lawn after a long summer weekend. He has broad shoulders, rigid bearing, maybe ex-military. Or maybe his father was a cop. He stares at me sternly. Finally, he says: "I want to ask you about your company. About what you do."

"What we do?" I say. "Well, it's pretty complicated, actually . . ." I think about it, take a deep breath. "And it's a bit technical . . ."

Napier pipes up, "Hold on, Kip." He steps forward. "You don't have to answer that."

The agents turn to Napier, as if noticing him for the first time. "And you are?" Crosby says.

"Ed Napier. I'm an investor in this company. I also serve on its board of directors. Pythia is developing some very exciting technology, but I'm afraid we need to keep it a secret. For competitive reasons."

"I see," Crosby says. He squints at Napier, then looks to his partner, as if to say: Is that who I think it is?

Agent Farrell says, "Wait a second. You're Ed Napier? *Las Vegas* Ed Napier?"

"That's right."

"I was just at The Clouds, last weekend."

Napier gives his thousand-watt smile. "No kidding. How'd you do?"

"Lost two hundred bucks."

"That's all we took you for?" Napier says, with his big booming voice. "Sounds like you need to come back this weekend!"

The FBI agents laugh. Napier laughs. Even I try to laugh. Peter stands in the corner of the room. He is not laughing.

"Well, Mr. Napier," Agent Crosby says, "the reason we're here is to investigate some of your employees. Agent Farrell and I serve on the CCTF—sorry, Cyber Crime Task Force. We've gotten reports about computer hacking efforts originating from your company's IP addresses."

"I see."

Crosby continues: "The targets are online brokerage houses. Datek, E-Trade, Schwab." He raises his palm. "Now don't get me wrong. We're not accusing anyone in this room of hacking computer systems. But sometimes employees use their company's facilities to commit crimes."

"Ah," I say.

"So we were hoping we could get a list of all the employees at Pythia. That's the name of the company, right?"

"That's right," I say.

"And then we could cross-reference that list with our own list."

"Your own list?"

"Felons, criminals, people with shady pasts."

I look up and notice Peter. He's staring at me, as if to say: *People like you.*

I say, "Of course."

"Then we'd like to talk to each employee. It would be completely voluntary. Just a few minutes each. You know, sometimes just having the FBI show up at your door scares the bejesus out of people, makes stuff spill out."

"Right," I say. "The thing is, we use a lot of contractors here. About ten of them. They're not all employees, strictly speaking."

Crosby says, "But you know who they are."

"Sure."

"Well that's fine. Then a list of them, too."

I clear my throat. "What exactly does the FBI think these hackers are doing? Why online brokers? Are they stealing money?"

Agent Farrell says, "We're not sure. That's why we want to talk to people. Figure it all out." He points to his skull, to demonstrate where all the figuring is about to take place.

"Okay," I say. "I'll get a list together for you. It'll be ready later today."

Agent Crosby steps toward me, hands me a business card. I look at it. It is stamped with an embossed gold-foil FBI seal, an eagle clutching arrows. Very authentic. You can buy fifty business cards exactly like these for $34.95 at businesscards.com. Trust me, I know.

"When it's ready, you can call and fax it over," Crosby says.

"Roger," I say. "Will do."

Napier says, "Listen, if you gentlemen need something to do this weekend, why not come back to The Clouds? I'll comp you both. Great penthouse suites. Thirty-sixth floor. Bring your wives."

Farrell says, "I'm not married, actually."

"Even better," Napier says, and winks. "I'll comp you for that, too."

Crosby laughs. "I don't know . . ."

"Really," Napier says. "Here's my card." He reaches into his pocket, takes out his own pile of business cards. He hands one to

Crosby and one to Farrell. "Call my assistant, Clarissa, anytime. This weekend, next weekend, whenever. Tell her who you are. She'll make arrangements. Maybe I'll see you there."

"That's very generous," Agent Crosby says, "but I'm afraid we can't do that. Accepting gifts from someone involved in an investigation . . ."

"Am I involved in an investigation?" Napier asks.

"A little. For now."

"Well, then," Napier says. He shrugs. "Maybe when this is all over."

"Yeah," Crosby says. "Maybe." He nods. But I notice it: The agent's body language has changed. He's no longer stiff and aggressive. His shoulders have slumped, his posture is relaxed.

See how to become a billionaire? When someone investigates your criminal activity, offer them penthouses and hookers. And all this time you thought it was brains and hard work.

The two agents turn to leave. Farrell reaches for the door, stops with his hand on the knob. He turns to Peter. "Just for the sake of my notes, what's your name?"

Peter, who was pale when the FBI entered the room, has now assumed the appearance of week-old snow: grayish white, slowly melting. "Me?"

"Yes."

"Peter," he says. "Peter Room."

Farrell takes his notepad from his pocket, scribbles something. "Peter Room," he repeats. He turns to Jess and Toby. "And you two?"

"Toby Largo," my son says.

"Jessica Smith."

Farrell nods. He write down the names. He clicks his pen closed, slides it into the spiral wire binding of his pad, replaces it in his pocket.

"Thank you," he says. He nods to Agent Crosby, and the two men leave.

*   *   *

Sixty seconds later, after we watched the FBI Pontiac pull from our parking lot, Peter makes an announcement. "That's it," he says. "I'm done."

"You're done?" I say.

"I quit."

"Peter," I say. I look over to Ed Napier, meaningfully. "Not now."

"I don't care about him," Peter says. "I'm not going to jail, for you, him, or anyone else. I'm out of here."

Napier says, "Peter, calm down. Those two guys are clowns. Trust me. They're digging. If they had something, they'd arrest us. But they have nothing."

"If they have nothing, why did they come here? How did they know about Datek and the brokers?"

"Maybe you weren't careful," Napier says.

"Fuck you," Peter says.

"Whoa," I say.

Napier raises an eyebrow. For the first time since I met him, he speaks softly, half to himself. "Watch yourself, Peter."

"Watch myself? What are you going to do about it? Beat me up?"

Napier keeps smiling.

I say, "Peter, please treat Mr. Napier with respect."

"Sure," Peter says. "You want respect? Here's respect." He looks at Napier. "Respectfully, I want to let you know—" He turns to me. "That I'm out of here." He walks to the door. He opens it, pauses at the threshold. "By the way," he says, turning to us, "if you think I'm going to leave evidence lying around, pointing to me, you're out of your mind."

He leaves, slams the door.

"One thing I've noticed," Napier says, as if he's continuing a different conversation, "is that these computer guys are arrogant little shits. They always think they're the smartest guys in the room."

"In Peter's case," I say, "it's true."

"We'll see," Napier says. He's looking into the distance,

thoughtfully. If I had to guess what he's thinking, it would be: Should I have Peter killed now? Or later?

Napier says, "What did he mean when he said he wasn't going to leave evidence around?"

"I don't know," I say.

Napier looks at Jess. "Jessica?"

"I have no idea," she says.

I say, "Peter's been acting strange these last few weeks. He's been nervous about getting caught."

Napier nods. Finally he says: "Peter now has other things to be nervous about."

Later, after Napier leaves, Toby and I take a taxi to Hank's Service Station on Willow Road, to retrieve my Honda at last. I pay cab fare for what I hope will be the final time, settle up the bill with Hank (the insurance deductible of five hundred dollars), and then we are off, speeding along Willow to go back home. With the con approaching its climax—four more days, tops—I am feeling munificent, and mull over taking Toby out to dinner.

Toby is in the back seat, with his leg cast propped on the gearbox near my elbow. He stares out his passenger window, thinking quietly. This is a new side of Toby that I was previously unacquainted with: thinking, quiet. It is a side of him I wish I had seen more of, growing up.

He says finally, "It's called a button, right?"

"What's that?"

"When you have imaginary FBI agents show up at your office, to scare the mark. To put pressure on Napier."

"Is that what you think?" I say.

"You really should tell me, Dad," Toby says. "I thought the whole idea was to teach me about cons."

"The whole idea," I say, "was to prevent you from getting killed."

"Which you've done."

"So far."

More silence as Toby stares out his window. Finally, he says, "So am I right? Is this a button? The FBI agents aren't real, are they?"

"No," I say, "they're not."

"Just actors?"

"Just actors."

"They were good," Toby says. "Very convincing."

"Thank you."

"I like the muscley black guy. Nice touch."

"I thought so."

"And the shaved head. Very Kojak."

I turn left at Middlefield, head into Palo Alto. On the horizon, I see rain clouds—unusual for this time of year. Typically, Northern California has two seasons: Wet and Dry, and never the twain shall meet. Recently, though, in the past few years, it has begun raining in the summer, and staying dry in the winter. I believe this is all part of God's cosmic plan to Screw With Your Mind. Entire religions have been founded to explain why God would want to do such a thing. But I am untroubled by the question. A con is a con, no matter who perpetrates it.

Toby says, "And what about Peter?"

"What *about* Peter?"

"He's just acting, too, right? Part of the con?"

"Toby, you ask too many questions."

"I'm curious."

"You know what they say about curiosity."

"I just think it's strange, is all."

"What?"

"Being part of a con, and not knowing what's going on."

"Don't be insulted," I say. "It's for your own good. The less you know, the better."

Toby grunts. This may be a gesture of agreement, perhaps even a sign of growing maturity in my son, that he accepts, finally, that some things are unknowable. Or perhaps it is merely a grunt, an involuntary clearing of the throat, a choke on swallowed phlegm.

CHAPTER THIRTY-TWO

The big question, in every con, is how to end it. It's easy to steal money from someone; it's the getaway that's the problem. You don't want your mark going to the police or—in the case of rich, powerful, and frightening men—hunting you down on their own, chasing you to the ends of the earth.

Ideally, when it's over, your mark should be unaware that he's been conned. He should think his exciting venture failed due to a misunderstood phone call, or bad luck, or poor timing. He should be anxious, in fact, to try the con again! The sign of a great con, then, is one in which you can play your mark two or three times in succession, with increasing stakes, until you have taken everything from him. If your mark walks away unaware that he has been played, then you have succeeded, and you should be proud.

So how to get rid of a mark once you have his money? The button, which Toby mentioned, is one way. You run a button like this:

You set up the con over several weeks. You allow your mark to slowly learn that, by participating in an illegal scheme, he can make vast amounts of money, risk-free. You let your mark win a few times, to start the greed dripping into his veins. He wins a few horse races, thanks to "intercepted" telegraph messages, for example. Or he makes a million dollars in the stock market, thanks to an illegal router box hidden in a manhole in Manhattan.

You watch as your mark's excitement builds. You can practically see his lips moving as he does the math and counts the money he is about to win . . .

Then you set up the blow-off. There will be one more big bet, in which the mark will be able to make his fortune. But of course he must gamble everything he has.

So he bets on a horse . . .

Or he buys a million shares of stock . . .

Or he purchases a winning lottery ticket from an unsuspecting old woman . . .

Whatever the con, here's what happens next: The mark wins. His horse comes in first. His stock triples in price. He knows, in other words, that he is only minutes away from claiming his prize—millions of dollars, vast riches! But the moment he tries to redeem the winning racing ticket, or tries to liquidate his stock portfolio, or whatever he needs to do, something unexpected happens. A visit from the FBI, perhaps? A tail by a local uniformed policeman? Or a phone call from the district attorney?

Typically, the police burst into the betting parlor, threatening to arrest everyone. The mark escapes—just barely, without getting caught. He thanks his lucky stars. He is sad that he is unable to claim his prize, that he lost his betting stake, but relieved that he is not in prison, branded a criminal, his life in tatters.

The mark thinks about how close he came to beating the odds, to winning a fortune. He longs for the day when the roper will call him on the telephone and offer him an opportunity to try their scheme again.

Now *that* is a great con. When the mark doesn't know he has been conned. When the mark wishes for the day when he will be fleeced again.

So Toby is right about Agents Farrell and Crosby. They do not really work for the FBI. They work for Elihu Katz, or one of his friends, or one of his friend's friends. They are con men, just like me. They are based out of Los Angeles. You can hire them for five hundred dollars a day each, plus expenses, plus a small slice of the take distributed at the end of the job. I don't know much about

"Agent Farrell" and "Agent Crosby," but I think I remember hearing that they were unemployed soap opera actors, and that Agent Crosby even had a part on *Days of Our Lives* for exactly two weeks, playing a doctor, until the writers decided he was "too black" and killed him off in a freak tractor-trailer jackknife-through-the-hospital-cafeteria-window accident. As far as I know, none of Agent Crosby's con victims has ever recognized him as the man on TV. White Middle America is so frightened of being accused of thinking that "all black men look alike" that it overlooks the obvious fact that the FBI agent threatening jail time was on television performing brain surgery just a few months earlier.

It is gratifying, in a perverse way, that Toby has discerned the mechanism of this con so quickly. He knows what we are trying to do to Napier. He knows, instinctively, that the FBI's appearance in our office this afternoon is the setup, the preparation for the final button.

My son, Toby, has good instincts. Part of me is proud of this. And part of me is disappointed. And part of me, I must admit, is just a little bit frightened.

CHAPTER THIRTY-THREE

Toby and I return home, vegetate in front of the TV for an hour by watching World Wrestling Federation SmackDown! (exclamation mark part of the show's title, not an indication of my own enthusiasm) and then decide to walk into Palo Alto for burgers and beer.

The night is warm. A breeze blows from the west, sweeping in from the foothills, carrying the smell of dust and rosemary. I feel the rain coming. For a moment, three blocks after we set out, I think about returning to the apartment to retrieve an umbrella, but then decide to keep going—the restaurant is only four more blocks—and to risk it. Life is an endless series of gambles, tiny and vast. Every time you walk out of your house, or get in your car, or try to rip off criminals—it's the same: You take a chance. Get wet, get killed. Always playing the odds.

Toby is skipping along on his crutches beside me. "I get this off in a week," he says, meaning his cast.

Unsure of what to say, I try, "Good." Not sufficiently paternal, I decide. I add: "Must really be looking forward to it."

"Hell, yes," Toby says. "Try wearing a cast for six weeks in the summer."

"I'd rather not," I say.

"Then don't piss off the Russians."

"Good advice," I say.

We eat at Gordon Biersch, a three-location Bay Area chain that brews its own beer and caters to programmers and Stanford kids. With school out and half its clientele missing, the place is empty. I have one too many beers, but I'm feeling good, that the con is going well—no surprises—and decide to live a little.

An hour and a half later we return home. Toby goes straight to the head, starts pissing with the bathroom door half-open. Classy.

I decide not to say anything. Instead, I walk through my apartment, pulling the curtains shut, the coda for the day. In fifteen minutes, I will fall asleep. In three days, I will be on a plane heading somewhere far away, and warm—maybe Phuket Bay, maybe the Maldives. Even if the con goes perfectly, and the mark doesn't know he's been conned, it's never smart to stick around. Out of sight, out of mind.

Toby returns from the bathroom, too quickly.

"You gonna wash your hands?" I say.

"Jesus, Dad, I'm twenty-five years old."

"A twenty-five-year-old who just took a piss."

"It's been in my underwear all day long. Cleanest part of my body." He thinks about it, decides it's not worth a fight, shrugs. He hobbles back into the bathroom. I hear the sound of water, and the soap dish scraping the tile basin.

There's a knock on the door. I look through the peephole. It's Mr. Santullo's Arabian grandson. I open the door. I think he's going to hassle me about something, maybe that I need a business license to sell vitamins out of my apartment. Or maybe he'll reprimand me for drinking highballs with Mr. Santullo and helping with his bills.

But he has a different agenda. "Hey, Kip," he says. "Can I come in?"

I stand aside, let him pass. He stops in the front hall. "I wanted to let you know something," he says. "Two guys came by while you were out tonight."

"Guys?"

"FBI agents. They showed me a badge."

I'm relieved. I know instantly it's "Agent Farrell" and "Agent Crosby," playing their part perfectly. On the chance that my mark is having the apartment watched, he'll see the FBI snooping around. One more true-to-life detail. Perfect. I make a mental note to give them a little extra when the con is done. They're good. They deserve it.

"What were their names?" I ask. "Agent Farrell? Crosby?"

The Arabian squints, looks uncertain. "I don't think so," he says. "Something different."

"Black guy? White partner?"

He shakes his head. "No. Both white, a man and a woman. Here—I have a card." He reaches into his pocket, hands me a business card. It looks a lot like the business card that Agent Farrell handed me, except that it is printed on a heavier matte stock. You're not going to get fifty of these for thirty-five dollars at business-cards.com. In order to get a card like this, you need to work for the FBI. The real FBI. The card says: "Special Agent Louis Davies" and lists a San Francisco Federal Building address.

Now, for the first time, I feel a falling sensation, the pit of my stomach clutched by my throat. This is not right. There is no Special Agent Louis Davies in my con. Not that I hired, anyway.

The Arabian says, "He had a warrant. He searched your apartment."

"Did he?" I look around the apartment. Nothing seems out of place. Then I look at the computer monitor resting on the card table. It should display my bouncing-vitamin screensaver, which automatically appears after twenty minutes of computer inactivity. But instead the screen shows my computer desktop. Someone has been on my machine in the past twenty minutes. Looking for something. But what?

The Arabian says: "I asked them if they wanted to talk to you. They said no."

"Thanks for telling me."

"That's the strange thing," the Arabian says. "They *told* me to tell you."

"They did?"

"They said, 'Be sure to let Mr. Largo know we came by.'"

"I see."

Toby appears in the living room behind me. "What's going on?"

"Nothing," I say. I pat the Arabian on the shoulder. "Thanks," I say.

"Sure . . ."

I realize that the Arabian is staring at me. "What?" I say.

"Nothing."

"Tell me. What?"

"It's just . . . Your teeth. They're two different colors."

"Are they?"

"Sorry." He shakes his head. "Keep the card." He turns and leaves.

Toby says: "So what does that mean?"

"I'm not sure," I say.

"You're not sure? I thought you know everything. You plan everything. I thought there's no loose ends."

"I guess there's a loose end," I say. My mind is racing. I'm trying to figure it out. Are those real FBI agents, snooping around? Why? What are they looking for? How much do they know? Why are they interested in me? Could they possibly know about my con?

"That's not very comforting, Dad," Toby says.

"No, it's not."

"I mean, this is not exactly impressing the hell out of me."

I look at my son, try to smile. How can I respond to that? I walk toward the bedroom. "I get the bed tonight," I say. "You take the couch." I close the door, and try to go to sleep.

At night, it rains. In the morning, the radio news jockey reports that rain this time of year is "freakish" and wonders what it means.

CHAPTER THIRTY-FOUR

But like they say: The con must go on. Once you start, it's a treadmill, and you can't get off. When two loose ends show up at your door with a search warrant, you can't throw up your hands and say, "That's it. I quit." You're in the middle. Napier has three million dollars of Sustevich's money. You owe the Russian mob twelve million. You have two days to pay it back. Otherwise you're going to be one of the first to try the brand-new drink that's the talk of the Moscow club scene: the Acid Highball. Take one part hydrochloric acid. One part ginger ale. But ginger ale optional. Shake. Stir. Drink. Die.

Okay. Now it's the morning. Toby and I are driving to work. I've forgiven him for acting like a snot-nosed shit. He's my son after all. That snot-nosed shit thing he does? That's from me. I think back to when I was twenty-five. Running Pigeon Drops with my own father. Hated his guts. Probably made a few snotty comments of my own, whenever he wasn't in jail. Did I? I try to remember. I've spent the last thirty years blotting out the memory of my father, who failed me in every way possible: taught me crime instead of fishing, never paid for squat, then dropped dead and left me and Mom with nothing.

I've been successful at forgetting about him. Now he's just a dark presence at the edge of my memory, a story I hardly bother to tell or think about. But of course he's the subtext for my entire life. You never figure this out until it's too late. Here I am, fifty-four years old, on the downside of my arc, heading toward my own end, and just now, driving in my car to commit a criminal act with my *own* son, I realize that everything I've ever done—*everything*—has been a reaction to my father. My attempt at leaving his world, my returning to it; my leaving Toby, my going back to him; my grasp at redemption, and my failure, so far, to find it.

Can you tell I'm feeling sorry for myself? That's what happens to men like me. We're superheroes, in total control of every thread in our lives. The moment someone introduces a rip into our meticulous plans, we panic and flail. Calm down. That's the only way to pull off this con. Stay calm. Keep your eye on the prize. You're almost done.

Bad news, when you start talking to yourself. A warning sign.

CHAPTER THIRTY-FIVE

Instead of going to the office, Toby and I drive into the city. We head downtown, to Montgomery Street, an impossibly narrow road that serves as both the eastern border of Chinatown, and the main artery of the financial district. It's studded with dim sum shops and orange traffic cones. Steam rises from the manholes. Cars double- and triple-park, sometimes up on the sidewalk, sometimes in the middle of the road. The street is both impassable and unavoidable. To get anywhere downtown, you need to drive it, but you do so at your peril, and curse yourself for trying.

I honk and weave, take Montgomery to Sansome. Our destination is the Transamerica Pyramid, the iconic triangle at the center of the San Francisco skyline. We park underground, sign in at the security desk, and are handed paper visitor's badges we must pin to our shirts. We go to the eighteenth floor, to the office of Rifkind, Stuart, Kellogg, a law firm I have selected on the advice of Elihu Katz.

In the Rifkind Stuart waiting room, Jessica is already there, waiting for us. "I gave our name," she says. "Peter's not here yet."

"No," I say. "Peter's not coming."

She nods, as if she expected this answer. I go to the reception desk, speak to the hot brunette who looks like she just stepped out of a *Playboy* shoot. Lawyers always have the best-looking receptionists. Never got any growing up, during the long dry years of high school, college, then law school. Finally, twenty years after starting, they make partner and it all pays off. In the form of a raven-haired girl with collagen lips and nice breasts. "I'm Kip Largo," I say, "and this is Toby. My party is here now."

The brunette presses a button on her PBX. "Harris, Mr. Largo's party is here."

She removes her earpiece, stands. "This way, please."

She leads us down a short hall. I see Toby ogling her ass as she walks. She takes us to a conference room, all windows, with spectacular views of the Bay eighteen floors below.

"Can I get you some water?" she says.

I decline quickly on behalf of my team. What I want to avoid is Toby flirting stupidly, embarrassing me.

"Mr. Stuart will be right with you," she says. She leaves.

"Hot," Toby says, after she goes.

"Sit down," I say to Toby.

Harris Stuart shows up two minutes later. Despite his grand and WASP name, he's short and bald, Slavic-looking, shaped like a Russian Matryoshka doll—big round bottom leading up to a glossy tapered head.

"Pleased to meet you, Mr. Largo," he says. He shakes my hand. "Elihu Katz is a good friend of this firm."

Maybe that's code for something, maybe not. Elihu Katz has been around a long time. In his years running his own big store, conning both men of great repute and complete unknowns, he has used lawyers for all sorts of things: both to make trouble and to get out from under it. What I know about Rifkind, Stuart, Kellogg is what Elihu told me: that they will be very agreeable about whatever I request, no matter how unusual it seems.

We sit down at the table: me, Toby, and Jess on one side, Mr. Harris Stuart on the other.

"I know your time is valuable," Stuart says, "so I won't waste it. I've looked into your request. There is a shell company available, and it's pretty clean. The owner is amenable. We could do the deal quickly—two hundred and fifty thousand, plus legal. I'd say less than three hundred thousand, all in."

"That sounds fine. What is it?"

"It's a company called Halifax Protein Products."

"Protein products?"

"They made fish oil," Stuart explains. "They used to harvest cod liver oil, fatty acids from fresh innards, that kind of thing."

"Can you make a living doing that?"

"Apparently not," Stuart says. "They've been defunct for three years. No operations since ninety-six. But they've kept their filings in order, and they're still listed on the Nasdaq OTC. No trading volume to speak of."

"Sounds perfect. Can you get it done today?"

"Before lunch."

"What a country," I say, half-joking.

But Harris Stuart nods seriously. "Yes," he says. "It really is."

In twenty-four hours, I will be the majority owner of a company called Halifax Protein Products, which trades on the Nasdaq under the ticker symbol HPPR. Later today, when I sign a few papers and have Rifkind, Stuart, Kellogg file them with the State of Delaware secretary of state and with Nasdaq, we will issue ten million new shares of stock.

The value of each share of stock ought to be approximately zero dollars, since HPPR no longer engages in any kind of business and serves no customers. The cod liver oil business never panned out the way the company founders (company flounders?) expected.

Halifax Protein Products is what is known as a shell company— a paper entity that does nothing, except exist. It has value only because the previous owners of the company continued to file the necessary paperwork to keep their company listed on the Nasdaq stock exchange.

You may ask why anyone would want to buy stock in a company that used to harvest cod liver oil, but which now does nothing. Surely this would be a foolish investment, ranking up there with investments in Internet companies that lose one dollar for every fifty cents' worth of sales, or companies that give away services for free in the hope of making money sometime in the distant future. And indeed it would be a foolish investment. Unless, of course, you knew that HPPR was about to rise from ten cents per share to ten dollars per share.

If you knew that was about to happen, then you'd want to own a lot of shares of HPPR. You'd try to buy as many as you could. As many as you could afford.

It was important for Toby and Jess to be at the meeting with Harris Stuart. That, too, is part of the con. Part of what I've been planning since day one.

I suppose I got the idea from the Dot Com Kid in the Blowfish bar. Back when this story started, what seems so long ago . . .

The kid tried to con the Italian guy, the man with the meaty hands and the low-rent signet ring. Remember? He said to the man: Here's a forty-dollar pot. How much will you bid to win the forty dollars?

And the big dumb guy thought: Forty dollars? I'll bid thirty dollars to win the forty-dollar pot!

Same idea here. How much would you pay to own HPPR, if you knew HPPR would rise to ten dollars per share? Would you pay five dollars? Seven dollars? Hell, even nine dollars?

I suppose that's where I got the idea.

But now, descending in the elevator from the office of Rifkind, Stuart, Kellogg, I realize something. That the Dot Com Kid tried to pull off a similar scam, but found himself pushed down on a bar top, having his neck squeezed and the air forced from his lungs. He was nearly killed. It was only my last-minute intervention that saved him.

So yeah. You have to wonder. If I find myself pushed backward atop a bar, being choked to death, who the hell is going to come to *my* rescue?

CHAPTER THIRTY-SIX

Back in the office, Peter is missing.

He failed to show up at our meeting downtown at the lawyer's. He is not in our office. He doesn't answer his home number or his cell phone. His cubicle has been cleaned, emptied of photos and music CDs, just a tangle of wires where his notebook computer used to sit.

And now this: Jess walks up to me with a sealed envelope. On the front, in Peter's handwriting, it says: "Kip Largo."

Jess hands it to me. "I found this in the conference room, on the foosball table."

Jess is looking at me with a strange expression. That she knows I'm setting her up, but feels obligated to go along. Her expression is somewhere between curiosity and resentment. Curious about where I'm taking her, resentful that I didn't tell her beforehand. But—as I will try to explain to her later—it's for her own good.

I slide my finger under the lip of the envelope, and feel that the adhesive is still wet. Peter probably wrote and left the note while we were at the lawyer's office. Within an hour, he'll be on a plane, to somewhere far away.

At least, I hope so. For Peter's sake.

I open the envelope, pull out a single sheet of paper. It's a handwritten note on green graph paper, the software programmer's stationery of choice. I silently read Peter's letter.

"Call Napier," I say to Jess.

"What does it say?"

"Call Napier," I say again. I fold the note and put it in my pocket.

For the first time in the eighteen years that I have known Jessica Smith—née Brittany Diamond—she looks at me with something approximating hatred. Because now her suspicion has been confirmed: that I do not trust her.

Her anger and hurt seem genuine. But I tell myself that she has been conning men for twenty years—of course her reaction seems genuine. She's a professional. That's her job.

Napier shows up twenty minutes later with two slabs of muscle in tow. All the fake politeness of recent days—the strained deference to my team, the bright smile, the boyish enthusiasm for our scam—is gone. Now he's the old Napier—the Napier who supervised my dental work in the concrete room of his house, the Napier who threatened to hunt each of us down and kill us if we betrayed him.

"What's this about?" he says, sweeping down the corridor. His two goons follow behind him like a cape.

"Peter," I say. Napier approaches me; I hand him Peter's note. The note says:

Sorry Kip—
You need to stop. This is dangerous. The routers will be shut off soon. Sorry.
—Peter

P.S. I'm taking a long vacation. Please don't bother trying to find me.

Napier crumples the note, sticks it in his jacket pocket. We walk into the conference room and join Jess and Toby, who are sitting at the table, silent.

Napier asks, "What does that mean? 'The routers will be shut off'?"

"It means: Game over."

Napier squints at me. He's trying to figure it out.

I explain: "The boxes that intercept the orders . . . the one I showed you in Manhattan? They're programmed to check into our office every forty-eight hours. It's a security feature. If they don't receive the correct security code, they shut down, erase their own memory."

"Then make sure they receive the correct security code . . ."

"It's not that easy. Peter erased the program."

"He *erased* it?" Napier looks at me like I'm an idiot. "You let him erase it?"

"I didn't *let him*. He just did it."

"That little shit," Napier says dreamily, but I can tell from his face: He's not even thinking about Peter anymore. He's on to other things—like trying to figure out how to salvage the scam.

"How long do we have?" he asks, finally.

Toby says, "The routers checked in last night. So Peter must have erased everything this morning."

Napier says, "So we have until tomorrow night."

"Until tomorrow night?" I say. "To do what?"

Again, Napier gives me a look—half-hate, half-pity: *How stupid can you be?*

"To make money," he says.

"You don't understand," I say. "It's over. In two days, Pythia won't work anymore. None of us are programmers. We can't re-create it. We need Peter."

"We have until tomorrow night before the system shuts down, right?"

"That's true," I say.

Napier says, "Okay then. That's all we need. One more day. Tomorrow we follow Pythia's advice, make big trades. One more day. It's all I need."

After Napier leaves, Toby says, "Now I understand. That's how we steal his money without him knowing."

Jess says, "Well *I* don't understand." She's still annoyed at me for keeping secrets.

Toby smiles, starts explaining the con enthusiastically. This may be the first time in his academic life he's had a natural affinity for a subject—he's finally the smartest kid in the class. He says: "Tomorrow Pythia is going to tell Napier to buy a stock. And we all know which stock it's going to recommend."

Now Jess understands. "Ah," she says. "HPPR. Which Kip already owns . . ."

"Dad paid three hundred grand for the whole company. Now he owns ten million shares of stock. How much are you going to sell it for, Dad?"

I shrug. "I don't know. How does ten dollars a share sound?"

Toby smiles and nods. It's official: I'm the Coolest Dad in the World. "So you sell ten million shares to Napier for ten dollars a share. You walk away with one hundred million of his dollars. He's left holding worthless stock. And he never even knows you're the one who took his money."

"I suppose he could try to investigate, go to the SEC," I say. "But he'd have to explain why he was intercepting federal wire communications and manipulating stock prices. So I doubt he'll make much of a fuss."

I can tell from Toby's face he's enthralled by the whole con. "How brilliant is this?" my son asks. "You pay three cents a share; you sell it for ten dollars a share."

"Yeah," I say, quietly. "Irrational exuberance, I guess."

CHAPTER THIRTY-SEVEN

A "cacklebladder" is con man's lingo for a rubber bladder filled with warm chicken blood.

A cacklebladder is yet another way to blow off a mark after he has been trimmed. During the last few moments of a con, a con man hides a cacklebladder in his mouth. At the moment that the mark loses everything, one con man lunges at the other, brandishing a pistol. "How could you bet on the wrong horse?" he screams. (Or "How could you buy the wrong stock?" Or "How could you place all your money on red? I said black!")

A shot goes off. The con man falls to the ground. The mark leans over to look at him. A stream of warm blood spurts from the con man's mouth, splattering the mark. The other participants in the con rush into the melee, pull everyone apart. The "dead body" is removed. The mark is instructed to run—to get out of town—to speak not a word of what he has seen, lest he somehow get tangled up in what has proven to be not just a financial scam, but also a murder . . .

Cacklebladders work well for everyday marks—greengrocers from Omaha, accountants from Poughkeepsie. But their effect is less certain when your mark is a criminal, someone accustomed to blood spurting from mouths, someone familiar with murderous violence. The point of the cacklebladder is to shock your mark into submission.

But how do you shock someone for whom blood and pain are everyday occurrences, trifles distributed to business associates without thought, objects of whimsy?

CHAPTER THIRTY-EIGHT

It is the night before the end.

Tomorrow we will finish the con, and take tens of millions of dollars from our mark, and then I will board a plane. I will wait until it's over to decide my final destination, and to decide whom I will bring along. Planning is helpful, when it comes to ripping people off, but dangerous when it comes to getting away. It's risky to tip your hand. To let people know where to find you. And it's even more risky to buy a second airline ticket—to trust someone before the game is done and the masks are removed.

Toby and I watch TV. Too loud. Mental note to self: After this is over, buy a television with a working volume control.

But now I have a sudden fear. Am I like one of those rednecks who—upon winning the lottery—decide to splurge . . . on a top-of-the-line double-wide?

So maybe I should aim higher than a television.

"Jesus Christ, Dad," Toby yells. "When the hell are you going to fix this TV?"

No. First things first. A decent television.

Instead of wrestling, Toby and I watch CNBC. This is the cable television financial network, where stock prices scroll along the bottom of the screen, twenty-four hours each day. Compared to the gray and monotonous anchormen, the green and red scrolling text, slow as a train of ants across a picnic blanket, is weirdly compelling.

Toby wants to watch wrestling. I tell him that he certainly can do so. When he lives in his own apartment.

"Jeez, Dad," he says, "I thought you *wanted* me to stay with you."

I don't bother to salve his hurt feelings. On the television, the anchorman finally comes to the news story I've been waiting for. In the graphics box beside the anchor's head appears a close-up of Ed Napier, smiling broadly as if—off-screen and cropped from the picture—a hooker is blowing him with great gusto.

The anchor says: "In the continuing saga of the redevelopment of the Las Vegas Strip, today Ed Napier announced that he was increasing his bid for the Tracadero hotel. The new bid includes ninety million dollars of cash."

"Ninety million dollars," Toby says. "I wonder where he's planning to find that."

"Yeah," I say. "I wonder."

The anchor continues: "The Eurobet Group, a consortium of European and Japanese investors that is competing with Napier for control of the site, indicated that they would try to match Napier's offer. Tracadero management could not be reached for comment."

Toby says: "You'd think he would wait to get the cash before he spends it."

"You'd think," I say. "But that's not how rich people think. They always assume they're going to win. Maybe that's why they're rich."

"Yeah, maybe," Toby says. For about two seconds, he mulls over the wisdom I have shared with him. Then he says: "Come on. Turn on wrestling."

At ten o'clock, I pat my son on the shoulder, tell him good night, and head to the bedroom. Within minutes, I drift to sleep.

I wake to the sound of my cell phone ringing. I reach to the nightstand, unfasten it from the charger, put it to my ear. "Yes?" I say.

"Kip, it's me." Jessica Smith.

"What's wrong?"

"Nothing." She stops, pauses. "Well, something. I need to talk to you."

I look at the clock. Eleven-thirty. "Can't it wait? It's late. Tomorrow's a big day."

"It's important."

I rub my eyes, sit up in the bed. "All right. I'll come to your place." She gives me the address. In minutes, I skulk out of the apartment without waking my son, and start driving forty minutes north on 280.

She lives in Noe Valley, in a two-family Victorian in which she has the back entrance. It's about ten degrees cooler here than in the city, and the night is wet with fog. I knock gently on the glass in her door. She opens it within seconds, as if she has been sitting behind the door all this time, anxiously waiting.

"Thanks for coming," she says. She refastens the chain on the door and leads me up a narrow flight of stairs, into a sitting room. The floor is unvarnished pine, the walls painted yellow, with built-in bookshelves loaded with expensive glossy art books and hardcover novels. I don't know what I was expecting—maybe piles of porno tapes from Aria Video, or contact sheets with thumbnails of naked women, or dildos rolling around the floor. But certainly not this. Past a half-wall, I see her kitchen. On the counter: a Mr. Juiceman electric juicer, a toaster, and a well-thumbed two-pound cookbook called *How to Cook Everything*.

On this countertop, I see into the intimate corners of her life—the quiet domesticity: juice in the morning, two slices of toast, a nice home-cooked meal at the end of the day. All that is missing, alas, is me. I think again about that marriage proposal, which I delivered to her just two months ago in her office, and which she studiously ignored. Once again, it seems appealing. Would it be strange to marry your fellow con artist? I've known her since she was nineteen. Half a lifetime. Maybe that's the best kind of love: dull familiarity, boring sameness. Maybe it's the search for novelty and excitement that ruins us. By definition, novelty disappears the moment you find it. Familiarity can only grow richer.

She leads me to the couch. I sit.

"You want a drink?" she says.

"No thanks."

She sits beside me. "We need to talk."

"I'm here. Talk away."

She says: "I'm upset."

She waits for me to say something. I try: "Upset?"

"You don't trust me."

Her accusation catches me off guard. I was expecting warm intimacy, maybe even some making out on the couch. Now I understand: I've been called here for a fight.

"Of course I do," I say.

She launches her indictment. She's been preparing for this, rehearsing. It sounds like a prosecuting attorney's summation. "You came to *me*, Kip. You needed my help. I agreed. You asked me to put aside my own business for a few months; I put it aside. You asked me to sleep with Ed Napier; I slept with Ed Napier." She reaches across the couch, touches my forearm. "I've done everything you've asked."

"You have."

"Then why do I feel like I'm always three steps behind you? Why won't you tell me the con?"

"I have told you—"

"You knew Ed Napier would discover who you really are. You *wanted* him to. But you didn't tell me that was the plan. And the FBI agents you hired—why didn't you tell me about them? And Peter—getting upset, disappearing? That's part of your con, too, isn't it?"

"What's the difference?"

"How would you feel, if I didn't trust you?"

"Hurt. But I would understand."

"How does the con end, Kip?"

"I told you—"

"I know," she says. "You can't tell me. For my own protection."

"Right."

"You know what I think? You never trusted me. Not since the beginning."

"That's not true," I say.

But she's right. I haven't trusted her since that night, two months ago, that she called me on the telephone. It was too convenient, calling suddenly—out of the blue—after not speaking to me for years. Calling at the exact moment I was formulating my plan. Things like that just don't happen. Not in my world.

"Tell me how it ends, Kip. After tomorrow, you're going to get on an airplane and go somewhere far away. Who's coming with you?"

"Whoever wants to."

"Can I come?"

"I would love that," I say. Which is true. I would love to marry you, Jessica Smith. I would love to get on the plane with you, and sit down beside you, and travel somewhere far away, and start a new life together.

If only I could be sure that you are not the one who is going to betray me.

"Then tell me," she says. "Be honest with me. Tell me how the con ends. Show me you trust me. Start now. So that we have no more secrets."

"We'll always have secrets."

She smiles. In an instant, her face changes; her eyes glaze like a shower door sliding closed. Now she looks past me, to a future where I play no part. She says: "I think you should leave now."

"Jess." I try to think of something to say. But I can't. So I rise from the couch.

She leads me back down the staircase, to the door of her apartment.

"I'll see you tomorrow," she says. Her voice is cold, emotionless, professional. Before I can answer, the door closes behind me.

You may wonder why, if I didn't trust her, I asked her to be part of the con in the first place. I will tell you. It's true that I did not

trust her. But having an enemy inside your camp is the most certain way to control them. It's like a piece of string that runs directly
from you to your foe. The question is: Who is doing the pulling,
and who is being pulled?

And finally, there is always the chance, however slight, that she
really did call me out of the blue. Things like that happen, right?
So, just in case, it's nice to have her around. Later, when this is all
over, maybe I'll try that marriage proposal one more time.

As I drive home, I think about the three women currently in my
life: Celia, Jessica, and Lauren Napier.
Each of them makes me unhappy in a different way. And yet,
on a night like this, driving through the fog on 280, back to my
apartment, I wouldn't mind sharing a warm bed with any one of
them.

CHAPTER THIRTY-NINE

At seven o'clock in the morning, Toby and I are both awakened by the garbage cans rattling outside our window—Thursday is garbage pickup day in Palo Alto.

Our simultaneous waking means we compete for the bathroom. It's true that Toby is hobbled by a leg cast and crutches, but what he lacks in speed he makes up for in wiles. He meets me in the hall near the bathroom door. "Your apartment. You get it first," he says, waving his hand magnanimously. "Let me just grab my toothbrush . . ."

He walks in, shuts the door. I hear the lock click.

"Hey," I say.

"You snooze, you lose, Old Man," he calls through the door.

I shake my head, walk away. I have to piss. My son does not understand male biology. I look forward to the day he is as old as I am, and his prostate has grown to the size of an avocado pit, and he wakes in the morning with a submarine ballast full of brine.

I head to the living room. The phone rings. I go to the kitchen, pick up the handset.

"Hello?" I say.

"Mr. Largo?" I know the voice. Russian. Cultured. Effete. The Professor.

"Yes."

"You know who this is?"

"Of course."

"Do you know what tomorrow is?"

"Friday?"

"Yes," Sustevich says. "And it is also three days before you need to repay your debt to me. Do you remember how much you owe?"

"Let me see," I say. I pretend to pause, think about it. "Hmm. Good thing I wrote it down on the back of a 7-Eleven receipt. I must have it here somewhere. Hang on . . ."

"Twelve million dollars."

"Fine," I say. "I'll take your word for it."

"You will be able to repay it?"

"I gave my word."

"Yes, I appreciate that," Sustevich says. "But you must understand, in my line of work, sometimes a man's word is not his bond."

"I understand. But don't sweat it. I'll have it."

"I hope so. For your sake, and for your son's."

"You know," I say, "I'm having second thoughts about my son. You can have him. You need a house boy? Someone to keep you company in that big old mansion of yours? How many bathrooms do you have?"

"Mr. Largo? Have you been outside yet? Have you checked your garbage cans?"

I feel the room grow cold. "Check them . . . for *what?*"

"There's a message there. A warning. Shall I stay on the line while you go look?"

I don't answer. I drop the telephone receiver to the floor, where it thumps against the carpet and begins twirling— unwinding like a newborn infant hanging grotesquely from an umbilical cord.

I run from my apartment, past the row of rosebushes, to the front of the building. My penis flaps in my boxer shorts—I pass a neighbor walking her toy poodle, an old woman I've nodded and waved to for the past five years—and she turns away from me, mortified. I look down; the lips of my underwear are spread wide open; my graying pubic hair displayed like stylish fur trim. I pull my underwear fabric closed, keep going.

Around the side of the house: the three garbage cans. The

old-fashioned kind—steel, dented, twenty years' worth of bangs and kicks and drops.

I pull the top off the first can. The lid creates a vacuum as I lift—the side of the canister is sucked inward. Finally, it gives, and the top comes off. Inside I see one white trash bag. I smell old fish. I drop the lid to the ground. It clatters with a metallic racket.

I pull open the second lid. Inside: a black plastic garbage bag and a grease-stained pizza box, folded on the diagonal to fit in the trash can.

I push aside the second can, turn to the third. The lid is firmly planted on the canister. I pull. Another momentary vacuum—the lid refuses to give. Then it comes off, surprisingly fast, so that I have to take a step back to keep my balance.

The garbage can is stuffed with white plastic trash bags. On the top bag, I see the warning that Sustevich left me. It takes me a moment to figure out what it is. Then I realize: it is a long red ponytail, ending in a clump of bloody skin and gristle. Human hair and a human scalp, deposited on the trash bag like a cherry on a sundae.

The long red ponytail belonged to Peter Room.

Goddamn Peter Room. I told him to get out of town. He hung around a minute too long, never believed my warnings. It all seemed like a big game to him: pretending to predict the stock market, pretending to be scared of fake FBI agents, pretending to storm out of the office and quit . . .

He enjoyed the drama—the acting. He didn't understand: In a Big Con, some people aren't acting.

I run back to my apartment and go to the phone. Toby is leaving the bathroom as I enter. "Okay, I'm done now—" he starts to say. Then he sees the blood drained from my face, and the *thing* in my hand with the long red hair. He stops suddenly, takes a step back. "What the hell . . ."

I ignore him, bend down, pick up the telephone. "You son of a bitch," I say.

"But I was doing you a favor," Sustevich says. "No loose ends."

"He wasn't a loose end," I say. "He was part of the con."

"Well, how was I expected to know *that?*" Sustevich says. His tone is one of amusement, as if he's talking about accidentally double-booking a luncheon date. "He stormed out of your office, didn't he?"

"Where is he now?" I say.

"Oh," Sustevich says, "long gone. We don't want law enforcement officers to find his body. Not until you pay me back."

"Why did you do it?"

"Consider it a warning, Mr. Largo. Now you see that this is not a game."

"I never said it *was* a game."

"Sunday, Mr. Largo. Twelve million dollars. Fish tacos, then."

He hangs up.

I drop Peter's scalp into a plastic Barnes & Noble shopping bag, and double-knot it like a bag of dog poop. Later, on the way to the office, Toby and I will stop at a Dumpster behind the old Intuit office park. There, among scrap-paper detritus and empty laser toner cartridges, Peter's scalp will find its final Silicon Valley resting place.

CHAPTER FORTY

How did Sustevich know that Peter Room was a loose end? How did Sustevich know that Peter stormed from my office, quit my con?

Could someone have told him? Of course someone did.

But who?

In my heart I know, but before I act, I must be sure.

CHAPTER FORTY-ONE

After depositing Peter's scalp in the Dumpster, we drive to the office. I say to Toby, "Don't tell Jessica."

"Don't tell her what?"

He knows what I mean, but he wants me to say it out loud. "Don't tell her about Peter."

I don't want her to know because I'm not sure how she will react. I can't afford to have Jessica freak out, go ballistic. I can't afford another loose end running around. For her sake and for mine.

"Dad," Toby says, "I think you owe her the truth."

"You think that, do you?" I say. "Good to know."

At that he's silent.

When we get to the office, Jess is already there. She doesn't say hello. Still mad. "I wrote the press release," she says, "just like you asked." She hands me a piece of paper.

PALO ALTO, Aug. 28 PRNewswire—Halifax Protein Products today announced a corporate reorganization and shift in strategic focus. The company, which has been publicly traded for the past seven years and which has been a food-service vendor, announced that it will change its name to Zip Internet Marketing and will become a major e-commerce player and content aggregator. The company will create a vertical business-to-business

portal focusing on community building and e-commerce technology enablement . . .

By the end of the first paragraph, my reading slows to the speed
of a jeep in foot-deep mud. I can't go on. I say, "That's perfect. Put
it on the wire."

The press release is camouflage, a distraction. Later, people will
ask questions. Why did the price of HPPR rise from three cents to
ten dollars in only a few days?

Fortunately, anyone curious will be able to point to the news in
the press release—that Halifax Protein has become Zip Internet
Marketing, that a fish oil company has metamorphosed into a
"business-to-business portal" and "content aggregator." The sky-
rocketing stock price will be regarded as yet another example of Internet mania, and not evidence of a hundred-million-dollar con.

At eight-thirty, I'm seated at my desk, waiting for Napier to
show up, and for the con finally to end. I sense Jessica standing behind me.

She says: "You know, it's strange."

"What?"

"Look at this." She reaches over my shoulders to type into my
keyboard. I feel her breasts lightly brush my back. I suspect she is
being mean, doing this on purpose, to say, *See what you never will
have?*

I close my eyes. For a moment, I try to imagine being in bed
with her, after this is all over. But can it ever be over?

"See?" she says. I snap out of my reverie. She has brought up a
stock chart on the screen—symbol HPPR, Halifax Protein.

"What?"

"The stock is already rising. It went from three cents to five dollars in the past twenty-four hours."

"Your press release. The whole business-to-business e-commerce
thing."

"It didn't hit the wires yet. It doesn't get published for another half-hour."

"Strange," I say.

"Who the hell would want to pay five dollars for a worthless fish oil stock?"

"Good question," I say.

CHAPTER FORTY-TWO

Do you know the con involving the priceless pooch?

Here's how it goes. A guy walks into a bar. He brings a dog with him. He says to the bartender, "Hey Mack, can you do me a favor? I have a job interview across the street. Can you watch my dog for sixty minutes while I'm gone?"

The bartender says sure, what the hell, I'll watch your dog.

"But listen," the dog owner says, "he's a prize-winning dog, so please keep an eye on him." And with that, the dog owner leaves the bar.

A few minutes later, a well-dressed gentleman walks into the bar. He's got a Rolex and a spiffy suit. Reeks of money. He takes one look at the dog tied to the bar stool and he says, "My God, that dog is beautiful. It looks exactly like Muffy, the dog I had as a child. I'd love that dog for my *own* son." He approaches the bartender. "Listen, bartender, I'll buy that dog from you. Name your price. A thousand dollars? No, wait. Make that two thousand dollars."

The bartender says, "Sorry pal, can't do it. It ain't my dog. But the owner is coming back in about an hour."

The rich guy looks at his Rolex. "An hour? I can't wait that long. But maybe you can do me a favor all the same." He hands the bartender his business card. "Here's my card. Just give it to the dog's owner and have him call me."

"Sure thing," the bartender says. And the rich man leaves.

An hour later, the dog's owner returns to the bar. He's in tears. "That's it," he says. "It's over. Another job rejection. I can't afford the rent anymore. It's hopeless." He looks down at his dog. "And I certainly can't afford to take care of *him* anymore." He looks at the bartender. "Listen, I know it's a lot to ask. But the dog seems to like you, Mack. Why don't you keep him? Buy him from me. A few hundred bucks. What do you say?"

The bartender has a choice. Either he can reveal that he holds the business card of a stranger willing to pay two thousand dollars for the dog, or he can decide to keep that information secret. Most bartenders choose the second option.

So the bartender agrees to pay a few hundred dollars for the dog, thinking he can call Daddy Warbucks and resell the dog for a couple grand within minutes.

The transaction done, the dog owner leaves the bar.

Alas, the bartender discovers, too late, that the phone number he has been given is defunct, and the dog he paid three hundred dollars for is a mutt that was picked up for free from the pound.

CHAPTER FORTY-THREE

Now it is time to sell my own mutt for more than it is really worth.

Napier shows up at nine o'clock. No goons this time, as we agreed.

Walking down the hall, he rubs his hands with childlike glee. "All right, then," he says. "Let's make a hundred million dollars or so."

He marches into the conference room, looks around, sees Toby and Jess. "Who knows how to operate this thing?" he says.

"I'll do it," I say. I walk to the front of the room, pull down the projection screen. I reach under the conference table, feel for the power switch, boot up the computer. Toby limps over, turns on the projector.

"It's going to be a little different today," Napier announces. "You tell me which stock to buy, then I call my guy, who trades it for my own account. Not that I don't trust you."

"That's fine," I say. "What about my cut?"

"Your cut?" Napier says. He smiles. "Right, your cut. We'll deal with that later." My expression must indicate less than full confidence in this. He says, "Don't worry, Kip. My reputation precedes me. I always follow through."

Napier's reputation does indeed precede him, the way a hearse precedes a funeral procession. It is a reputation littered with grandiose promises and broken deals, hurried last-minute settlements before litigation, and—in the case of business associates who prove too stubborn—ominous and sudden disappearances. In other words, Napier is the kind of man from whom you want your cash up front, before services are rendered.

But today apparently this will not be the case. Napier leans over the conference table, pulls the speakerphone toward him. He dials a number.

"This is Derrick," the voice on the phone says.

"It's me," Napier says. "Are you ready?"

"Locked and loaded."

Napier turns to me. "Let's get started." He shuts the door to the hallway.

I walk to the computer keyboard, type the command that I've watched Peter type a half-dozen times before:

```
>pythia -n=1
```

A green stock chart appears on the screen: HPPR. The chart tells the strange story of a fish stock that, twenty-four hours ago, was trading at $0.03 per share, but which, since then, has risen steadily to $6.20. Above the current price and to the right, Pythia draws a red target circle at the $9.95 level.

Napier looks at the screen, nods. "Okay," he says. He calls into the speakerphone: "I want you to buy whatever quantity is available of symbol HPPR, limit price eight dollars, good till cancel."

From the speakerphone, "Derrick's" disembodied voice repeats: "Mr. Napier, for your account ending 9612, we will be buying Harry Peter Peter Robert, limit price eight dollars. This is an iceberg order, displaying quantity bid equal to quantity asked, up to the limit of eight dollars, good till cancel."

"That's right," Napier says.

"Your order is being relayed to the Nasdaq system now . . ."

The speakerphone makes a loud static pop. The lights flicker, as if deciding whether or not to call it a day, and then, decision made, shut off. The Pythia screen goes black.

"What the hell . . ." Napier says.

He's being backlit by the sun streaming through the windows behind him. With the shadows on his face, it's hard to read his expression.

Then: "Freeze! Freeze! Freeze!"—men's voices, loud, maybe amplified.

Everything happens at once. The door of the conference room bursts open, and two men tumble into the room wearing Navy flak jackets with a big yellow "FBI" embroidered on front and back. Each fans to an opposite side of the door, and falls to a crouch. They sweep their pistols back and forth, aiming from me to Napier, to Toby, to Jess.

Now two more men appear in the room—calmly walking—it's agents Crosby and Farrell. Crosby and Farrell keep their pistols up and pointing to the ceiling.

Finally, another agent enters the room—older, with gray hair, wearing a tweed jacket and leather elbow patches, like an Ivy League English professor. He walks slowly, purposefully, as if he does this sort of thing—busting into start-up companies' conference rooms—all the time.

"Hands up!" Agent Crosby yells.

I put up my hands. So do Toby, Jess, and Napier.

"Kip Largo," the gray-haired agent says, "you are under arrest."

"Under arrest?" I say. "For what?"

"Wire fraud, securities fraud, racketeering, Section 2511 interception of electronic communication. You have a minute? Pull up a chair, I'll read the list . . ."

"Wait," I say, "this is a big misunderstanding."

"Mr. Largo," the gray-haired agent says, "anything you say can and will be used against you. You have the right to have an attorney present. If you can't afford an attorney, one will be appointed for you."

"Shit," I say. The first two agents into the room now approach me. They handcuff my wrists behind my back. "Ouch," I say.

"Okay," the gray-haired agent says. "Let's get everyone downtown . . ."

Napier says, "Gentlemen, please. Hold on a second. I have nothing to do with this."

The gray-haired agent turns to Napier. "Who's he?"

Agent Crosby says, "Ed Napier."

"Hello, Agent Crosby," Napier says. He smiles warmly, as if he's welcoming a guest to his hotel. "What's going on here?"

Agent Crosby shakes his head. "Your partner is involved in a criminal enterprise."

"Is he?" Napier says. "I had no idea. I'm just a venture capitalist, not a private investigator."

Agent Crosby turns to the gray-haired agent. "We don't need him, do we?"

"Is he on the list?"

"No."

Gray Hair nods. "Cut him loose. You know where to reach him?"

"Yeah," Crosby says.

"Okay," Gray Hair says to Napier. "We'll be in touch later. You're not planning on going anywhere, are you?"

"Maybe Las Vegas. I own a few hotels there . . ."

"Right," Gray Hair says. He's not easily impressed. "I'm staying at the Comfort Inn up the street. Guess we have something in common, after all." He turns to Crosby. "What about the others?"

Crosby says: "Toby Largo, Jessica Smith . . ." He looks up at me. "Where's Peter Room?"

I shake my head. "Unavailable," I say.

"Okay, let's go," Crosby says. To Napier: "You better scram."

Napier looks at me, as if debating whether to say something—a threat, perhaps; or a request to talk later. But he decides, in the end, that discretion is best, and he says nothing. Threats, apparently, can wait. He nods and walks quickly from the room, before the FBI changes its mind.

Meanwhile, as Napier exits down the hall, the show goes on. Gray Hair says loudly: "Read these two their rights."

Crosby begins to recite Miranda rights for Jess and Toby, while, at the far end of the hall, we hear the office door open and

Napier scurry out, quiet and sheepish for the first time since we've met.

When Napier's cherry-red Mercedes pulls out of the parking lot, we continue the charade for another five minutes, in case Napier returns for forgotten keys, or in case he has instructed his men to watch us from afar. I have heard stories: about con men too eager to call it a day, who break out in whoops and hollers, or even begin to divide their take into equal portions, while their victim is listening, just a few feet away. Seems hard to believe, that you could work so hard to rip someone off, and then blow it all in a fit of stupidity, greed, and laziness—but then again, isn't this what the whole con business proves—that human nature *is* stupidity, greed, and laziness?

And so: Toby and Jess are escorted out of the office, pale-faced and near tears, into the back seat of a waiting black sedan with tinted windows. I am escorted after them, into the back seat of a second dark sedan. As my car pulls out of the parking lot, I see two FBI agents wrapping our office door with yellow police tape that says "POLICE LINE—DO NOT CROSS" and setting orange traffic cones around the nearby parking spaces.

As we start down Bayfront Expressway, past the stinking salt ponds, the man in the front passenger seat turns around to face me. It is Elihu Katz.

"You still have the right to remain silent, you know."

"Elihu," I say. "This is a pleasant surprise."

"I love the endings best. Always have. Nothing like seeing their face. How did it go?"

"Not sure yet," I say. "It's not really the end."

"No?" He looks at me, probing for more. He wants me to explain, but I can't. Not yet.

Instead, I look around the sedan. Built into the rear console is a mini-bar, stocked with cans of Coke and a half-filled bottle of Stoli. "Cool car," I say.

Elihu nods. "Yeah. Got you a discount. Now that prom season is over, you can get these cheap."

"Nice work," I say. "Looks very FBI."

"Ehh," Elihu says, and shakes his hand back and forth, to say *so-so*. "I figured it was better than a white stretch. Could have gotten those even cheaper."

"Good call," I say. "Don't see many FBI guys in white stretch limos."

"Yeah," Elihu says. He turns back around. He reaches to the floor, pulls up a black leather attaché case. He hands it to me over the seat. "Here you go," he says. "Careful with this. Not insured."

I nod.

We drive in silence.

I check in at the Fairmont Hotel in San Jose, under the pseudonym Kyle Reilly. I pay cash for three nights in advance. I've instructed Toby and Jess to check in to separate hotels at opposite ends of the Peninsula. I explained that I will contact them in three days, after I'm certain that we've successfully blown off our mark.

Upstairs in my room, I turn on the TV and head to the bathroom, where I take a long piss and a warm shower. At first, it's a relief to be alone—not to have Toby around—and to be able to urinate when I want, to walk into the bathroom and not find my shower towel dropped into a wet pile on the floor.

But then I decide to head down to the hotel restaurant and grab a beer and a burger, and I suddenly realize that it would be fun to have Toby along—to enjoy his cynical humor, to verbally spar with him, to roll my eyes at his relentless libido. For the past two months, he has been—for better or worse—my constant companion, my pal. I'm closer to him than I have ever been in my life. And I think it's funny, and probably deep and meaningful in some metaphysical way that eludes me just now—that it took my committing a crime to bring me closer to my son, and that—despite my desire not to repeat my own father's mistakes—here I am, aping my father's actions twenty years after his death, unable to escape his clutches even now.

*   *   *

On the TV, I'm watching the green and red stock ticker scroll across the screen, and the CNBC anchor says: "In news from the gaming industry, today the Eurobet Consortium announced that it would not match Ed Napier's bid for the Tracadero hotel site on the Las Vegas Strip. The withdrawal of Eurobet from the bidding process now opens the way for Ed Napier to purchase the site and build on it the largest hotel in the United States."

You know what else I'm thinking, as I sit here alone, in the empty restaurant, eating my burger and drinking my beer? That a successful con is like a meal. It's only fun when you have someone to share it with. What good is it if you're alone in a hotel, without someone to talk to?

Back in my room, I place the black attaché case that Elihu Katz gave me on the hotel bedspread. The duvet is orange and brown, with fabric as thick and crusty as day-old French bread, spread with dried seminal discharge from hundreds of guests, the bedspread's floral pattern camouflaging tracks from dirty shoes and skid marks from luggage wheels that have rolled across the world's filthiest tarmacs.

I open the attaché and remove three brown paper bags, each the size of a baseball. The paper bags are crinkled and wrapped tight, like the remains of a half-eaten office lunch hastily tossed into the trash. Gently, I unwrap one of the bags, spread the paper at the aperture, and pour the contents into a neat pile on the bedspread. I stare at a small mound of loose diamonds, a mix of one and two carats, like a tiny sand castle. The diamonds sparkle even in the energy-efficient gloaming of the hotel bulb. There are five million dollars' worth of gems in each bag.

I carefully scrape the diamonds into the first bag, picking up the stragglers one at a time, with my index and thumb. I twist the bag closed, replace it in the attaché. I open the second bag and pour the contents onto the bedspread. Another five-million-dollar sand castle. I return the contents to the bag, and then check the third.

Diamonds are the currency of choice for men like me: small,

fungible, anonymous. And they're beautiful, too. But it's important not to grow too attached. Soon they will be out of my hands, and I will give them to Andre Sustevich.

Tomorrow I will give the diamonds to the Professor, and thereby settle my debt.

It's not every day that you steal money from a man, and then use it to repay him what you owe. You have to admit: That's elegant. A piece of work of which I can justifiably be proud.

On Monday, even though my business with Sustevich will be done, and my debt repaid, Sustevich will start to have a sinking feeling. It may mirror the sinking stock price of HPPR. When the market for HPPR disappears on Monday morning—when almost no rational investor is willing to buy the stock, and the situation returns to normal—the price of Halifax Protein will drop like a stone, back to where it started—to maybe three cents a share. Those eight million shares that Sustevich bought, for an average price of six dollars a share—in giddy anticipation of being able to resell them to Napier for ten dollars a share—will, like the priceless pedigreed pooch that turns out to be a mutt—prove worthless.

CHAPTER FORTY-FOUR

At ten o'clock in the evening I rent a car at the San Jose airport and drive north to Woodside to meet with my accomplice.

Cons are like marriage. Everyone believes in the romantic fairy tale, about how, if you look hard enough, you can find the perfect partner, someone who complements you and makes you magically complete. But the reality is more mundane. Usually you hook up with whoever is around at the time you need to get going.

And so it was in my con. Desperation, and greed, make for strange bedfellows.

I drive up to the gate of his mansion, stop at the security booth. It's the same guard as last time, the middle-aged man who led me into the compound for one of my several rounds of dental work. "I'm here to see Mr. Napier," I say.

The guard nods. "Take the road up to the house, park in the circle." He walks to the gate, pushes it open.

The moon is three-quarters full—enough light to see. I drive slowly up the gravel road. Every ten yards foot lamps illuminate a small circle of ground. Over the crest of the hill I see the Spanish house, the limestone and red clay roof. It's lit from below with bright spotlights. I pull into a parking circle twenty yards from the loggia. I'm greeted by a man in a suit. His face is familiar. He's the bruiser that kicked out my front tooth. He looks at me in the moonlight.

"Your teeth look good," he says.

"In a bright room, the color's a little off," I explain. I feel compelled to say: "Thai dentist."

The bruiser probably hears: "Tie dentist"—as if I am requesting that he bind and gag Dr. Chatchadabenjakalani and beat him up. So I explain: "You know, Bangkok."

The bruiser nods and smiles lasciviously, as if I've said something dirty.

"Forget it," I say.

He leads me up the flagstone path, into the arcade, past the rattan furniture and potted red bougainvillea plants, and into the sitting room. Napier is there, leaning over the billiards table. He's wearing a cotton sweater and khaki slacks. This is the first time I've seen him without a suit.

The bruiser backs out of the room without a word. Napier doesn't look up at me. He pulls back his stick and snaps it into the cue. The white ball slams without spin into the four ball, which flies straight into the corner pocket. That's Ed Napier summed up in one flick of the wrist: His shots are hard, brutal, direct. No soft banking rolls. No light touch.

He starts lining up the next shot: the five into the middle pocket. Without looking up at me, he says, "And so, a job well done."

"Yeah," I say.

Napier slaps the cue; the five ball whizzes across the felt and drops into the leather net of the pocket.

Finally Napier looks up at me. He leans his stick upright against the side of the table. "You don't sound happy for a man who's just gotten away with twenty million dollars."

I shrug. I want to explain that this victory comes at a personal cost. My worst fears have been confirmed. But why bother? Napier's not the kind of man who dwells on betrayal. He just deals with it. With a flick of the wrist. Hard, brutal, direct.

"How are your teeth?" he says.

"So so."

He stares at my teeth. I smile like a sixth-grader on Picture Day.

"You look like my grandmother, may she rest in peace. Different colors."

"I'll have it fixed."

"Sorry about that," Napier says. "Jackie got a little . . . enthusiastic."

"Like wrestling," I say.

"Sorry?"

"Nothing." I think about sitting on my couch with Toby, watching Killer Eight Ball and Frankie the Fist. That was fun, while it lasted.

"Let's drink," Napier says. He walks to the mosaic tiled bar at the side of the room, pours two glasses of scotch. He hands me one. "Scotch," he says. He raises his glass. "To success."

"To success," I say. I drink.

Napier says, "Ahh," and puts down his glass. "Stay for dinner?"

"Sure."

He cocks his head, leads me into the dining room. The table is set with two places, on white linen. We each walk to a chair. He says, "Looks like I'll win the Tracadero."

"Yeah, I thought you would. I don't think Sustevich is in any position to match you. He'll have his hands full with damage control. Angry partners wanting to know what happened. How he lost the deal. How he lost all their cash."

Napier says, "Those Russians can be difficult. Take it from me. I know."

We sit down. I gesture to a third spot at the table, one that is conspicuously missing a place setting. "I take it your wife won't be joining us?"

Napier shakes his head glumly. "I'm afraid not. She's had a bit of an accident."

"I see."

"So you were right about her, too."

"Not something I like being right about."

Napier shrugs. "I always suspected. But what can I say? She was super-hot. A great fuck." He pauses. "As you know."

I think about that night in The Clouds, about the black semiglobe eyes-in-the-sky in the ceilings of the casino. I think about Lauren Napier's room on the thirty-third floor, the tatami mats, her legs wrapped around my waist, her painted toenails that looked like Red Hots.

"Yeah, sorry about that," I say. "I guess I got a little . . . enthusiastic."

Napier smiles.

That was my first clue: Napier's wife. It was a bit strange, wasn't it, that she happened to find me in a bar one afternoon? That she offered me a hundred thousand dollars to set up her husband? That she had a sob story ready about being beaten silly and scared for her life?

And then, a few days later, to learn that my own son owed money to a Russian mobster? Hey, lucky break: My son desperately needed money, and Lauren Napier was offering it! My stars were certainly aligned.

Those kinds of coincidences probably wouldn't register with most people.

But men like me, we get feelings in our bones. A coincidence is a sign from God, a clue that must be treated with respect.

When did I figure out that it was Sustevich who was behind Lauren Napier? That it was the Professor who wanted to ruin Napier, in order to snatch the Tracadero, and perhaps other pieces of Napier's empire? I'd say I knew for sure the moment the Professor allowed me into his Pacific Heights mansion. He was too polite, too interested in investing in my con. Guys like me are used to being treated like shit. Treat us any better than that, and we're immediately suspicious.

So Sustevich, in a frenzy of greed, found out how I was going to set up Napier, and he decided he wanted a little piece of that action, too. It wasn't enough for Sustevich to watch me destroy his enemy. The Professor also wanted a little vig on the side. As I knew he would.

Using the Russian mob's money, Sustevich started buying up HPPR. Since I was the only owner of the stock, he essentially paid me. On average, he paid six dollars per share for a stock he thought would rise to ten dollars. That would have been a good investment, if only it were true.

Unfortunately, he will soon learn that he paid six dollars for stock that is worthless. I will split with Ed Napier the proceeds—about twenty-five million dollars for each of us—less the money we owe Elihu Katz for the fronted diamonds.

The diamonds are a distraction. Sustevich lent me six million; I will pay him back fifteen million. When the Professor and I part ways, he'll think I'm the best investment he's ever made. In the meantime, without his even knowing it, I've stolen him blind.

This is as Ed Napier and I agreed to, so many weeks ago.

Finally, you have to wonder.

How long ago did Sustevich start planning his *own* con? Napier met Lauren—the woman who would become his wife—four years ago, at a fashion show. Was she already Sustevich's employee? Did the Professor know, even then, that Ed Napier would become his eventual target?

Perhaps it was not such a cunning leap. If you are the Russian mob, anxious to gain a foothold in Las Vegas, to wash your money clean, to make millions more in the process, you know who stands in your way. You know that Ed Napier is the King of Las Vegas. To win the crown, you will need to remove it from his head. So you start planning years in advance, by handing Napier a new queen, a beautiful young girl who is destined to betray him . . .

Back in my hotel, I check my home answering machine. I will not return to my apartment—not for a while, perhaps not ever.

The first message on my machine is from Celia. "I'm just checking in," my ex-wife says. "I haven't heard from you. So . . . either one of you—call me." *Either one of you.* It's official: She's calling the apartment of Kip and Toby. Father and son. It has the makings of a charming Friday night sitcom. Young ne'er-do-well moves in with hardworking Dad. *But get this*— (I picture the eager studio exec pitching the series to his bosses) —*the old guy, he's a con man. See? Brilliant.*

The second message is from Mr. Santullo's Arabian grandson. Even before he finishes saying "Hello Kip" I know something is wrong. He says quietly: "I would have told you in person, but with everything going on . . . Just in case you didn't know, my grandfather died last night. We're having the funeral on Saturday, at St. Mary's at one o'clock. If you can come, I'm sure he would have liked it."

I hang up the phone and think about that night, just weeks ago, that I had drinks in Mr. Santullo's apartment. My landlord was a good man. He lived a long life. At the end of it, he was alone, the winner of an actuarial contest in which you find out, too late, that winning means you've lost. That you've outlived your friends, and your wife, and even your daughter. That you are abandoned, taken advantage of by people looking to make a buck, people for whom your remaining days are an inconvenient hurdle between them and lucre. I suspect that the old man is shuffling around heaven right now, in a terry-cloth bathrobe and a wife-beater undershirt, with a highball glass in his hand. I wonder: Will I meet the same fate as Mr. Santullo? Will I, too, die alone, abandoned by those around me, because they could not trust me, and because I could not trust them? I hope Mr. Santullo keeps a second highball glass ready for me, wherever he is.

CHAPTER FORTY-FIVE

On Saturday, against my better judgment, I leave my hotel and drive to Palo Alto to attend the old man's funeral. When I walk into the church, I think I've come to the wrong place. It can't possibly be a funeral: Nobody's here.

But then I see the mourners up front, barely two rows of them—a handful of the frail and elderly, a few younger faces I recognize—the Arabian, and his wife; our neighbor with the poodle; the guy with the eye patch down the street.

It's obvious that the priest doesn't know Mr. Santullo, perhaps never even met him; and he sticks with safe generalities: about how Mr. Santullo brought much joy and love to the people he touched during his many years on the earth, and that he is now at God's side.

At the end of the funeral, I leave the church without exchanging words with anyone. I know I ought to get back to San Jose and my hotel room before anyone in Palo Alto sees me. I'm only one day away from boarding a plane and leaving California. This time tomorrow, I will be in the air, heading to someplace as of yet undetermined—but certainly someplace warm, someplace where the economy depends heavily on rum-based drinks.

I descend the church steps, cross the street, fidget in my pocket to find my car keys. I press the remote. My rental Ford Escort chirps happily.

As I place my hand on the car door handle, I know something is wrong. At first, I am unsure of what. Then I realize: no traffic.

It's Saturday at noon, downtown Palo Alto, a block away from the Whole Foods supermarket. The street should be filled with yuppies in Volvos, software kids in the New Beetles, heading over to stock up on quinoa and free range chicken. Instead, the street is empty—silent. I look two blocks down the road and see, in the distance, a yellow police barricade and a uniform shooing cars away. I turn around. A sedan with tinted windows rides slowly toward me, the wrong way up a one-way street.

I think about running. Too late. The voices are just ten feet behind me. "Mr. Kip Largo! Freeze!"

"FBI! Put your hands up!" a female voice says.

Without turning, I raise my palms over my head. Across the street, the mourners from Mr. Santullo's funeral straggle from the church and start down the stairs. I see the Arabian and his wife. He's looking curiously at me, trying to figure out what's going on. Then his brain *clicks*, and you can almost see the expression on his face change from curiosity to disgust: He can't believe I'm being arrested at a funeral.

Neither can I, buddy, I want to tell him. Before I can, my wrists are pulled behind my back and snapped with a plastic band. My head is pushed down like a spent jack-in-the-box and I am shoved into the waiting sedan.

I'm chauffeured by two stone-faced men in suits who ignore my attempts at conversation. We drive south on 101, thirty minutes to San Jose, and pull into the underground garage of an office tower on Bascomb Street. We take the freight elevator up to the fifteenth floor, just me and the two marble statues in suits. Neither looks at me during the ascent. The elevator chimes and the doors open, and I'm led down a short hall to a gray double-door without signage. One of my handlers gives a little shave-and-a-haircut knock on the door. The door opens.

We walk past a bank of desks, some occupied by serious-looking men, some empty. I'm taken to a windowless room with a table and four chairs. One of my captors takes a pocketknife from his pants and slices through my plastic handcuffs.

He says, "Please have a seat, Mr. Largo."

"Am I under arrest?" I say.

"Please," he says again, in a tone somewhere between patience and menace, "have a seat."

I sit down on the wire frame chair. The agent nods. "We'll be right with you."

The agents leave.

I'm left alone in the room for a few minutes, probably so I'll have time to get nervous and talkative. Finally the door opens, and two new agents appear. The first is a woman in her forties, with blondish gray hair, cut short, and a navy pants suit. She looks like a soccer mom who just stepped out of her Chrysler minivan. She smiles pleasantly when she enters the room, as if she might offer me a peanut butter and jelly sandwich. "Mr. Largo, I'm Agent Warren," she says. I notice that when she stops smiling, the corners of her mouth stay wrinkled long after her lips relax.

The other agent is a thin man, in his forties, with closely cropped dark hair, skin pulled tightly across his skull, and bright blue eyes. The effect makes him like a very, very surprised skeleton. He introduces himself as Agent Davies.

He says, "Mr. Largo, do you know why you're here?"

"Let me ask you something," I say, ignoring the question. "Are you guys real FBI?"

"Real FBI?" Agent Davies says.

"Yeah. Am I being conned? Is this a button?"

"A button?" Agent Warren says.

Davies shakes his head. "Mr. Largo, I assure you: We're the real thing."

"Yeah, but how do I *know* that?"

Agent Davies reaches into his pocket. "Here," he says. "I have a business card." He hands it to me.

"Oh," I say. I examine the card carefully. "A business card? You didn't say that." I reach into my own pocket, pull out Agent Crosby's business card. I hand it to him. "See? Mine's nicer."

Davies squints at the card. "Who's Agent Crosby?"

"Black guy. Shaved head. Ever work with him?"

Davies thinks about it. It takes about eight seconds, and then he realizes I'm yanking his chain.

"Mr. Largo, please," he says. "Let me start again. Do you know how you got here?"

"Well," I say slowly, "when a man and a woman love each other very much, like my mommy and daddy, a man puts his penis—"

"Mr. Largo," Davies says, "I don't have a lot of time. Please. I need your help."

This is the first FBI-like thing I've heard all day. No threats of prison sentences or violence, no bluster. Just a decent request. I slump back in my chair. "Okay, I'm sorry," I say. "Start again."

"In the interest of time," Davies says, "let me get to the point. You're not under arrest. Not exactly. Not yet. I may change my mind about that at the end of our conversation today."

"I see."

Davies says: "At first we couldn't figure out what you were up to. We spent a lot of time on that damn vitamin site of yours. What is it?—MrVitamin.com? Ordered a thousand dollars' worth of beta-carotene, before we realized it was legit." He shakes his head. "Nice site, by the way."

"Thanks."

"My wife is a Web designer. I should hook you guys up."

"Okay," I say agreeably. I pat my pocket. "I got your card."

"Anyway, it took us a while. Then we finally figured it out. You stole money from the Russian mafia."

He looks at me. I say nothing.

"I'm not one hundred percent sure how you did it," Davies says, "or why you did it, or how much you took. I don't think I *want* to know. The truth is, it couldn't have happened to a nastier bunch of guys."

Davies waits for me to say something. But I refuse, either to confirm or deny what he has said. This might be a trap. So I sit quietly, and stare.

He continues: "Unfortunately, your little caper has caused me and my partner—and the ten other members of my task force—a serious problem. We've been working on Andre Sustevich for the past nine months. We've been building a case against him, piece by piece. Drugs, prostitution, racketeering, you name it. We were about a week away from closing down the entire Sustevich organization."

"So what's stopping you?"

"You," Davies says. "Whatever you did—is stopping us."

"I don't understand."

"Sustevich's bank account is drained. He's disappeared. Maybe he's on the run. Or maybe he's dead."

"Like you said, it couldn't have happened to a nastier guy."

"I'm afraid it's not that simple. The United States government has now spent nearly six million dollars building a case against Sustevich. This is a big deal. Our boss's ass is on the line. Our boss's *boss's* ass is on the line. Thus: My ass is on the line. You know what that means?"

"I'm getting a sense. Is my ass on the line?"

He points at me, the universal semaphore meaning: *Bingo, shithead.*

"Look," I say, "I'm not admitting that I had anything to do with Andre Sustevich. But if I did, I would guess that he gambled with other people's money, and he lost. Everything. So maybe he's hiding from some angry Russian partners."

Davies says, "But you're still missing my point."

"What's your point?"

Agent Warren, my new FBI Den Mother, interrupts. "Maybe I can explain," she says. She speaks in a soft, gentle voice. "I think what my partner is trying to say is: We're going to arrest someone . . . for *something*. We're not going to shut down the investigation and come up empty-handed."

I'm starting to see where this is going. "Ah," I say.

"So the question, Mr. Largo," Mother Warren says, "is whether we make an arrest for stock manipulation and securities fraud, or whether we make an arrest for prostitution and racketeering. Truthfully, we'd prefer to prosecute Sustevich. But if we have to, we'll prosecute our second choice."

"Me."

Agent Warren shrugs. She has the expression of a mommy gently scolding her kid with a tummy ache: *See what happens when you eat too many cookies?*

I try one more time. The safest strategy, whenever you are accused of anything—whether cheating on your wife or on your taxes—is: deny, deny, deny. "Listen, guys, I want to help you. I really do. But I have no relationship with Andre Sustevich. I have nothing to do with him."

Agent Davies's face says: This is getting tiresome. He reaches into his jacket pocket, removes a microcassette recorder. He places it on the table in front of me. "I want you to listen to something." He presses play.

Out of the speaker comes a tinny voice, audible over the rushing-water sound of static. The recording has a compressed quality to it—all the same volume—the telltale sign of a telephone intercept.

I don't recognize the first voice. It's a man with a thick, messy East European accent—like sour cream dripped over blintzes. He says: "But Kip Largo is a criminal. He's uncontrollable."

I recognize the second voice instantly: dignified and careful, a crisp Russian accent. The Professor.

"Don't worry about Mr. Largo. He can't surprise us. I have an employee within his organization."

"And who is this employee?"

On the tape the Professor says: "Let's just call the person 'Vilnius.'"

"Vilnius? Can you trust this Vilnius?"

"I don't need to trust Vilnius," Sustevich says. "I *own* Vilnius."

Agent Davies reaches down, presses the stop button.

He looks at me.

"So?" I say. "What am I supposed to say?"

Agent Warren says, "Don't you care?"

"Of course I care. If it's true. But men like Sustevich say a lot of things."

"Do you know who it is?" Agent Warren asks.

"No," I admit. "Do you?"

She shakes her head. I feel relieved. I don't want to know. After all, the possibilities are few. And none will make me happy.

Agent Davies finally gets to the point he's been tacking toward for the past ten minutes. "So," he says, "here's the deal. Give us Sustevich. If you can't do that, give us Vilnius. Whoever he is. Or she is."

"And if I say no?"

"Then you're looking at Strike Two and three more years in Lompoc."

"That's not a very appealing choice," I say.

Agent Warren shrugs. *No it's not, dear, but now you've learned a very valuable lesson.*

"If I help you," I say, "then I walk?"

"For now," Davies says. "I can't make any promises about what happens next month if people start getting interested in you, or if we turn up something else that you've done that we don't know about. Which is why you might want to disappear for a while."

"And let's say—just for the sake of argument—let's say that I have some property that once belonged to Andre Sustevich."

"Like what?" Davies says. "You swiped an ashtray from his mansion?"

"Something like that."

"Well," Davies says, looking to Warren for support, "I think it's safe to say that, if you hand us someone from Sustevich's organization, we're not going to worry too much about whether the Professor got fleeced."

I smile. "You guys are cruel."

"Are we?" Agent Warren says. "I think we're being very fair."

I say to her: "Where were you fifty years ago, when I needed you most?"

She squints at me, shakes her head—doesn't understand.

"Forget it," I say. "Long story."

Did I always know that there was a Vilnius?

I suspected it, of course. And my fears—or my hopes, depending on how you look at it—were justified, as soon as I saw the stock price of HPPR rise. When HPPR went from three cents to six dollars—even before our press release went out, even before Ed Napier was told to buy it—I knew that someone close to me was working for Sustevich.

I suppose I always knew. It was just too convenient, after all, that Jess called me when she did. That she reinserted herself into my life at the exact moment I was going to launch my con. That she me made me fall in love with her again.

There's no such thing as a coincidence like that. A coincidence is God telling you to watch your ass.

CHAPTER FORTY-SIX

On Sunday morning, I take the black leather attaché case that Elihu gave me, and head down to the hotel lobby. I walk outside, ask a bellhop to hail a cab for me. He flips a toggle; a green light illuminates under the hotel awning. Twenty seconds later, a taxi pulls up.

I slide into the cab. "Sixty-five Cahill Street," I say. "The Amtrak station."

The cab driver, a middle-aged black man, says: "You got it." He starts his meter and pulls into the traffic.

We get to the station five minutes later. I say, "Can you wait? Keep the meter going. I'll be one minute."

The cabbie nods. I get out of the cab. The Cahill Street station is an L-shaped building, with railroad tracks running along the bottom of the L, and a bus depot along the vertical. The exterior walls of the building are happy red and brown bricks, with a bright red clay roof.

Inside, the station seems bigger. It's built in Italian Renaissance style, a grand 1930s project designed to put the city's unemployed to work, with a waiting room two stories tall, Caen stone walls, marble wainscoting. Above the ticket counter, a mural showing San Jose during the year the station was built, back when the city was not the southern extremity of something called Silicon Valley, but rather an agricultural depot, a convenient terminus for rail lines that carried California prunes and apricots to markets back east.

I head across the marble floor, to the far side of the lobby. The public address system is switched on, and a voice—or something like it—echoes through the hall, either announcing the departure of a train, or the arrival of a train, or maybe of a bus, on either track five or perhaps track nine. The PA system seems to date from the station's construction, too.

At the far end of the room I find the lockers. These are the new kind—keyless—that allow you to set your own three-digit combination. I insert a five-spot into the bill reader—enough for twenty-four hours. I read the printed directions on the inside of the locker door and attempt a dry run: closing the locker while still empty, then unlocking it with my combination—9-1-1, which I think is somehow equally clever and memorable. I wonder if Sustevich will agree.

Satisfied, I deposit the briefcase into the locker. I shut the door and leave fifteen million dollars' worth of diamonds in the train station lobby. I don't look back.

In the booth of a Vietnamese noodle shop down the street, I dial Andre Sustevich's cell phone. A voice answers—not the Professor's. I recognize it.

"Hello, Dmitri," I say. "How's it hanging today?"

"Yes," Dmitri says, "good."

"Bad news, Dmitri," I say. "I'm afraid I won't be having that drink with you, after all. That acid? I'll take a rain check. Professor around?"

"Hold on, please," Dmitri says. I hear the sound of Russian being spoken, a clatter as the phone is handed from one person to another. After a moment, the Professor comes on the line.

"Mr. Largo, where are you?"

"I was about to ask you the same question. I stopped by your house, hoping for a drink. You cleared out of there mighty fast."

"Just temporary," Sustevich says. "A few logistical issues to work out." There are more Russian voices in the background, and then I hear highway sounds—a horn from a passing big rig, the rush of tires on asphalt. Even the Professor himself sounds different than

I remember him: harried, out-of-breath—as if he were literally on the run. That veneer of sophistication which I'm so used to was apparently left behind, like his appliances, in the Pacific Heights mansion. Send Russian hit men and a squad of FBI agents after someone, and sangfroid grows warm fast.

"I see. Well, listen, Andre, I have some good news. The money I owe you? I have it. I left it for you at the San Jose Amtrak station, in a locker. You have a pencil?"

Rustling sounds. I picture the Professor reaching into a glove compartment, tossing aside an old pack of Soviet chewing gum—Big Red?—to find a pencil. "Yes, go ahead."

"The Cahill Street station. Locker 1440. The combination is 9-1-1."

"I see."

"There's fifteen million dollars' worth of gems in the suitcase. That's three million more than I owe you, to cover any transactional costs. So keep the change. Buy something nice for Dmitri—I'm thinking maybe a pashmina or some earmuffs?"

"That's very generous of you."

"So, we're Even Steven, right? Once you pick up the gems, we're done with each other."

"Yes," Sustevich says.

"And you won't bother me again? Neither me or my son?"

"You have my word," Sustevich says.

"No more scalps in garbage cans," I say. "No more random freaky murders."

"As you wish."

"Send my regards to your boys. Especially Dmitri."

"Mr. Largo, allow me to say: You were a pleasure to do business with."

"Hey, Professor," I say. "Allow *me* to say: *pa shyol na hui.*"

"Ah, very good, Mr. Largo," Sustevich says. "Fuck off, to you, too."

CHAPTER FORTY-SEVEN

I call the telephone number that Agent Davies gave me. He answers on the first ring.

I say: "The San Jose Amtrak station on Cahill Street. You know where that is?"

"Yeah."

"Locker 1440. Inside there's a black attaché case that contains fifteen million dollars' worth of diamonds. Sustevich is on his way to pick it up. Either him or someone who'll lead you to him."

"Locker 1440, Amtrak Station," Davies repeats, probably for the benefit of whoever is in the room with him.

"Whoever opens that locker works for Sustevich," I say. "That's your arrest. Okay? Am I off the hook?"

"Lead us to Sustevich," Davies says, "and you're free."

CHAPTER FORTY-EIGHT

Why do I feel compelled to watch the end?

Why am I here in the lobby of the Amtrak station, hiding in a phone booth, pretending to chatter to a friend while I keep a lazy eye sweeping the lobby floor, watching the FBI agents as they try, hopelessly, to act nonchalant, to blend with the crowd of backpackers and vagrants, businessmen and Japanese tourists?

Maybe I am here for the same reason that Elihu Katz wanted to be in the front seat of my limousine, on the morning I concluded my own con: Because the endings are best, because I want to see her face.

So: Am I the betrayer or the betrayed?

The phone call I made to Sustevich, telling him to pick up fifteen million dollars' worth of diamonds from the locker a hundred yards from where I stand has set in motion a chain of events that can end only one way.

Sustevich is no fool. He still has that knack for self-preservation which has allowed him to survive in his brutal world.

He will not appear in person today. He will send "Vilnius," a person he trusts, because you can always trust what you own.

He will send Jessica Smith.

I suppose I shouldn't be surprised. It's true that I've known her for eighteen years, and loved her for as long, but it's not as if we met at a church potluck, or volunteering at the Red Cross blood drive. She was a hooker I solicited one rainy night in L.A., and introduced to a life of cons and double crosses. How much money did we steal together? How many lives did we ruin? How many men did we break and shatter?

So: How can I be surprised when it turns out that the woman I love is betraying me? She is a con woman. What did I expect?

I suppose I knew all along. How else could I have expected the con to work? It required a betrayer in our midst. It's exactly as you learn on Sundays: Without Judas, there can be no salvation. To be saved, you must first be betrayed.

How will it end for her? There is little mystery. In the next few minutes she will enter this nest of FBI agents, and walk to the locker at the far side of the lobby, and punch the three-digit combination into the keypad. As soon as the door springs open, the lobby will come alive: that businessman in the far corner, with the suspicious earpiece; that woman in the bulky overcoat; that Asian man reading the paper—and maybe a few more I can't recognize—will swoop down and arrest her.

She will be trundled to a gray room, the first in a long series of gray rooms that will be her world for the next ten years. Then men will threaten and bluster, prosecute and harass, until she gives them what they want: Sustevich. And then she will wind up in prison anyway, whether she gives up the Russian or not, because that is the way the FBI works: When it spends six million dollars on a crime task force, there needs to be a crime. Someone must be arrested, and prosecuted, and locked away for a long time. Who gets caught is immaterial. What matters is that the god of justice is given his sacrifice, and that the public learns a lesson, that crime hardly ever pays.

At one o'clock I see a figure walk across the Amtrak lobby. The betrayer. The afternoon sun streams through the station's atrium windows, washing the marble floor white and bathing the Caen stone walls, so that the figure is a dark shadow in the backlight, a smudge with a limp.

A limp.

When I see Toby hobbling across the floor on his crutches I am momentarily addled—it is so unexpected that I forget why I am here, who I am waiting for—and my first instinct is to step from the phone booth and shout a greeting. Then the pieces fall back into place, and I fully understand everything: that Toby has been working for Sustevich since the beginning, and now the Professor has sent his student to this train station for one last errand.

How did Toby fall into Sustevich's grasp? Maybe it was exactly as my son claimed—stupid gambling debts, sixty thousand dollars' worth—and then the wily Russian was pleasantly surprised when he learned whose son he owned. Once Sustevich discovered that he controlled the son of Kip Largo, con man, he used Toby to manipulate me, to launch a con to ruin his nemesis, Ed Napier.

But maybe Toby is right about me. Maybe I never give my son enough credit. Maybe it was not Sustevich who discovered Toby. Maybe it was Toby who went to Sustevich. Maybe my son had a proposal for the Russian: He would manipulate his con man father to help Sustevich acquire the Tracadero. Maybe there never was a gambling debt. Maybe it was pure brutal ambition—my son's ambition—to score at his father's expense.

Now I recall that night in Las Vegas, when I walked downstairs to the bar and saw Toby cuddling with Lauren Napier—and the look he gave me, when I told him to leave. Could he have been fucking her the whole time? How long was he with her before I had her? How long had he been planning to use me?

But what about the cast and the broken leg? The injury was real. Was the violence, too, part of his con, a wrestling injury, like the ones we watched together on TV—real, for the sake of the drama? What kind of man tells thugs to break his leg, to make a con look real? Perhaps the same type of man who gets punched in the mouth to make a con look real. Maybe Toby and I are not so different, after all.

The more I think about it—Toby's quiet hangdog looks, his begging to stay in my apartment, his wanting to be taught how cons work—the more I admire my son. He played it just right. He was never a threat. It takes determination and confidence to play the dope. How much do you have to hate your father in order to betray him?

Yes, I think Toby and I are not so different, after all.

So he's hobbling across the floor, toward the locker and the diamonds. When he opens that locker, the next ten years will be set down before him, as if the concrete prison walls themselves will be tossed from the sky, one after another, landing with finality on each side of him, penning him in darkness.

Can I let that happen to my son? Can I fail him again?

How many times can a man fail, claiming to be a victim of circumstances beyond his control, before he realizes that circumstances are another word for the world in which we live? I think about my life with Toby. The milestones that most fathers regard as normal are missing. Instead, the milestones are of disappointment and failure: my betraying his mother when he was fourteen; getting kicked out of his home; letting him grow up without me; then the newspaper notoriety about securities fraud; the long prison sentence; the years of being locked in Lompoc while he grew from boy to man.

How many times can one man fail his son?

I think about my own father, and I know that the answer is: for as long as he is alive. There was no redemption for my father; no salvation. His failures simply grew, like a bizarre malignancy, for as long as he breathed. Even in his death, he failed us: leaving nothing, forcing me to turn my back on college and to rejoin his world of cons and rip-offs and crime.

This is the place where it will end. The failure that I have been, that my father was, that his father was. The failure that Toby surely will be, too, if I allow him to continue across the train station lobby, and open the locker door.

The FBI needs to arrest someone today; they have made that much clear. But it does not have to be Toby.

And as much as I'd like to get on that plane and go someplace warm, and have a rum drink, or two, or three, I guess that's not in the cards. Not today.

I pull open the telephone booth door, and the glass pane rattles in the wood frame. I step into the lobby. Toby is twenty yards from the lockers, but moving slowly on his crutches. I am forty yards behind.

It's an easy race. I start off across the lobby, and I see the FBI agents—the Asian man, and the woman with the overcoat—look at me curiously. Do they know who I am? Do they know who Toby is? No matter. I walk briskly across the marble tile floor. Now I'm in the middle of the atrium, walking too fast—so that everyone is looking at me—but no one can stop me.

I pass Toby from behind. As I do, I say, practically into his ear, our last moment of intimacy: "Keep walking and don't turn around" and I stroll ahead of him, without looking back at my son.

I head straight for locker 1440. I reach out to the keypad, and I press 9-1-1. I hear the lock mechanism click. I press the latch. The door opens. I remove the black attaché.

"Freeze freeze freeze!"

Their voices echo through the vast stone hall.

They come at me from all directions—people I never figured for FBI: two of the drunks that were lying on the benches, two of the Japanese tourists, and the woman in the bulky overcoat. They have guns out, pointing at my face. I gently lay the attaché case filled with fifteen million dollars' worth of diamonds at my feet, and I slowly raise my hands above my head.

As the FBI agents swarm toward me, I look past them, and I see my son, continuing to walk coolly through the lobby, toward the exit. As he pivots on his crutches, he turns momentarily toward me, and his face is caught in a beam of sun from the atrium windows. It's hard to read the expression. At first I think it's puzzlement, maybe curiosity. Then I see something else. I'm not sure what. I know I will think about this expression for years to come, and will try to figure it out. What is it? Relief? Gratitude? And somewhere in the back of my mind, I wonder:

Is it disgust?

CHAPTER FORTY-NINE

I have time to think about things now.

Seven years, maybe out in five, if things fall my way. And there are other possibilities. Elihu Katz is a minor contributor to one of the candidates for California governor. The Democrat is a bit of a dark horse, but if he wins, and then does a lousy job, and then gets turned out of office after one term, I may find myself one of the beneficiaries of a last-minute flurry of gubernatorial pardons. Admittedly it sounds like a long shot, but in my situation you need to hope.

Needless to say, Agents Warren and Davies were not happy that I turned up at the Cahill Street station instead of Sustevich, or instead of one of his men. But they were phlegmatic about it. They never did find Sustevich: He simply disappeared, and left his briefcase full of diamonds behind. Whether the Professor is comfortably ensconced in a dacha outside Moscow, reading tracts on economics; or if he was killed by the angry stakeholders of "Eurobet" is still a topic of some debate. But it hardly matters. The FBI's six-million-dollar task force was a smashing success nonetheless, for it was able to announce a major arrest: a career white-collar criminal who manipulated stock prices and committed securities and wire fraud. All my profits from the scheme—some twenty-five million dollars—were disgorged and will be used to fund future white-collar fraud investigations. Somehow, my partner, Ed Napier, escaped attention and prosecution. Maybe he was accidentally overlooked. Or maybe those million-dollar campaign contributions, to both parties, are valuable, like casino chips you save for the last big bet.

Speaking of casino chips, Napier recently completed the Tracadero deal, using cash I helped him raise. Demolition on the old site starts next month, and a new casino, The Inferno, thematically based on Dante's poem, will be complete in two years. It is said that the employees will dress in red and will carry pitchforks and shoes with specially fitted cloven hooves.

For what it's worth, Napier has been a gentleman. He sent a letter to me here in Lompoc, full of innuendo, in which he said, essentially, that there will be a job waiting for me when I get out, assuming that I don't make a stink about him and what we did together. Even without his letter, I wouldn't have caused trouble—it goes against my code; it's not what you do to your partner.

And I won't need Napier's money when I get out. To the dismay of his family, Mr. Santullo changed his will a few weeks before he died, and he left his Palo Alto property to me. The Arabian and his wife have gone to court to contest the will. They accuse me of manipulating the old man. Their evidence: that I helped him pay his bills. My lawyer says that—despite the fact that I am a con man, and in prison for fraud—I have a good shot at keeping the property. If I ever get my hands on it, I should be able to sell it to a developer who will, I'm sure, build an office building on the site where Mr. Santullo as a young man used to entertain his friends and drink highballs. If it works out, I'm expecting a cool two million dollars in cash.

Jessica Smith has not visited me, or written, or called. I wrote her a letter when I first arrived here, but I have not yet received a response. I think she is angry: angry that I used her, and that I never told her the truth about the con. But how could I? Until the very end, I wasn't sure if she was the one trying to con *me*.

This is what I explained in my letter to her. I thought she would understand. After all, she is a professional. This is what we do for a living. We mistrust. We cheat. We pretend.

But as I said, she has not written back. However, I have not given up. Each day, and each mail call, brings new hope.

Toby has not contacted me, either. I try to be philosophical about this. I think maybe my son needs time to figure out how he feels about me. At some point in the past, surely it must have been hatred. Why else would he have tried to con his own father?

But over time, perhaps his feelings will change. Every year I spend here in Lompoc is a year that Toby lives free, a year that Toby can simply carry on with his own life, unburdened by me or the choices I've made.

Finally, I suppose it shouldn't matter what Toby thinks of me. My choosing to come here, in his place, is my own reward, my own redemption. It shouldn't matter whether Toby knows this, or not.

Right?

My ex-wife, Celia, visited the other day. It's funny, isn't it, that in the end, she's the only one I have left. She said she was still living with Carl, but that she has her doubts about him and is thinking of leaving. She said Toby moved back to Aspen, or somewhere farther east, and calls her occasionally, out of breath and full of boyish enthusiasm about some new venture or idea he's kicking around—a coffee shop where you are given a book with your latte and must complete a quiz before leaving; a dance club where the floor is a giant mattress; a home delivery service for cigarettes and beer.

I asked Celia if Toby ever mentioned me in any of his phone calls. She looked down at the table for a moment, thought about it, and then looked up. "Yeah," she said. "Toby loves you."

And even though I knew she was lying, it was still good to hear.

BIBLIOGRAPHY

People who read *Con Ed* often ask where one learns how to pull off a con. One reader wondered (flatteringly, I admit) whether at some point in my past I myself was a con man. Alas, the reality is much less interesting. A lot of a writer's work entails reading the work of other (in my case, more talented) writers. I am thus extremely indebted to the following authors and works:

Faron, Fay. *Rip-Off.* Cincinnati: Writer's Digest Books. 1998.

Hyde, Stephen, and Geno Zanetti, eds. *Players.* New York: Thunder's Mouth Press, 2002.

Marlock, Dennis M. *How to Become a Professional Con Artist.* Boulder, CO: Paladin Press, 2001.

Maurer, David W. *The Big Con.* New York: Anchor Books, 1999.

Sifakis, Carl. *Frauds, Deceptions, and Swindles.* New York: Checkmark Books, 2001.

ABOUT THE AUTHOR

Matthew Klein graduated from Yale University in 1990. He attended Stanford Graduate School of Business, in Palo Alto, during the Internet boom years, but he dropped out of school a quarter shy of graduating, to help run a technology company he founded. He lived in Silicon Valley for almost a decade and started several technology firms, which collectively raised tens of millions of venture capital dollars, and employed hundreds of people . . . before they went bankrupt and disappeared. Although Matthew is not a con man, some of his prior investors might disagree. Today he lives near New York City, with his wife, Laura. He writes novels and runs Collective2.com, a trading-related software company.